BEST FRIENDS

A Selection of Recent Titles by Julie Ellis from Severn House

AVENGED

BEST FRIENDS

DEADLY OBSESSION

GENEVA RENDEZVOUS

THE ITALIAN AFFAIR

NINE DAYS TO KILL

NO GREATER LOVE

SECOND TIME AROUND

SINGLE MOTHER

VANISHED

VILLA FONTAINE

WHEN THE SUMMER PEOPLE HAVE GONE

BEST FRIENDS

Julie Ellis

severn House

This first world edition published in Great Britain 2000 by
SEVERN HOUSE PUBLISHERS LTD of
9–15 High Street, Sutton, Surrey SM1 1DF.
This first world edition published in the U.S.A. 2000 by
SEVERN HOUSE PUBLISHERS INC of
595 Madison Avenue, New York, N.Y. 10022.

British Library Cataloguing in Publication Data

Ellis, Julie, 1933-
   Best friends
   1.Detective and mystery stories
   I. Title
   813.5'4 [F]

   ISBN 0-7278-5534-4

All situations in this publication are fictitious and
any resemblance to living persons is purely coincidental.

Typeset by Palimpsest Book Production Ltd.
Polmont, Stirlingshire, Scotland.
Printed and bound in Great Britain by
MPG Books Ltd, Bodmin, Cornwall.

For Tess Karsh, a lovely lady.

One

This was one of those exquisite June days that are brilliant with sun without being steamy and that would segue into a glorious burnt orange and shocking pink sunset within hours. The kind of day she treasured, Kathy Marshall thought as she gazed from her shop window into the early afternoon in this mid-sized town fifty-two miles east of Binghamton – with no indication of the trauma it would shortly bestow on her.

On the last Monday of the month she would open her second health food shop back home in Madison, two hours away in central New York state. To confirm the actual date she turned to the wall calendar – and froze.

Seventeen years ago today – when she was twenty-nine, Marcie five and Linda seven – she became a single mother. That was the day Glenn announced, *'I can't take this marriage trap anymore. I'm suffocating.'*

She'd clung to her typing job, fighting to support the kids. She took Glenn into court at regular intervals to collect the meager child support that was part of their divorce agreement. Even when his career soared – after his third marriage – he was a delinquent father. She'd worked her way up to executive secretary – and six years ago defied reason. She quit her job, moved here from Madison, and opened the shop.

She felt almost like an expatriate returning home. Eleven years ago she had still been hurting from the divorce, but these years of building the shop had given her fresh confidence, a sense of worth. The demons had been put to rest. At forty-six she was a whole person again.

It was going to be great to be home again – and in the same town as Marcie and Frank. That was a major reason for opening the second shop in Madison. She was fond of Linda's husband David – living with Linda in Seattle – but she adored Frank. Marcie and Frank had the perfect marriage. And with Jill so capable she knew this shop would be in good hands.

1

"Jill, I'm taking off." She reached for her purse, fished for her car keys. "Close up, please?"

"Sure thing." Jill's smile was warm. She was thrilled at knowing she'd soon be in charge of the shop. "I love that Carole Little outfit." Slacks and top in a soft olive green backgrounded print – the green emphasizing Kathy's emerald eyes. Jill surveyed Kathy's slim yet curvaceous figure with admiration. "The colors are great with your hair." Short, auburn-tinted blonde, framing delicate features that belied her age by at least ten years.

"Thanks, Jill." Today she was in a glorious, upbeat mood. "See you in the morning."

She was reaching for the door of her latest-model white Taurus when she heard the phone ring in the shop. From habit she paused, waited while Jill picked up the phone. A moment later Jill beckoned her inside.

"It's Marcie," Jill said, oddly anxious.

Kathy reached for the phone, Jill's air of anxiety registering in her mind. "Hello, darling."

"Mom, something awful's happened!" Marcie's voice was unsteady, harsh with shock. "Frank's dead!"

"Oh, my God!" Kathy's mind tried to assimilate this. Frank – Marcie's husband of one year – was never sick. Marcie joshed about his being a fitness nut. "An accident?"

"He was murdered—" Marcie's voice broke. "I walked into the den – and there he was, lying on the floor, his head in a pool of blood." She began to cry.

"Marcie, talk to me," Kathy pleaded. "Marcie, please!"

"Mom, the police are holding me. They think I killed Frank." She collapsed into convulsive sobbing.

"Marcie!" Kathy called out frantically. "Marcie!"

"I don't think she can talk any more." A strange voice – edged with cautious sympathy – came to her over the phone. "But she asked to call you."

"I'm her mother." Kathy struggled for calm. *This is unreal.* "Tell Marcie I'll be there in two hours!"

Jill hovered beside her in alarm. "What's happened?"

"Frank's been murdered . . ."

"Oh, Kathy!" Jill's face was drained of color.

"Who could do such a thing? Frank is – was – such a caring, giving person." Kathy closed her eyes for a moment in anguish.

"The police are holding Marcie on murder charges. I have to go to her—"

"Don't worry about the shop – I can handle things here."

"I'll stop by the apartment and pack a few things." Kathy ordered herself not to fall apart. *Marcie needs me.* "I don't know how long I'll have to be there. I'll call you tonight."

She drove to her apartment, threw clothes into a valise. Call Angie, she told herself. Angie and she had been close since the first grade. She and Angie and Ellen – they'd always been there for each other in crises.

In the pleasant kitchen of the modest ranch house she and Joe had bought almost sixteen years ago, Angie opened the refrigerator, brought out the remains of last night's chicken, to be cut into strips and added to pasta, then reached into the freezer compartment to bring out a container of the tomato sauce. After a long day in the real estate office she wasn't in the mood for elaborate cooking. Joe – bless him – understood.

They ought to think about replacing the fridge, she thought uneasily – but with both girls in college they dreaded any unbudgeted major expense. Even with college loans, higher education was rough on the average family.

The phone was a jarring intrusion. With a sigh she reached to respond. Probably Joe, calling to say he'd be late again. He was so conscientious about finishing a job by the day he'd promised. The other contractors in town took on half a dozen jobs, jumped from one to the other – and everybody had to wait.

"Hello—"

"Angie, it's me." Kathy's voice telegraphed catastrophe.

"Kathy, are you all right?"

Kathy paused for a long, labored breath. "I can't believe what's happening . . ."

Cold from shock, Angie listened to the torrent of words that poured from Kathy. Subconsciously, part of her zoomed back through the years to the murder thirty-one years ago that had cemented their closeness into eternity.

"Angie, could you get over to the police precinct? Try to see Marcie? She sounded so dazed. She couldn't talk to me – beyond telling me the bare facts."

"I'll go right over," Angie promised.

"I'm leaving now. I should be in town in two hours."

"Hang in there, Kathy. Marcie's going to be all right."

But how could Marcie be all right when Frank – whom she loved – had been murdered?

Her valise in tow, Kathy left her apartment, hurried back to the car. She glanced at her watch as she settled herself behind the wheel. It was just past six. Under normal conditions – at off hours – she'd make it to Madison in just under two hours. Was she going to be caught in home-going traffic? Please God, not tonight.

For the first forty minutes, traffic moved with reasonable ease. Kathy struggled to absorb what had happened. Frank was dead. *Who murdered him? Why? How can the police believe Marcie had killed him?* Marcie, who was involved in fights against cruelty to animals, in battles against child abuse, in a battle to save wetlands for endangered species.

Now cars were inching along. Kathy churned with impatience. Stop off at that gas station a quarter-mile down the road and call Ellen down in New York. Ellen and Angie had stood by her during the ugly divorce. Later they'd helped her get started with the shop. At any crisis they were together. But she didn't want to remember that other death – thirty-one years ago – that had bound them together forever.

Marcie would need a lawyer, she pinpointed, willing herself not to fall apart. Angie would know who to call. Angie knew everybody in Madison.

Would Marcie be allowed bail? The vision of Marcie being held in a prison cell was devastating.

In the living room of the three-bedroom Upper West Side Manhattan apartment she had shared with her husband and two children for the past fourteen years – since Ted was three weeks old – Ellen Courtney stared at Phil in a haze of bewilderment and alarm. In the morning he was to drive Ted and Claire out to his mother's house in Montauk. They were scheduled to spend six days there before leaving for their summer tours. What did he mean – '*I'll stay out there with Mom, too. Maybe I'll go back for another four or five weeks after the kids take off.*'

"What's this about staying out at Montauk with Mom?" She tried to sound puzzled rather than upset. When they were out there for

4

the Memorial Day weekend, Mom had said something vague about Phil's being terribly uptight. But it was close to the end of the school year – most teachers were uptight by then.

"I'm not teaching summer school this year," Phil pointed out, avoiding eye contact. "And you know how I love Montauk."

"I won't be able to get away until some time in August." *Phil knows that.* "I'm finishing up the new book – final revisions."

"I'm not telling you to come with me." He was striving for casualness. "Hell, you don't need me here. You'll be working your butt off, just stopping to order dinner sent in. It's always that way when you're on the last few weeks of a book."

"You make me sound like a monster." But echoes of past fears infiltrated her mind. In the first year of their marriage Phil had written a novel that spent four weeks on the *New York Times'* bestseller list. Then he'd had a block for over three years. The second book had gone nowhere. After that – with Ted almost two and Claire due in weeks – he'd gone back to teaching. He couldn't support a wife and two children on the three thousand dollar advance he'd just been offered. "I'm always there for you and the kids."

"Your body's there but not your mind," he said with strained humor. "Look, I understand. You finish your book, and I'll lie on the deck at Mom's house and gaze at the ocean."

Now Mom's exhortation – delivered years ago – filtered into her mind. *'I think it's brave of you to give up your nine-to-five PR job to try to write paperback novels – but if you make it and Phil's tied down to teaching, you're going to have problems. It'll be a terrible blow to his ego.'*

Can't he understand that if it wasn't for his support – financial and emotional – I wouldn't have been able to pursue a writing career? What I earn makes life more pleasant for the four of us. It's security for the future. Money for the kids' college years.

"Look, I'll pick up dinner." Phil punctured her introspection. "What would you like?"

The phone rang before she could reply.

"I'll get it," Ellen said. Fighting for poise, she picked up the receiver. "Hello."

"Ellen, something insane has happened." Kathy's voice – sharp with pain – came to her.

She listened in horror while Kathy reported what had occurred in Madison less than two hours ago.

"I'll drive up tonight," Ellen broke in. She could make it in two and a half hours. It would be at least seven or eight o'clock before she could be on the road – by that time the rush hour traffic would be over. She hesitated. "Where will you be?"

"I'll be at Angie's," Kathy told her. "Come there."

Two

Her foot on the brake pedal, Kathy swore under her breath. What was the tie-up now? Then she realized the delay was caused by rubbernecking – one car had sideswiped another, though it appeared no one was hurt. A police officer directed the merging traffic – but everybody had to see what was happening, she thought in a rage motivated by anxiety.

Cars were moving again, she observed with relief. Her turn-off was just ahead. Should she have called Glenn? Marcie was his child, too. No. Marcie would prefer that she didn't. Marcie had never forgiven him for walking out that way. Five months after a 'quickie' divorce he married an eighteen-year-old cocktail waitress. Three years later he divorced her. He married Ronnie a year after his second divorce, joined her father in business and his career soared.

She'd sweated out those early years, terrified of any financial emergency. Grateful that her mother had left her the house – the monthly mortgage payments mercifully small. But any house repair was a crisis. At rare intervals Glenn would send splashy gifts for Marcie and Linda. He'd paid for Linda's college – at a state university – but told her it would be her turn when Marcie was ready for college.

Was it wrong to harbor such intense resentment for the closeness between Glenn and his second set of children? He'd never had time for Linda or Marcie. But he adored his two kids with Ronnie. They were just the ages now that Linda and Marcie had been when he walked out on them.

Was it always rotten for children when their parents divorced? The children and one partner were the casualties. The one wanting the divorce came off scot-free. Ahead of the game. At least, in many instances.

With relief Kathy approached the exit that led into Madison. She'd been born and raised here, she thought with nostalgia. Her parents had been born here. Mom and Dad had a wonderful marriage. She'd loved their house. Mom was always so pleased that she and Angie

7

and Ellen made it their hang-out all through the school years. During their freshman and sophomore high school years Leslie, too, had been part of their tight little clique. Mom had been so good to Leslie during that awful time when her mother died. All at once a protective wall jutted up in her brain. She didn't want to think about that time. Especially not now.

Dusk was settling about the town, providing a spurious air of serenity. Driving past the cemetery she remembered with fresh horror that Frank was dead. Life had seemed so beautiful for him and Marcie. His architectural office was beginning to acquire substantial clients. Marcie loved her job. In another year or two they planned to start a family.

Why did something so awful happen to Frank? He was involved in trying to set up a Senior Citizens Center in Madison. *'Because my grandmother's Senior Citizens Center was so important to her,'* he'd explained in tender recall. Frank was not close to his parents, but he'd adored his maternal grandmother, who died when he was twelve. He fought along with Marcie to stop development on the wetlands at the edge of town.

She'd been so happy to see the girls settle into stable marriages. It had become an obsession with her to know that her daughters did not repeat her failure. Let them know the joys her own mom and dad had shared. *The good marriage.*

Mom and Dad were buried in this cemetery – Dad killed by a hit-and-run driver when she was a high school senior. Their lives were turned upside down. Mom knew nothing about business. *'Kathy, Dad took care of everything. I never even had to pay a bill, write a check.'* The man Mom put in charge of the store – where she herself began to work as a saleswoman – ran the business into the ground. *'He was stealing every day of the week – and I didn't know how to stop him.'*

That was another generation of women – they lived in a different world. Yet she remembered what Angie had told her about a fight with Joe when she'd railed against Joe's ambivalence at her working: *'The trouble with you, Joe, is that you have this fantasy about a wife in a frilly apron staying home with the kids.'* Joe had said, *'Isn't that every man's fantasy?'*

In town she drove to the police precinct. Her heart pounding, she parked, headed for the entrance. Did Marcie even realize the impact of being held for murder? She must be in shock over Frank's death.

8

Frank's murder, her mind taunted. She shivered, a hand on the door. This wasn't real. It was something that happened to other people – headlining the supermarket tabloids.

In a waiting-room on the third floor she spied Angie's slightly plump figure sprawled at the end of a utilitarian wooden bench. Her pretty face reflected her anguish.

"Angie—"

Angie leapt to her feet, rushed forward, hugged her in a tight embrace.

"Kathy, they wouldn't let me see her. But the officer in charge said you'd be able to see her in a little while."

"I can't believe this." Kathy shook her head in bewilderment. "I keep thinking, 'It's a nightmare – I'll wake up and it'll all be over.'"

"She'll need a good lawyer." Angie was always the clear-headed one, Kathy thought. "I called Jeffrey Stevens at his house – he's the best criminal attorney in the county. He's standing by to talk with you."

"First I have to see Marcie. What about bail?" she asked Angie in sudden hope. "Can I arrange for that?"

"This is a murder charge," Angie said gently. "I don't know if bail will be allowed. Or when. But the lawyer will know – talk to him about it."

They waited in the dreary reception area – with detectives striding in and out of doors at the rear. Were they all involved in investigating Frank's death? Murder didn't happen often in Madison.

Angie went to the coffee machine, brought back styrofoam cups of coffee for them. At last an officer behind the front desk beckoned to Kathy.

"You can see her now." He gestured to a passing police officer. "Murphy, take Mrs Marshall to the conference room. Your daughter will be brought to you," he told Kathy.

Kathy walked into the small bleak room. A table and two chairs were the sole furnishing. A small fluorescent light fixture dangled from the ceiling. Kathy sat down. Moments later a police matron appeared with Marcie, dazed and pale.

"Oh, baby." Kathy leapt to her feet, held out her arms to Marcie.

Why didn't the matron leave them alone? Kathy railed in silence while Marcie – in her mother's arms – poured out the horror of the evening.

"I was talking to him twenty minutes earlier – and then I came downstairs to put up dinner – and he was dead." Marcie was beyond tears now, in a straitjacket of grief. "He'll never talk to me again – never hold me in his arms. What will I do with the rest of my life?"

"Darling, the first thing is to get you out of here on bail. I'm seeing a lawyer tonight. He'll want to talk to you." She tried to sound calm. Reassuring. "You're not alone."

She clung to Marcie's hands, listened while Marcie reiterated her feeling of desolation at a life without Frank. Then the matron signaled their time was up. Marcie was led away – into that area beyond where Kathy couldn't go but could visualize. She stood motionless for a moment, then hurried out to join Angie. She'd call this lawyer, talk with him as soon as possible.

At the house she delayed phoning only to exchange a warm embrace with Joe, Angie's husband, then called Jeffrey Stevens. She was relieved that he understood the urgency of the situation, instructed her to come right over to his house.

"I'll go with you," Angie offered. "We'll take my car."

Jeffrey Stevens lived in a new, exclusive suburb unfamiliar to Kathy. Angie found the house – a scaled-down version of a French Normandy chateau, set on two beautifully landscaped acres. They left the car and headed up the flower-lined flagstone path to the entrance.

"He's going to be expensive," Angie warned.

Jeffrey Stevens met them at the door, led them down a carpeted hallway to his home office. In a corner of her mind Kathy was aware of the four-drawer file cabinets that flanked one wall, the copier, the fax machine. Angie had said Stevens's practice extended into the whole county.

She and Angie sat in the chairs across from Stevens's huge leather-topped desk. He listened to her tortured explanation of what had happened, then reached for the telephone.

"Let me call downtown and see what I can learn." His tone was compassionate yet brisk.

Kathy leaned back in her chair, fighting against panic. She had to be strong, in control – for Marcie's sake. Everything about this house warned her that Steven's fees would be high – as Angie had said. Still, she had no concept of what this might be. But she would manage.

"All right, I'll be in touch," he wound up and put down the receiver. Now he turned to Kathy. "As you know, she's been brought in on murder charges. She was found standing over the body. Blood on her hands. Her husband suffered three blows to the head. The report hasn't come through yet, but they suspect the fingerprints on the murder weapon – a replica of Rodin's 'The Thinker' – will be hers." *I gave Frank that for his birthday last month.* "Next door neighbors heard them in violent argument shortly before he was murdered." The two women who'd bought three years ago, Kathy pinpointed. Grace and Tim Mitchell, on the other side, were away on vacation. And Grace and Tim were like family. They would never have made such a statement. "They'd been fighting at intervals for the past two days, the neighbors said."

"Every married couple fights sometimes," Kathy stammered. "Frank and Marcie were very much in love."

"What about getting her out on bail?" Angie asked.

"It's too early for that. She hasn't been arraigned yet. And not until she's been indicted by a grand jury can bail application be made. In murder cases it's difficult to arrange for bail – but we might be able to handle that." He appeared annoyed at Angie's presence. "Before we proceed any further, we have to discuss my fees."

"Yes." Kathy nodded. She could borrow on the house, as she'd planned to do for the new shop. Her heart pounded while she waited for him to continue.

"My fees run from two hundred and fifty to three hundred and fifty dollars an hour. If this should prove to be a lengthy case, then you'll be billed at the lower figure. I have to tell you, though, that a murder case can run in the neighborhood of two hundred and fifty thousand dollars. I have to pay for the services of private investigators, a paralegal. Each of the investigators bills me at one hundred and fifty dollars an hour, the paralegal forty dollars." He paused – not surprised, it seemed, at her shock. "You don't have to pay it all upfront," he soothed. *How can I ever pay money like that? Can Glenn come up with that?* "But I'll have to have a retainer of twenty-five thousand dollars within the next forty-eight hours, or I can't afford to schedule the time for the case." His face was impassive, his eyes opaque grey marbles.

"I'll have to talk to my bank about a loan on my house," she managed after a moment.

11

"Of course, the court will provide Marcie with a public defender if she can't afford a private defense attorney."

"I'll talk to my bank," Kathy reported, still reeling. *This is insane.* "I'll get back to you."

Kathy and Angie left the house, walked in taut silence to the car.

"I can't believe what I heard." Angie was furious. "No wonder he lives in a house like that – and drives a Jaguar." They'd seen a Mercedes and a Jaguar in the garage. "Why are my kids wasting their time studying to be teachers?" Her two daughters were both at State, pursuing degrees in education. "We'll find another lawyer – they can't all charge such insane fees!"

"You said he was the best." Kathy was striving to be realistic. "I want the best for Marcie. I'll talk to the bank about enlarging my mortgage." She'd paid off the mortgage, then borrowed to renovate before Marcie and Frank moved in. The house was almost fifty years old. It had needed a lot of work. "I'll call Glenn and tell him he's got to help." But panic was setting in again.

"Most lawyers I know just deal with real estate," Angie admitted. "But I'll ask around for somebody else."

Joe met them at the door, prodded them into the living room. There were times, Kathy understood, when Angie was embarrassed by Joe. She'd gone through college to earn a bachelor's degree that led nowhere, in truth – and six weeks after graduation had married Joe. He was a marine fresh out of the Vietnam war with a rash of medals. But he was also a construction worker – when Angie's circle of friends consisted of teachers, graduate students planning on becoming tax accountants, doctors, architects. He was a contractor now, working with his own crew. Angie recognized that he was often what she called 'kind of rough around the edges'. But Joe had heart, Kathy always told herself – and tonight it shone from him.

"Tell me everything that happened," he ordered with the same compassion Kathy remembered from the traumatic period of her divorce.

He showed no surprise at the figures Jeffrey Stevens had quoted.

"It's shitty," he conceded. "Sometimes I think the courts exist just to make lawyers rich. Nobody's going to be cheap." He ignored Angie's glare of reproach. "But Angie, what about Scott Lazarus? He's a whole different breed."

"Scott's a real estate lawyer," Angie reminded.

"Who's Scott Lazarus?" Kathy gazed from Angie to Joe.

"He was a criminal lawyer tied up with some major firm in New York. He handled some of their most important cases, was a big wheel in the field. Then about five years ago he got sick of the whole rat race, wanted a more relaxed lifestyle. He walked out of the firm – his wife divorced him – and he came here to practice less nerve-wracking law. Mostly real estate, wills, personal injury. Angie sold him his house. He's one of the sweetest guys we've ever known."

"I didn't know he was a criminal lawyer." Angie was ambivalent.

"He never talks about it. Only when I was putting that new roof on his house, we got to yakking about life in Manhattan and all – and he kind of opened up about some famous cases he'd handled. Angie, you're close with Scott. Ask him about handling Marcie's case."

"It's too late now," Angie hedged, glancing at her watch.

"Call him," Joe insisted. "The worst he can do is say 'no'. Call him!" Joe crossed the room for the cordless phone, brought it to Angie.

Tense and anxious, Kathy sat at the edge of her chair while Angie talked with Scott Lazarus.

"I realize you don't practice criminal law anymore, Scott – but I've known Marcie all her life. Her mother and I have been best friends since we were little kids. I took her over to talk with Jeff Stevens – he figures his fee could run to two hundred and fifty thousand dollars. Marcie's family isn't in that league—" Angie listened now to Scott's response. "Sure, Scott – I understand. I'll talk with you tomorrow."

Kathy's eyes clung to Angie as she put down the phone.

"What did he say?" Joe demanded.

"He said it's been over five years since he handled a criminal case – and that at this time of night his brain kind of shuts down. He'll talk to me about it in the morning. He said he'd call around eight."

13

Three

E llen glanced at the clock on the dashboard. Damn, it was past eleven – she'd expected to be driving into town an hour ago. But she'd waited to have dinner with the kids and Phil. Dinner was their special time together as a family. No TV, no stereo, no CD player. Family time.

Why couldn't she ever wash away the guilt that she was a working mother? The kids weren't deprived because she pursued a career. That's what paid for their private schools, fancy summer vacations, the two months in Europe last year.

Again she felt a deluge of unease. *Was* her marriage in crisis? Was she too wrapped up in her work to notice? How could Phil talk so casually about spending four or five weeks at Montauk when he knew she had to be in the city? Kathy always said, '*At least two of us made good marriages.*' Meaning Angie and her.

This whole situation was unbelievable. *Frank dead – and Marcie accused of his murder.* Tears filled her eyes as she remembered their wedding – a small, quiet celebration, so unlike Linda's glitzy affair. The love that they radiated had been beautiful. Kathy had always been anxious about Marcie – so sensitive, so emotionally fragile. But then Frank came into Marcie's life – and she'd stopped worrying.

Kathy said Marcie's parents-in-law had never liked her. They'd been shocked when Marcie and Frank lived together for three months before they were married, blamed Marcie – Kathy said – because Frank wouldn't accept a job with a prestigious Manhattan architectural firm that they'd arranged. Marcie had wanted to live in Madison, wanted Frank to establish himself there – and he'd gone along with that.

She remembered the elder Loebs at Frank and Marcie's wedding. They'd been cold, stand-offish – aliens present under duress. Frank's father was retired now – he and his wife divided their time between a condo in Manhattan and another in Florida. His sister was married and lived with her husband and two children in Westchester. Frank's sister and her husband hadn't bothered to come to the wedding – though as close family they'd been invited.

With relief Ellen approached the cut-off that led into town. She hadn't truly lived in Madison since she went off to college, but it still occupied a special place in her heart. The growing-up years were forever there in your subconscious.

She drove past the immaculate, summer-garbed cemetery. Nostalgia closed in about her. Her parents were buried there, like Kathy's and Angie's. She was glad that they'd lived to see Ted and Claire. For a few years the kids had four doting grandparents. Now there was just Phil's mother – but she was a wonderful woman. A marvellous, loving grandmother, a great mother-in-law. Mom's words when they were out at Montauk over the Memorial Day weekend tickertaped across her mind now: '*Phil seems so terribly tense, Ellen.*' Had Mom been trying to warn her that her marriage was in trouble?

Kathy sat at the round oak table in the dining area and forced herself to eat the mushroom omelet that Angie had just made for her. Who would want to murder Frank? she railed in silence. Frank and Marcie weren't on drugs or alcohol. They weren't ruthless, overly ambitious professionals. They were *good*.

Joe brought three mugs of coffee to the table.

"There's a car pulling up outside." Joe put down the mugs and moved quickly from the kitchen. "It's probably Ellen."

Moments later Kathy and Angie heard Joe greeting Ellen at the front door. Then Ellen was in the kitchen, rushing to embrace first Kathy, then Angie.

"Kathy, I know things are awful now – but they'll work out," Ellen said with determined optimism.

The three women huddled around the table while Joe went to pour a mug of coffee for Ellen. Haltingly Kathy brought Ellen up to date, explained that they were praying that Scott Lazarus would agree to handle Marcie's defense – and at a fee that was manageable.

"If there's a problem about money," Ellen said, "I can raise a good chunk on the condo. We paid off the mortgage last year – it's free and clear. And what about bail?"

"We won't know for a while if it'll be allowed," Kathy told her. But this was a murder case, her mind taunted. Bail was not often granted.

"We'll see this through together." Angie managed a shaky smile. "Kathy, make Marcie understand that. We're there for her, too." They sat drinking endless cups of coffee until Joe insisted everyone go to bed. Kathy lay sleepless in the small bedroom that was Angie's younger daughter's room. Both daughters were working for the summer at a resort hotel up at Lake George. Kathy was haunted by visions of Marcie, locked in a cell, grieving for Frank with no one to comfort her.

Lying in the darkness of the bedroom, she tried to plot the course ahead. In a corner of her mind she remembered other crises where the three of them had come together. Involuntarily she allowed her mind to dart back thirty-one years – to when their close little clique had extended to include Leslie. The other time murder had entered their lives.

That was the experience that had knit them together forever. She and Ellen and Angie. Leslie's father had moved away with her not long after her mother's death. Still on the police records as an unsolved murder. But don't think about that time.

She slept at intervals, awoke to daylight – grey, but distinctly morning – filtering between the drapes at the bedroom windows. She turned to inspect the clock on the night table. It was a few minutes past six. She heard muted voices down the hall. Joe would have to be at a construction site by eight a.m., she realized – and last night he'd said that was a forty-five minute drive from Madison.

She forced herself to remain in bed. Don't disturb Angie and Joe's usual morning routine. Not until she heard Joe's car pull out of the driveway, was aware that Ellen and Angie were talking in muted voices in the kitchen, did she arise and prepare for the day.

By ten minutes to eight the three women sat in the dining area and made a pretense of eating breakfast. The phone rang. A jarring, discordant sound they'd been waiting to hear. Angie picked it up on the second ring.

"Hello—" Her voice was breathless with anxiety.

Kathy uttered a silent prayer. Please God, let Scott Lazarus take on Marcie's defense. Joe said he was tops as a criminal lawyer. He'd hated the pressure, but he was among the best. And Angie was sure his fee would not be a shocker.

"Yeah, we can do that, Scott." Angie managed a hopeful smile for Kathy. "Sure, we'll be there." She put down the phone. "He wants us to meet him at his office at nine thirty. That'll give him time to talk with the District Attorney's office before we arrive."

"Is he willing to defend Marcie?" Kathy asked, hopeful but uncertain.

"He wants to talk to you," Angie told her. "But I think he'll do it."

At nine thirty-five a.m. Kathy and Angie sat with Scott Lazarus in his small, utilitarian inner office. Ellen waited in the reception room. The three women had been shaken by the headline of the *Madison Daily News* that had leapt up at them from the receptionist's desk: 'Architect Murdered, Beautiful Young Wife Held.'

"We won't be interrupted," Scott assured Kathy and Angie. "I told Pam to hold all calls."

On sight Kathy liked him. A soft-spoken, gentle man with silver-streaked dark hair and compassionate brown eyes, he still managed to exude an aura of strength. Handsome in a quiet fashion. Kathy could envision him winning over juries. But he still hadn't said he would handle the case.

"Scott, I think you've met Marcie and Frank," Angie said in sudden recollection. "At that meeting last month to protest a variance on the wetlands at the edge of town. Frank was the young architect who spoke so eloquently against allowing development out there."

Scott nodded in recall. "I thought his name rang a bell."

"Will you handle the case?" Angie pursued.

He nodded. "I may be a little rusty, but we'll put up a good fight."

"About your fee," Kathy began uneasily.

"We'll talk about that later. It won't be a rough problem." Kathy knew Angie had told him about their encounter with Jeffrey Stevens. "Right now we have a lot of work to start in motion. I spoke with the District Attorney's office. I'll go over to check out the—" He hesitated, almost apologetic. "To check out the crime scene. I'll talk with Marcie later this morning. I'll try for a quick arraignment." His voice softened. "She'll be held for a grand jury hearing. On what the District Attorney told me, I'm afraid she'll be indicted. The man who walked in and found Marcie standing over the body is an attorney. He's claiming he had an appointment to meet Frank to discuss a divorce action."

Kathy stared at him in disbelief.

17

"That's a lie!" she lashed back. "Frank and Marcie never talked divorce – they had a wonderful marriage. He's lying!"

"I'll put an investigator on him. We'll find out why he's lying," Scott promised and pondered for a moment. "It could be some misunderstanding. Being a divorce attorney, perhaps Matthews took it for granted Frank wished to discuss a divorce. I'll talk with him."

"You'll want a retainer," Kathy interrupted. Let him use as many investigators as he needed! "How much should that be?"

"Fifteen hundred will be fine," he told her. "I'm waiting to hear what the fingerprint people come up with – but let's not be surprised to learn that Marcie's fingerprints are on the murder weapon. It was an item in the den – she'd probably touched it somewhere in the course of the day."

"What about bail?" Angie asked.

"We have to wait until she appears before the grand jury. Then I'll prepare bail application. I don't know that it'll be granted." He confirmed Kathy's fears. "But we'll start immediately to work for it. We'll need letters – a bunch of them – from well-respected people in town, who'll attest to her good character. Who're convinced she won't flee from trial."

"That'll be a snap," Angie assured him. "Marcie was born and raised here – she's very well liked. A dedicated social worker."

"About life insurance," Scott began and paused. "I have to ask this because the prosecution is sure to explore this subject. Did Frank carry a heavy policy naming Marcie as beneficiary?"

"They carried no life insurance on each other," Kathy said. She understood – he wanted to rule that out as a possible motive. "I'd tried to persuade them to buy insurance while they're young and the premiums are low – but Marcie had a thing about it. No life insurance, she insisted."

"I'll see that she's held in a private cell," Scott told Kathy. "Not in a holding pen."

"Oh God . . ." Kathy shivered. She hadn't realized Marcie might be sharing space with others – hookers, drug addicts, petty thieves.

"She'll be all right," Angie insisted. "Marcie is a survivor."

"I'll try to have her brought before an arraignment judge quickly," Scott repeated. "Hopefully we can make it today. Fight for an early grand jury hearing. And once she's indicted, we'll go after bail."

Four

Marcie – small, appearing almost fragile – sat at the table in the tiny lawyer-client conference room and struggled to comprehend what the lawyer her mother had hired had just said to her. Short, auburn hair framed a face that was a replica of her mother's – her eyes the same emerald green. Her mind was fuzzy from grief and lack of sleep.

"But that's insane," she whispered. "Frank and I never talked about divorce. Frank had no appointment with a lawyer to talk about that—"

"You know this Eric Matthews?"

"Yes. We've been working with him on a fundraising campaign. To build a senior citizens center here in town. And on a committee with him to fight re-zoning of the wetlands tract." *Why is he lying this way?*

"We'll go before the arraignment judge as soon as possible. I'll ask that you be released – that's routine – but the judge won't agree. Then we have to wait for a grand jury hearing. I'll have a lot of questions, Marcie – but we'll let those wait for a couple of days. Oh – do you have a cat?"

"No. Frank's allergic." She closed her eyes in pain. "Frank *was* allergic—"

"I thought I heard meowing."

"The women next door have two cats . . . When can I see my mother?" she asked after a moment.

"I'll make arrangements about visitation privileges," Scott promised. "She'll be here tomorrow."

"Tell her not to call my father," Marcie said with sudden defiance. "I don't want to see him."

A matron took Marcie back to her cell. She sat on the hard bench across from the bunk and allowed her mind to wander back to the sunny afternoon – just over a year ago – when she and Frank were married in the small garden behind the house. The only guests had been Frank's mother and father and Linda and David – and Angie

19

and Joe Santini and Ellen and Phil Marshall because they were like family. And Grace and Tim Mitchell next door – 'Aunt Grace' and 'Uncle Tim' to her and Linda.

Mom felt so uncomfortable that I wouldn't let Dad know I was being married. I didn't want him at my wedding.

Frank's parents hadn't even stayed for the wedding dinner. As soon as the ceremony was over, they'd climbed into their white Cadillac and headed back for New York. She closed her eyes, hearing Frank's voice.

'Mom and Dad wonder sometimes if there was a switch at the hospital, and they got somebody else's baby. I wouldn't play the game the way my sister did. Mom said I have a bad attitude – I got it from my "West Side liberal friends" at my fancy private school.'

Their wedding had been a simple affair – the way she and Frank wanted it. Linda insisted on the big scene – with bridesmaids and flower girl and a mob of people watching. But now Frank was dead. His parents would come here and claim his body for burial. *But they can't take away the love Frank and I shared. That will live forever.*

The small, drab room that housed Madison's night court was filled to capacity. Anxious family and friends of those awaiting arraignment – some exuding nervous bravado – shifted in their seats. One hand clutching the other, Kathy sat at the edge of her seat – Angie and Joe at her left, Ellen on her right. At intervals Scott Lazarus turned to offer a reassuring smile. Still, Kathy thought in anguish, he was sure Marcie would be held for a grand jury hearing.

Scott Lazarus had prepared them for the usual night's catch of hookers, drug dealers, petty thieves. The judge wore an aura of bored martyrdom. But tension was high among the onlookers.

Kathy stiffened to attention. Scott was on his feet, preparing to present Marcie's case. *Poor baby, she looks so scared – and I can't do anything to help her.*

Scott was eloquent in his insistence that Marcie was a loving young wife who had walked in only moments after her husband was murdered. Kathy noted the pair of local reporters were avidly scribbling into their notebooks. This wasn't a routine night court arraignment. This was a prospective murder trial – a rare occurrence in Madison.

As was happening so often in the past few days, Kathy's mind darted back through the years to the death of Leslie's mother thirty-one years ago. For just that one year Leslie was part of their inner circle. *Is what's happened to Marcie some weird retribution for what we did all those years ago? Will something awful happen to the three of us?*

Kathy flinched while the ADA from the District Attorney's office enumerated the charges.

"Marcie Loeb was discovered hanging over her husband's body. Local attorney Eric Matthews admits he was there to discuss divorce proceedings. The two women residents of the house next door report hearing 'violent verbal battles' between Marcie and Frank Loeb in the course of the two days before the murder."

As Scott had warned, the judge ordered Marcie held for a grand jury investigation. Kathy exchanged an anxious glance with Marcie before she was led away.

"Scott will be with us in a minute," Joe said, glancing at his watch. Kathy remembered his alarm clock went off before six a.m.

"Everything went about the way we expected." Scott seemed determinedly casual as he joined them. He hesitated now. "Why don't we go to the restaurant across the street for coffee?"

"You two go for coffee," Angie said. "You'll drive Kathy home, Scott?"

"Sure thing," Scott agreed. The other three headed for Angie's car. Scott prodded Kathy across the street.

"Let me bring you up to date on what's happening," he said. "First of all, starting tomorrow you'll be able to see Marcie once each day until the grand jury hearing."

"Oh, that's good," Kathy said with relief.

"In a small town like this a lawyer in good standing can cut through red tape." His smile was reassuring. "I won't lie to you, Kathy. The grand jury is sure to indict Marcie. Her fingerprints are on the murder weapon. I know – they could have gotten there earlier. But fingerprints are there – and there was blood on Marcie's hands. And next door neighbors heard her fighting with Frank. That's enough evidence for the grand jury to hold her for trial."

"Why haven't the police looked for other suspects?" Kathy flared. "The real murderer is out there somewhere!"

"They have all this evidence." His voice was gentle. Compassionate. "They think they have enough to go to trial."

Kathy was silent until they were seated at a table in the sparsely populated restaurant and a waitress had taken their order. "Was Marcie able to be helpful?"

"She's in no state to be questioned. That'll have to wait a few days." He hesitated. "But she told me to tell you she doesn't want to see her father."

"Glenn wasn't the ideal father – he had no time for Marcie and Linda." Only for his second set of children. "Marcie was only five when Glenn demanded a divorce – but she was badly hurt. Both the girls were – though Linda snapped out of it after a while." Sometimes she worried that she was losing Linda to Glenn – especially after the splashy wedding he'd provided. She couldn't have handled that. "Oh, I'll have to call Linda tonight, tell her what was happening." No need for Linda to rush to Madison – not in her seventh month of pregnancy.

"I regretted that my wife and I never had kids – but she didn't want them." Pain in his eyes now. "Our marriage was dead before the end of the first year. Long before our divorce, we lived separate lives. When I decided to give up my New York practice to move here and settle into real estate law – with a huge drop in income – she wanted out."

"Marcie and Frank had such a wonderful marriage – that makes this situation all the more tragic." *I want to hold Marcie in my arms, try to comfort her. I know she's hurting.*

"If Marcie says anything to you about the fights she was having with Frank, please tell me," Scott urged. "I must know to defend her properly."

"Yes. I will—" *But I don't believe Marcie and Frank were fighting.*

Scott had said he hadn't pleaded a criminal case in over five years – but that wasn't a skill that disappeared in that short period. Was it? *Should I have tried to bargain with Jeffrey Stevens? Angie said he's the best criminal lawyer in the county.*

"Is there some chance of bail?" Kathy interrupted his assessment of the local district attorney. "Marcie's father is very well off – there's a possibility he'd come forward with collateral for bail." *I can't ask Linda and David – they have a huge mortgage on the house, loans on the two cars plus college loans.* "I have to call him and tell him what's happening." She couldn't allow him to read about Frank's death and Marcie's arrest in some tabloid. Even small town murder cases were hitting the national rags. "I'll do that tomorrow morning."

Churning with impatience and discomfort, Kathy watched the clock. No doubt in her mind that Glenn would not arrive at his office before ten a.m. She waited until fifteen minutes past to reach for the phone to call him. She dreaded this encounter – they hadn't spoken since Linda's wedding three years ago. *But I have to be in touch with Glenn – Marcie needs all the help she can get.*

Her heart pounding, she waited for a response to Glenn's private line, gearing herself for what must be said. She was startled when a feminine voice came to her – Wilma, his administrative secretary, she assumed. They'd spoken on rare occasions in the six years that Wilma had been with Glenn.

"Oh, he's in Europe," Wilma said. "He went with Ronnie and the kids. He'll be back Monday evening." She sounded uncomfortable. An ex-wife was an intrusion.

"Do you have a copy of his itinerary? This is important." *Why do I always get so uptight just talking with somebody in Glenn's office?*

"Sorry, he didn't leave any. He said he wanted to get away from everything for ten days."

"Thank you, Wilma."

Kathy put down the phone in a flurry of frustration, went out to the kitchen to make herself a cup of coffee. Angie was at her office. Ellen had gone over to the high school to talk to some of Marcie's former teachers about character reference letters. Angie would talk with Betty Williams – Marcie's boss at the agency – about a letter.

"Kathy?" Ellen called from the foyer. "I'm back."

"I'm out in the kitchen. Come have coffee with me."

Ellen strode into the kitchen with an air of triumph. "I have promises of a bunch of letters. Everybody wants to be helpful."

"I called Glenn." Kathy grimaced. "He's in Europe with his wife and their kids. He won't be home till Monday evening."

"Does Scott have a date for the grand jury hearing?"

"He's working on it. Oh, and he arranged for me to get into the house for some of Marcie's things."

"I'll go with you." Ellen said. *She realizes how painful this will be for me.* "Let's do it today. I have to drive back to the city in the

23

morning. My deadline. But I'll be up again in a few days." She hesitated. "What about Frank's funeral?"

Kathy exhaled a long, painful sigh. "Scott called to tell me. Frank will be buried this afternoon in a cemetery in Westchester County. In the Jewish faith burial should be within forty-eight hours. And Marcie and I can't be there . . ."

"I'm taking the four of us out to dinner tonight," Ellen said firmly. "None of us are in the mood to cook."

"You'll go with me to the house to pick up some things for Marcie?"

"Why don't we go now? Will I need a pass?"

"I have a pass for two." Kathy stared into space. "I ask myself, will Marcie ever be able to live there again?"

"She saw a lot of happiness in that house," Ellen reminded tenderly. The house where both Kathy and Marcie had grown up.

"That house has seen so much—"

"Remember that awful night when Leslie came to us there . . . ?" Ellen's voice faded away for a moment. "Sometimes I think back, and I ask myself, 'How did we dare behave the way we did?'"

"Every once in a while I think of Leslie and wonder what happened to her. We all exchanged letters for a while—"

Ellen nodded. "For a while."

"But then we were caught up in other things," Kathy recalled. "And maybe we wanted to forget."

In her small office in the District Attorney's suite, Lee Ramsey grasped the telephone and listened with a blend of disbelief and triumph while District Attorney Bob Miller delivered his message in his usual meandering fashion. She knew she had acquired her job as ADA because there had been loud accusations of sexism in the department. But for the fourteen months she'd been here she'd been given the lowliest of assignments.

"I've planned this fishing trip for months," Miller wound up. "Chuck's all tied up with that drug case. You handle the Frank Loeb murder from here on," he repeated with an air of indulgence. "At least, for now," he amended.

"Why for now?" she asked with calculated calm. "If I pick it up now, why can't I carry on?" Meaning, there could be another outburst of sexism charges if she was yanked off the case.

"Okay," he said after a moment. "You handle it. It's a snap. We've got a witness who walked in moments after she killed him. But don't screw up."

"I'll get a conviction," she promised. It couldn't be a tough case, she considered. If it were, Bob Miller would cancel his fishing trip. He gloried in winning convictions where the going was rough. But if the climate should change, she'd go for the jugular. She couldn't afford to lose her first homicide.

"I'll send the file with Deirdre," Miller wound up. "You're in charge."

Lee leaned back in her chair, her mind rushing ahead. Madison saw a fair amount of domestic violence – but rarely a murder. And this was a young, highly respectable, middle-class couple involved. A real attention-grabber. For an ambitious ADA the case was a plum.

She was ever conscious that she had begun law school at a time when others her age were already well established in their field. It hadn't been easy to begin law studies at thirty-nine – but that was when she'd known where she meant to go with her life. After the ugly divorce.

She glanced up with a start at the light knock on the door. Without waiting for a response, the secretary she shared with Miller and Chuck – the other ADA – pulled the door open.

"Here's the file on the Loeb case," Deirdre said, dropping it on the desk. Ten years her senior and on the job for thirty years, Deirdre harbored a perilously veiled resentment at Lee's placement in the office hierarchy. "And the boss said to tell you Frank Loeb's parents are here. He wants you to see them. They're real pissed," she warned with a malicious smile.

Lee tensed, sighed. "All right, send them in." She knew little about the case except for what she'd read in this morning's newspapers. Bob Miller communicated with his ADAs only when they were to be personally involved. She'd have to play it by ear.

She managed a swift glance at the slight contents of the file before Deirdre opened the door again. She rose from behind her desk as Frieda and Henry Loeb – both with deep Florida tans and resort town garb – walked into the office. Subconsciously she noted that their faces showed more rage than grief.

"I'm sorry about your son," Lee said, and Frieda Loeb bristled. "Please sit down."

The Loebs ignored her invitation. "We want that woman convicted!" Mrs Loeb said grimly. "She murdered our son!"

"She hasn't been indicted yet," Lee pointed out. "But we do expect an indictment."

"When?" Henry Loeb demanded.

"She'll be heard by the grand jury in a few days – they have to make the indictment," Lee emphasized. "But we have sufficient evidence to guarantee this."

"We're going home now to bury our son. But let us give you the real motive for his murder." Frieda Loeb planted both palms on Lee's desk. "We *know* why she killed him."

"It's for the insurance money," Henry Loeb pursued. "Frank carried a two hundred and fifty thousand dollar life insurance policy – with her as beneficiary. She killed our son for the insurance money."

Five

Kathy and Ellen heard a car pull up out front. It was twenty minutes past five. Angie was arriving home, Kathy surmised. Moments later Angie joined them in the kitchen.

"Why do we always wind up in the kitchen?" she asked with a wry smile. "If there's more coffee, I'll have a cup, too."

"Coming right up." Ellen rose to her feet, crossed to the coffee maker. "I'm taking us out to dinner tonight. When will Joe be home?"

"In about half an hour," Angie said. "Give him twenty minutes to get cleaned up."

"Do we need to make reservations?" All at once Ellen was uncertain.

"Honey, you've been away from Madison too long," Angie joshed. "You make reservations in Madison only at the fancy places and only on weekends."

How could she think about going out to dinner, Kathy thought in fresh anguish, when Marcie was confined in a jail cell? What was she thinking? How was she feeling?

"Do you mind if I call Montauk?" Ellen asked and Angie clucked in reproach. "I should talk to the kids and Phil."

"You said they're going off on some jazzy tours," Angie recalled. "The kids, I mean."

"Phil may stay up there while they're away," Ellen said after a moment. "I can't go out with him. You know me – I'm finishing up the new book. I can't uproot myself now."

Kathy sensed unease in Ellen. "Ellie, are you and Phil having problems?" she asked softly.

"Maybe." Ellen was contemplative. "I guess it's not an unfamiliar situation. He's upset that I'm doing well career-wise – and he's tied down to his teaching job and not writing."

"He hasn't written in years," Angie pointed out. "Except for five or six short stories."

"That's not entirely true—" Ellen seemed to be searching for

27

words. "He writes and tears up. He won't accept doing anything short of a blockbuster. Let's face it, publishing is becoming a business where middle-of-the-road books go nowhere. But I can't stop writing," she said defensively. "I'm doing well – and we've grown accustomed to a good lifestyle. There's college coming up for the kids. I don't want to stop," she admitted. "But why should my career put a crimp in our marriage?"

"A lot of women have asked themselves that," Angie said wryly.

"I'm scared," Ellen confessed. "I hear of marriages breaking up after long years – but I'd never thought it might be something that could happen to Phil and me."

"My going into business didn't always set well with Joe." Angie seemed to be driving herself to confide in Ellen and Kathy. Kathy was startled. As close as they were, Angie had never given them a hint of this. "Even though I waited until both kids were in school. I don't think he really accepted it until he realized it was my working that would make it possible for us to buy the house. Joe's warm and sweet and always there when I need him," she continued conscientiously, "but there were times in those early years when he resented having to wait for dinner sometimes because I got stuck at the office – or having to face up to the fact there were weekends in the rush seasons when I was showing houses and we'd have to settle for take-out food. When he was growing up, his mother was always there in the house to make sure meals were right on time and the laundry done, the beds made up, everything immaculate. His mother never went to work a day in her life once she was married – but then his parents never owned their own house. Not to this day."

"I don't think it bothered Phil until my income started to soar," Ellen conceded. "I think he feels guilty that I'm doing better career-wise then he is."

"It's the macho thing," Angie said. "We've moved in on their territory – and it hurts."

"It terrifies me to see Phil behaving this way." Ellen gestured in bewilderment.

"Ellie, fight to keep your marriage together," Kathy urged. "You have a major investment in it. The most important investment in your lifetime."

There was no way she could have held her own marriage together – Kathy fought guilt with reality. It had made her sick to feel her love turning to rage. Even now – all these years later – she couldn't relinquish resentment towards Glenn for what he had destroyed. He wasn't ready for marriage and parenthood during their years together. So he escaped, she thought bitterly, until he *was* ready. Leaving her to cope.

But what hurt now was the way Linda seemed to be forgiving him for all the years of neglect. Linda might have forgotten but Marcie remembered all the Sundays when they'd waited – eager, in their prettiest dresses – for a father who called at the last minute with excuses about another 'pressing appointment' or who simply forgot this was his day for visitation rights. Linda ignored the memory of crushed feelings when her father had forgot her birthday year after year because Glenn had put up a substantial chunk of the money required for her splashy wedding.

Ellen said between them they'd manage Marcie's bail money without Glenn. *Please God, let Scott Lazarus get Marcie out on bail.*

In the den of their pleasant three-bedroom, one and a half bath, barnyard red clapboard ranch, Fiona Matthews waited for her husband to finish his phone call. She understood the voice on the other end of the line was that of someone in the District Attorney's office. The call seemed to be about Frank Loeb's murder, she thought painfully. Eric never handled criminal cases – only divorces and real estate closings.

"Yes, I'll rearrange my morning appointments so I can be at your office by ten sharp." His tone was conciliatory in contrast to his exasperated expression.

"What was that about?" Fiona asked when he'd put down the receiver. Part of her mind was attuned to the sounds from the play-pen set up in the living-room, where their seventeen-month-old daughter played with their three-year-old son.

"I have to testify that I found Marcie Loeb hovering over her husband's body. I called the police. I know you like her – but I can't lie, Fiona."

Loud shrieks from the living-room invaded the den.

"I'd better get the kids to bed." Fiona hurried towards the door. "You aren't going back to the office again tonight, are you?"

"Not to the office," he said – and she sensed his reproach that she questioned the long hours he devoted to his work, the trips out of town. "One of my groups is meeting tonight."

Fiona knew his attendance at civic organizations and his bowling team brought in business. That was the way small town lawyers picked up clients, Eric said.

"I'll put dinner up as soon as we get the kids to bed."

Fiona's face softened. Eric was terrific about helping with the kids. But she and the kids saw so little of him. He kept lecturing her about how nobody could 'make it big' on a forty-hour work week.

She was so proud of him – of the kind of money he earned. Of course, most of his clients were working people. They couldn't afford the fancy lawyers in town. They didn't even have checking accounts – they paid in cash instalments. So they weren't rich and important. They paid their bills.

Not until the children were in bed and she and Eric were at dinner did Fiona broach the question that had plagued at her since Eric came home with news of Frank Loeb's murder.

"Eric, why did Frank Loeb ask you to come to his house to talk about a divorce? Why didn't he just come to your office like other people?"

"He said he was anxious to keep it from becoming an ugly situation. Every time he tried to talk to Marcie about divorce, she got hysterical. She'd never come to the office." He paused, exhaled a troubled sigh. "If I hadn't been caught at the office – if I'd been on time – he might be alive today."

"Eric, don't blame yourself." She rushed to console him. Even after six years of marriage she was awed by the fact that he had married her. She hadn't even finished high school. When her father died suddenly the beginning of her junior year, she'd quit school to help her mother support the family. "But I can't believe Marcie killed Frank. She's such a wonderful person—"

"Not everybody likes her," Eric refuted. "The folks over in Cypress Woods are up in arms about the way she's fighting to set up that house for juvenile delinquents – you know, kids who're into drugs and booze. Nobody wants that element in their neighborhood." He glanced at his watch, began to eat with a swiftness that told her he was anxious to be on his way.

"Eric, you're not going to that meeting of the Madison Militia, are you?" she asked in sudden alarm. She knew they met every other Wednesday night. Some of the things she heard about them scared her.

"God, no!" He grimaced. "I gave it a shot because I like to know what's going on in this town."

Her friend Josie – who lived next door – told her how the Madison Militia believed that the US government was being controlled by the United Nations – which meant to take over the world. They said Americans had to arm themselves to be ready for the day when UN tanks rolled over the United States to establish a 'one-world order'. She shivered. They sounded like such creeps.

Hunched over her computer, Ellen was all at once conscious of hunger. She glanced at her watch. It was past eight o'clock! Stop work, have dinner, phone Montauk, she ordered herself – then get back to the computer. She always felt so driven these last three or four weeks on a book. But this was an especially grueling session – anxious about her relationship with Phil, worrying about Marcie's situation.

She left her small, air-conditioned office and headed for the kitchen. There was part of a barbecued chicken and a salad in the refrigerator. That with tea would be dinner. She transferred food to a plate, settled herself at the table in the dining area.

The phone rang. She went to respond. Between six p.m. and nine p.m. most callers seemed to be somebody trying to sell something or to solicit funds for a philanthropic drive. Phil said she ought to let the answering machine pick up, but she never did.

"Hello—" Her voice was faintly sharp in anticipation. She listened to the opening spiel of the telemarketer. "I'm not interested, thank you." She heard the caller continue to talk as she put down the phone. Oh, she hated these nocturnal invasions!

She ate with unexpected gusto, stacked the dishes in the dishwasher to run later, and went into the living-room to make her two nightly calls – one to Montauk, to talk to the kids, Phil, and Mom, and the other to Kathy. She'd work over the weekend, she plotted. Monday the kids would come in with Phil. Tuesday morning Claire would leave for Canada with her group. Tuesday evening she and Phil would see Ted off for Madrid with his group at JFK.

Kathy said Marcie would go before the grand jury next Wednesday. That's when Scott Lazarus would petition for bail. Kathy would need her up there.

Julie Ellis

She dialed the Montauk number and talked briefly to Mom – who lovingly scolded her for not coming up to the house.

"Ellen, I can't bear the thought of you sweltering in the city when it's glorious out here," she lamented.

"I'll come out later in the summer," Ellen promised. "We're in a ghastly hot spell right now – not quite record-breaking but close. I stay holed up in the air-conditioned apartment, so I survive."

Now she spoke with Ted and Claire – both bubbling over with excitement about their summer tours but relishing their week at the beach.

"Okay, let me speak to Dad," she ordered at last. Why did she instantly tense when she was on a one-to-one basis with Phil? How could sixteen years of marriage go down the drain this way? *How do I stop it?*

They exchanged the usual bits of news, Ellen ever conscious that Phil had chosen to stay out at Montauk rather than in Manhattan with her.

"I'll drive up to Madison for a couple of days after we see the kids off," Ellen said. He'd made the point of saying he'd go back to Montauk. "Marcie's lawyer will try to get her out on bail. Kathy and Angie have collected a huge batch of letters saying how responsible she is and so on. The bail will be high, he warned. I told Kathy we'd put up the condo as security if she needed that. Okay?"

"Why ask me?" he said drily. "It's your money."

"It's our money." She struggled not to show her anger. *Why does he act this way?* "But I figured you'd want to help."

"Mom wants to talk to you again." He sounded relieved to break away. "Hold on—"

Phil walked out of the house and onto the deck. He stood at the railing and stared at the pounding surf. Remembering the first time he'd brought Ellen out here to meet Mom and Dad. In those days Montauk was their 'second home'. Ellen was working as a publicist for his publisher. He'd been nervous about that first meeting – but they'd hit it off so well. Mom and Dad had understood when he brought Ellen out for a weekend that he was serious about her.

That had been such a good time, he thought nostalgically. He was thirty-two and his first book had just hit the *New York Times'* bestseller list. He gave up his teaching job to concentrate on writing. And three months after he brought Ellen out here, they

32

were married. Right there on the beach – with family and close friends in attendance. *What went wrong with me after that?*

Ellen and Mom said he'd run into a writer's block because he was too anxious about following up the first book with a blockbuster. For three years he wrote and tore up the pages. But after Ted was born – and he and Ellen were so enthralled at being parents – he'd settled down and finished another book. It had been offbeat. His agent said publishers wouldn't know how to categorize it. When he'd finally got an offer, he knew he'd have to go back to teaching. How could he support his family on a three thousand dollar advance?

'You'll write anyway,' Ellen had insisted. *'On weekends and nights. Other writers do it – so can you.'*

But he couldn't do it. His output all these years consisted of half a dozen short stories. *Ellen* did it. She'd stayed home with the kids until Ted was five and Claire three. But right away she'd found a market with her first paperback. It hadn't paid much – but it was a beginning.

God, he felt rotten when Ellen worked so hard. She was compulsive about it – it was an addiction with her to see their income soar. With college tuition rising insanely she was anxious to see enough salted away to see Ted and Claire through college. On his salary they couldn't afford this apartment, the car, all the 'extras'. He was a parasite, he taunted himself – enjoying the good life on Ellen's earnings.

Lee had been at her desk for only a few minutes when Deirdre – her usual undertone of arrogance giving way to reluctant respect – came into her office to announce that there was a collection of newspaper reporters, local TV and radio people waiting to talk to her.

"The Loebs spread the word around before they left town that they're demanding a conviction," Deirdre explained. "You want to see them?"

"Sure." Lee's smile was casual. "They want news, we'll give it to them." Bob Miller wasn't bright sometimes – he had a way of antagonizing the press. It was important to be friendly with them. If she handled the press right, she could earn a lot of great publicity. They liked an ADA who would joke with them, give them more than dull facts. It was their job to hold readers and audiences – she'd liven up the scene for them, she promised herself with a flurry of exhilaration.

33

She walked out of her office with a confident smile, knowing she exuded glamour in an area where this was rare. Instantly she was flooded with questions. She blinked when a TV camera went into action.

"Okay, give me a break," she chided good-humoredly. "We're sure the grand jury will bring in an indictment when we present the facts. We'll win a conviction when we go to trial. The evidence against Marcie Loeb is indisputable." She paused, gazing about at the eager faces that surrounded her. Play this scene for everything it was worth. "Fact one: We have a responsible witness – a local attorney – who found Marcie Loeb hovering over her husband's body only moments after he was murdered. Fact two: her fingerprints are on the murder weapon. Fact three: neighbours heard her fighting with the victim for two days prior to the murder. Fact four: her husband was talking with an attorney about filing for a divorce. A divorce Marcie Loeb didn't want. And fact five—" She paused for dramatic emphasis. "Frank Loeb carried a two hundred and fifty thousand dollar life insurance policy – naming his wife as beneficiary."

Kathy heard the phone ringing as she stepped out of the shower. She hurried to pick it up, but it had stopped ringing. The blinking answering machine told her a message was waiting. She pushed the playback button.

"This is Scott Lazarus calling Kathy Marshall. Please give me a buzz as soon as you can. We need to talk."

Her heart pounding, Kathy dialed Scott's office. His secretary put her through to him.

"Hi, it's Kathy Marshall." *What's wrong? He said, 'We need to talk.'*

"Have you seen Marcie yet today?" he asked.

"No, I usually see her at three in the afternoon." *He's not bowing out of the case, is he?* Was he worrying about his fee? Joe said fifteen hundred wouldn't go far with a private investigator. "Did you want to see me right away? I can be there in ten minutes."

"That'll be fine." His voice was reassuring, though she'd been unnerved when she'd heard his message. "I need your help in getting through to Marcie."

"I'll be right there."

Driving into town she dissected their brief exchange on the phone. She understood Scott's problem. Marcie was so distraught about

Frank's death that she couldn't think beyond that, poor baby. The three times she'd seen Marcie, they'd just talked about Frank and how she'd loved him and how she was to survive now that he was gone. She barely seemed to realize that she was being held on suspicion of his murder.

At Scott's office in the converted white clapboard cottage right off Main Street his clearly sympathetic secretary ushered her right into his private office. He greeted her with a calmness that was comforting.

"Kathy, something has come up that I wanted you to hear from me before you read it in the newspapers or see it on a newscast. The DA's office just alerted me. Frank's parents went to the District Attorney's office and reported that Frank carried a two hundred and fifty thousand dollar life insurance policy in Marcie's name."

Kathy gaped at Scott in shock. He'd asked her about that – at their first meeting. "Marcie knew nothing about it! She had a strange obsession against their taking out life insurance. It was as though she didn't want to believe there might be a time when she'd be without Frank. Marcie didn't know!" But it was devastating evidence against her, Kathy realized. "It was like Frank to want to be sure Marcie was provided for if something happened to him."

"That's not good for our case. That's why I want you to help me get through to Marcie. I can't communicate with her." A touch of frustration in his voice now. "We need some answers. I know – she's still reeling from that awful moment when she walked in and found him that way. But we can't let too many more days pass before we start digging."

"What do you want me to do?" Kathy's throat was tight with anxiety. She hadn't felt this kind of horror since Glenn announced he was walking out on his family. "How can I help?"

"Make her understand that if I'm to defend her, she'll have to come back to reality, try her best to respond to my questions."

"What about Eric Matthews?" Kathy clutched at what plagued at her night and day. "Why did he lie about Frank's asking for a divorce?"

"I have an investigator on that. He's come up with nothing useful so far. Matthews has built up a good divorce practice in the six years he's been here. He—"

"But Frank wasn't seeing him about a divorce. No way!"

"I need to know what enemies Frank may have had in town. That's important."

"He and Marcie ruffled some feathers," Kathy conceded. "They've both been fighting to raise funds to build the Senior Center which some people here in town complain will raise taxes. And they've been passionate about the need to stop an outfit called Paradise Estates from building a multi-million dollar development on a seven hundred acre wetlands tract."

"I know there've been ugly words about the wetlands." Scott's smile was sympathetic. "I've offered to provide *pro bono* services for the preservation group."

"I can't understand why anybody in town is in favor of developing the wetlands. Ignoring the terrible environmental impact—"

"It all comes down to one thing. Money. Peter James convinced a segment of people that his Paradise Estates will bring a lot of jobs into town. That there'll be a large influx of fresh taxes and—"

"But haven't they seen what happened in a hundred other towns? Sure, we'll see more taxes coming in from those new houses and condos and shops. But what about the money the town will have to spend on roads, providing all the extra services? And with their own shopping mall, the residents there won't be spending money in the local stores!"

"We know those in favor of Paradise Estates building on the wetlands don't like Marcie." Scott was reaching for some source of rage they had not yet tapped. "I understand there's a group angry at her because of her efforts to set up a home for juvenile delinquents—"

"The two women next door carried on like mad," Kathy recalled. "They screamed about property values going way down."

"I want you to think about anybody else who might have bad feelings towards Frank and Marcie. Tell me whatever comes into your mind." Scott hesitated. "It may be necessary for us to find Frank's murderer in order to clear Marcie."

She nodded in mute comprehension. The evidence against Marcie was ominous. *All a matter of misinterpretation.*

"I'll do anything that's necessary," she told Scott. "Whatever you say." She struggled to clear her head. "I can raise money on my house – possibly my business—"

"We won't worry about money at this point. Except for Marcie's bail – if that can be arranged."

"Scott, get her out on bail, please. If she's home with me, she'll be able to unwind to some degree. To come up with facts that could be important."

"I've done some talking. But it'll be high," he warned yet again.

"Still, you're not afraid of her running off somewhere. The bail money won't be forfeited. Anyone who helps won't be concerned about that."

"Marcie won't run out."

"For starters," Scott pursued, "we must know who here in Madison was furious enough at Frank to kill him. Marcie can clue us in on that. You talk to her first. I'll follow up."

Alone in his office – remembering that he had a real estate closing in two hours – Scott went over in his mind each bit of evidence against Marcie. He hadn't told Kathy, but his personal probing had brought out that Marcie had been in therapy as a small child. To the District Attorney – who would surely track this down – that would mark her as possibly unstable. Another strike against her.

It was difficult to conceive of lovely, vulnerable Marcie committing an act of violence – yet as a lawyer he knew it was naïve to make such a judgement. His instincts told him Marcie was innocent – but were his instincts guided by how he felt about Kathy? He was unnerved by the way he was drawn to her. He'd thought once the coolness set in between Myra and himself – long before the divorce – that he'd never feel this way about another woman.

He was glad he'd had the courage to walk out on that high-powered practice. He'd been sick to death of the twelve-hour days, the weekends riddled with work or the professional socializing he loathed. All Myra had cared about were the fat fees he earned, his over-sized bonuses. But damn, he was burnt out before he was forty. What did he have out of his life? Not even a family. Myra never wanted kids – '*Who needs to be tied down like that?*' She didn't even want a puppy.

He often thought of his brother out in San Francisco – tied up in the same rat race as he, with two great kids he rarely saw. Why didn't George ever try to break out of the craziness? All of a sudden *he* had realized this was his last chance at a life that held some pleasure for him. So he was earning a quarter of what he'd brought home each week back in New York. He'd found time to be a human being.

Angie said Kathy had married very young, to a man who thrived on the career rat race. Their divorce had been nasty – she'd raised her daughters alone, had given up a safe, secure job to move out into her own business. Kathy Marshall was a woman who would understand his way of thinking.

It would break her heart if Marcie was convicted. How the hell was he going to keep that from happening? *The evidence is damning.*

Six

Kathy settled herself in the car again, disturbed by what Scott had told her about Frank's life insurance. Frank meant to protect Marcie – but he was providing the DA with a strong motive for murder. She sat behind the wheel debating about her next move. She couldn't see Marcie until three o'clock. Stop by Angie's office. Maybe Angie would be free for lunch.

She drove to Angie's office, parked and headed inside. She waved a greeting to the woman at the reception desk, then walked to where Angie stood pondering a map on the wall. "I thought you might be free for lunch." She glanced at her watch. "I guess it's early."

"That's good." Angie reached into a desk drawer for her purse. "Dottie, I'm running out for an early lunch. Okay?"

"Sure thing . . ." Dottie seemed to hesitate now. "I know everything's going to work out well for Marcie," she told Kathy. "Everybody in town is rooting for her."

Not everybody, Kathy's mind taunted. When she'd stopped for gas – at a station where they'd known her for years – her reception this morning had been cold. The *Madison Daily News* and the *Evening Journal* were nasty in their insinuations.

"Let's go over to Mulligan's," Angie suggested when they were outside. Mulligan's was a popular restaurant right across the road. "It won't be busy this early. We'll nab ourselves a rear booth where we can talk in privacy." Her eyes were searching Kathy's now. "You look uptight. Something new come up?"

"And not good." Kathy sighed. While they made their way across the road, she reported on the brief meeting with Scott.

As Angie had anticipated, Mulligan's was sparsely occupied at eleven forty a.m. They headed for a rear booth, focused for a few moments on the menu while a waitress hovered at their table. No one she knew, Kathy noted with relief, remembering the hostile air she'd encountered at the gas station.

She shivered, recalling the newscast she'd heard on the car radio en route to town. The newscaster had made Frank's murder sound so sordid – Marcie so guilty. What had happened to the old concept – innocent until proven guilty?

"Are you cold?" Angie was solicitous. "Restaurants always set the air-conditioning for men in jackets."

"No, I'm fine."

"Ellen called this morning. She'll be up here late Tuesday evening – after she sees Ted off for Spain." "Glenn will be back from Europe on Monday night. I checked with his office again," Kathy said. "I know Marcie doesn't want me to call him, but I have to do that. We may need him as backup when it comes to bail." If bail could be arranged.

"Between us – you and me and Ellen – we'll raise Marcie's bail," Angie said confidently, yet again. "Stop worrying about that."

At ten minutes before three Kathy was in the small conference room where she was allowed to see Marcie each afternoon. She couldn't erase from her mind even for this short, precious period the knowledge that the DA's office was building an alarming case against Marcie.

Then Marcie was brought into the room, and all she could think about was the anguish tormenting her baby. For a few moments she held her close, then prodded Marcie into a chair.

"Darling, I know how hard this is for you – but we have to talk about how to clear you of these insane charges. Scott says you're to go before the grand jury on Wednesday. That's when he'll apply for bail – but he needs your help, Marcie. He's determined to discover who killed Frank—"

"Please, God – yes!"

"But you have to help, Marcie."

"How?" Marcie whispered.

"Tell us who you believe wanted Frank dead."

"I *know*!" Marcie blazed with sudden strength. "Last night it came to me. I should have known right away. We'd been fighting about it for days. Ever since Frank told me he was planning to infiltrate their group. I was terrified something like this would happen."

"What group?" Kathy's voice was sharp, her mind in high gear. "The Madison Militia?" she pounced. The disgruntled group in town who noisily proclaimed 'We love our country but hate our government'. Most people ignored them.

"No." Marcie shook her head. "Frank said the Madison Militia were just a bunch of wackos. They're out in the open – they meet

40

every other week in a private room at The Rendezvous. Everybody knows who they are. This is a secret – paranoid – group. Like the Madison Militia they hate non-whites, Jews, Catholics and homosexuals. But they go beyond that. Frank says they claim the UN is trying to take over the world. They're arming themselves – right here in Madison – for civil war."

"In Madison?" They read about this happening in other small towns. But here in their own town?

"Frank had proof. He was terribly upset, scared what might happen. Somebody in town had got the wrong idea about Frank. You know his deadpan sense of humor. He said something and someone misinterpreted it. He was invited to come to a meeting. He told me they have a secret camp on some farm about eight miles out of town. They train there every weekend – as though they were in marine boot camp – and carry out secret maneuvers. Frank pretended to be interested in joining. He wanted to expose them. They must have found out. That's who killed Frank! A member of the True Patriots!"

"Do you know the names of some of the members?" Kathy prodded. *Make people understand this isn't an open-and-shut case of domestic violence. Something evil – beyond their comprehension.* "Who did Frank mention?"

"I wouldn't listen to him." Marcie was desolate. "I said I didn't want to know."

"Who introduced him to the group?"

Marcie shook her head. "I don't know. I was so upset when he told me he meant to infiltrate them that I just screamed at him. I was terrified. All I know is that they spend every weekend and some evenings in rugged, marine-style training. Like we've read about, Mom! Frank said they have enough weapons to outfit a small army. They must have realized Frank meant to expose them – and one of their members killed him!"

Kathy drove back to Angie's house. She was impatient to tell Scott about Marcie's suspicions. *This was what he wanted.* She parked in the driveway and rushed into the house. She dialed Scott's number. The phone rang five times before Scott's secretary picked up.

"I'm sorry," Pam apologized. "I was just finishing up a long-distance call on our other line."

"Is Scott there?" Kathy asked.

"He hasn't got back from his closing yet. It's running long. May I take a message?"

"Thanks, I'll call back," Kathy told her.

Thank God, the heat wave had broken. No need to turn on the air-conditioning. She knew – though Angie and Joe were careful not to point this out – that they were frugal about its use.

Before he left for work this morning, Joe had been out watering their small garden. She ought to go over to their house, water the flowers and shrubbery. Had the police released it yet? Was it still a 'crime scene'?

She'd ask Scott later about getting permission for the watering. How strange, she reproached herself, to worry about watering flowers when Marcie was behind bars.

Inside the house Kathy fought against a surge of claustrophobia. It was weird to have idle time on her hands this way. She was too uptight to read, daytime TV was a stranger to her. But idle time – a rare commodity in her life – ought to be put to productive use. *What?*

She'd make dinner tonight, she thought in sudden decision. Angie had a pasta machine. Prepare homemade pasta for dinner. Throw together a from-scratch tomato sauce. At intervals, Angie said, she baked a half-dozen loaves of Italian bread. *'They're always there in the freezer to spruce up a fast dinner.'* Kathy checked the freezer unit. Two breads there. Pasta with salad, a steamed vegetable and – for dessert – the lemon sorbet Angie kept in the freezer because it was low-calorie and she was always fighting weight. That would be a decent dinner.

She glanced at the kitchen clock. She'd wait half an hour, then call Scott again. She brought out the pasta machine, semolina, eggs, poured a little water into a measuring cup. Now she focused on mixing the ingredients, kneading. She cautioned herself to let the dough sit – covered with a dish towel – for ten minutes. Then she'd run it through the machine, hang the spaghetti on the drying rack.

But despite the activity she couldn't blot out of her mind the incriminating evidence the District Attorney's office was piling up against Marcie. Scott said the ADA who was handling the case was a woman. Was that an advantage for Marcie or the contrary?

Thirty minutes after her first attempt she paused to phone Scott's office again. He still hadn't returned from his closing.

"Shall I have him call you?" Pam asked. Kathy felt her compassion.

"Would you, please? He has the number, but let me give it to you again."

It was slightly past five thirty – the pasta drying on the rack, the sauce simmering, the bread defrosting – when Scott called.

"Scott, Marcie opened up to me – she has strong suspicions about who was out to kill Frank—" Her words tumbled over one another in her rush to pass on this first real lead. "I—"

"Why don't you meet me for an early dinner?" Scott said. "A working dinner," he amplified. "I had no time for lunch – I'm famished. Somewhere quiet, where we can talk."

"Fine," Kathy accepted. From the kitchen window she saw Angie's car pulling into the driveway beside her own. "Where shall I meet you?"

Angie came directly to the kitchen, sniffing appreciatively. "I don't believe it! You're making that marvelous tomato sauce of yours that Joe loves. He puts up with mine. And homemade pasta . . ." She gazed with a rapt expression at the rows of pasta drying on the racks.

"Dinner's ready to throw together whenever Joe arrives." Now Kathy told Angie about her visit with Marcie – and that she was meeting Scott for dinner to discuss this.

"We've all read about those paranoid organizations." Angie shuddered in distaste. "I read somewhere that after the Oklahoma City bombing, the numbers soared. But I never thought they might be right here in Madison."

"Not maybe – they're here. One of them probably killed Frank." *And we have to find out which one in order to clear Marcie.*

"I'll ask Joe if he's heard anything about them." Angie was somber. "He knows somebody in the Madison Militia. He never tries to argue with the guy – he thinks they're all kooks. You know that weathered shingle house at the corner of Cypress and Maple?"

"Yes." Kathy nodded.

"They're part of that scene. They came here three years ago from some place in the northwest. He lost his job in the lumber industry when all the trouble broke out about the timber barons stripping the national forests. His wife's uncle gave him a job in his hardware store here in town. They 'love their country but hate the government'.

Julie Ellis

Every holiday they bring out their flag. They have two kids – taught at home. There was a big stink when they refused to register their kids for school. When they were gung-ho to go to court over it, the Board of Ed backed down. Why give them a showcase? They claimed they didn't want their kids mixing with 'bad elements', meaning minority kids," Angie drawled with a mixture of contempt and anger. "African-Americans and Hispanics."

"And Jews," Kathy added grimly. It was rare that anti-Semitism showed itself in Madison – but there had been moments when she knew that to some people in town Jews were regarded as the enemy. "The KKK may be in abeyance, but a lot of those creeps have picked up their creed. Neo-Nazis, white supremacists – they're part of the picture." She checked her watch. "I'd better run. Scott will be at the restaurant in a few minutes."

"I'll tell Joe to keep his ears to the ground," Angie said. "He won't be happy to know terrorists are popping up in Madison. You know my flag-waving husband."

Walking into the spacious, multi-glassed restaurant where she was to meet Scott, Kathy understood why he had chosen this one. The room was sparsely occupied – this wasn't a dining spot that offered 'early-bird dinners'. The tab would be high. Only two tables other than the one where Scott sat waiting were occupied. Impatient to tell Scott what she'd learned, she followed the hostess – annoyed by her languid pace.

"Have you been waiting long?" she asked Scott when she was seated. He'd said he was famished, she remembered.

"Just a couple of minutes." He appeared casual, yet she sensed his eagerness to hear what she had to report. "Would you like a drink?"

"Thanks, no."

For a few moments they concentrated on the menu, gave the waiter their orders. When they were alone, Scott leaned forward.

"What did Marcie tell you?"

In rising excitement Kathy repeated her encounter with Marcie in full detail. Her own distress that Frank had put himself in such danger – and with such tragic results – was mirrored in Scott as she spoke. "She's convinced somebody from the—" She paused to retrieve the organization's name from her memory. "From the True Patriots murdered Frank. She wasn't talking about the Madison Militia – though we both think they're off the wall. This is a far-right

44

extremist group arming for violence – in secret. They're a tinderbox set to go off at the slightest spark. Somebody among the True Patriots must have realized that Frank was the last person in this world to be a fellow traveler – and was terrified they'd be exposed."

"I had no idea anything so extreme existed in Madison." Scott flinched as he considered this. "Sure, everybody in town knows about the Madison Militia – most people ridicule them. They're malcontents, sure the American way of life is being threatened. They hate gun control, taxes, the UN. To them our constitutional rights are being threatened. In some states they broadcast their sick messages through public-access TV. The estimate of their numbers ranges from five million to twelve million. But you're talking about those who've crossed the line – the extremist fringe."

"It's scary. Back in the sixties we talked out – in the civil rights marches and the anti-Vietnam demonstrations – but except for small revolutionary groups we didn't want to overthrow our government."

"We have the finest government in the world," Scott said softly. "Let no one forget that."

"But some people have."

Scott sighed. "So much has come out into the open since the Oklahoma City bombing. But you don't expect to discover terrorists in your own town."

"I don't understand all this talk about the government violating the Second Amendment rights," Kathy confessed. "You know, all the carrying on by the National Rifle Association that the Second Amendment guarantees their 'right to bear arms'."

"They *twist* the Second Amendment. It plainly states that 'a well regulated militia, being necessary to the security of a free state, the right of the people to bear arms shall not be infringed.' There's nothing said about *private* ownership of guns – not one way or the other. It refers to the bearing of arms as the right of a government-regulated militia. These extremist groups are not under government supervision – they're illegal."

"How do we track down the True Patriots?" Kathy was unnerved by the need for this.

"It won't be easy—"

"From what Frank told Marcie, they're hoarding guns and explosives, training members for military attack." Kathy shivered. "It's unreal."

"We must nail down members. Come up with evidence of what they're doing. Not just to clear Marcie. The town needs to know what's happening here."

Scott had Frank's kind of ethics, Kathy thought, clutching at this in admiration. But a moment later she was fearful.

"Scott, be careful. If they murdered Frank – and Marcie's sure they did – they'd kill again."

His face was taut. "I came here to Madison with the conviction it was a quiet, pleasant, small town – far from the violence of New York. We have to fight to make it that way again."

They grew silent at the approach of their waiter with water goblets, a basket of rolls. Scott reached hungrily into the basket.

"Forgive me." His smile was apologetic. "I'm famished."

"I'll join you." Kathy reached for a small hot roll.

"There are times when I come home from the office, and I hesitate to turn on the TV news because I dread hearing about the latest violence in the world."

"I remember when I was a kid and President Kennedy was urging people to build bomb shelters against a possible attack by the Soviet Union. My father and mother thought that was the joke of the western world. How could something like that happen here?"

"I'll stall for the latest date possible for Marcie's trial. Buy us as much time as possible," Scott said.

"Tell me about the grand jury hearing." Kathy tried to be realistic. "And about bail—" Call Glenn on Monday night, she reminded herself yet again. In case they'd need more money for Marcie's bail.

"Grand jury hearings are not open to the public," he began, and she was taken aback by this knowledge. "I'm preparing hard for the hearing, but I won't be able to get the case dismissed. She'll be held for trial. Right away I'll ask for bail."

"I've spoken with the rabbi at our synagogue," Kathy told him. "He's willing to be responsible for Marcie's court appearance – if bail is granted."

"It'll be a rough summer," he said gently, "but we'll all be working together."

They retreated from serious conversation at the approach of their waiter. Scott talked about how he enjoyed the lack of pressure as a Madison attorney.

"I lived with such madness in New York." His smile was wry. "Seventy hour weeks, tension at every turn. Even socializing was arranged with an eye on the career. My wife – my ex-wife," he emphasized, "reveled in that excitement. She could play the game. For me it was torture."

"And Marcie and I have dragged you back into the long hours and tension at every turn." Kathy's eyes reflected her gratitude.

"This is a one-time deal. I'll probably never handle another criminal case. But when Angie told me what Stevens was throwing at you, I knew I had to step in to help. Angie and Joe are special people – I knew her friends would be that, too."

"I can't tell you how grateful we are." She felt embraced in his compassion. Comforted. Glenn had run from troubled circumstances. Since she was eighteen, she'd had no one to lean on but herself.

"I'll have a lot of questions for Marcie. Do you feel she's ready to answer them?"

"I think so. More than anything else, she wants Frank's killer caught." She was conscious of an electric exchange between Scott and herself and was disconcerted by this. They talked about Marcie, but another, unspoken communication was reaching out between them. It was the drama of the situation, she told herself. The way some women fell in love for a little while with their obstetricians. "I suspect it's more important to her than her own freedom."

"She's going to beat this rap, Kathy," he vowed. "Hold on to that thought."

Seven

K athy paced about the deserted house on this late Saturday morning. Angie was at her office – this was one of the busiest days of the week for her. Joe had driven to a neighboring town to give an estimate on a job. At this moment – a glance at the clock told her – Scott would be sitting down with Marcie in the small conference room at police headquarters. He wouldn't push Marcie too hard, she reassured herself. And Marcie understood it was urgent for her to be open with Scott.

Joe kept telling her not to read the local newspapers – '*They blow everything out of proportion.*' Not to listen to the local radio news or watch the local TV news. But this morning's *Madison Daily News* carried an interview with the ADA that turned her sick. That woman was so certain she could win a conviction. Lee Ramsey's words to the press were etched on her brain.

The phone rang. She rushed to answer. It was too soon for Scott to be calling, she thought. He'd planned a long session with Marcie this morning.

"Hello." She was tense with alarm.

"I'd like to speak to Kathy Marshall, the mother of Marcie Loeb." A brisk male voice.

"This is she." Instantly she was wary. Some creep after a sensational news story for a TV tabloid? That would kill Glenn!

"I'm Gerald Nash, attorney for Frieda and Henry Loeb," he said. "My clients wish to take charge of their son's estate. His residence, his car, his—"

"Hold it right there!" Kathy blazed. "I own the house where my daughter and son-in-law lived! And just remember, my daughter is innocent until proved guilty – and that's not going to happen."

"You can prove the house belongs to you?" He was reluctant to relinquish this claim.

"I can prove it," Kathy assured him. "And if you have any further questions, direct them to our attorney, Scott Lazarus."

She slammed down the phone. She was cold, trembling. Frank's parents were impatient to get their greedy hands on the insurance he'd left to Marcie – that was what this was all about. How could such creeps have had such a fine son? A throwback to the grandmother he loved, she thought, fighting tears.

What did that ridiculous lawyer say his name was? Nash, she pounced in recall. What was his first name? Never mind, phone Scott and report this to him. But not for another hour – he was with Marcie now.

She'd told Nash to contact Scott – that Scott was her lawyer. He was, wasn't he? She waited impatiently for time to pass, then with a burst of energy she dialed his office. Belatedly she realized this was a summer Saturday. He probably wouldn't be going into the office today. But already he'd picked up.

"Scott Lazarus, good morning." Brisk and friendly.

"Scott, it's Kathy. I had a crazy phone call a little while ago . . ." In a rush to share she told him about Nash's objective.

"Slimy bastard. I'll take care of him. If anybody else approaches you, refer them to me. You did right," he approved.

"Was Marcie able to come up with anything helpful this morning?"

"It's difficult for her." Scott showed no anxiety. "But she's filling in the picture for me."

They talked another few moments, then Scott had to take another call. Kathy's mind lurched back through time to the other murder that had touched her life. To the horror of the death of Leslie's mother. The *Madison Daily News* had a field day with that, too. Leslie and her father moved away. The police listed it as an unsolved murder. She and Angie and Ellen never talked about it after a while – they needed to erase it from their memory.

Unnerved by the call from the Loebs' attorney, unhappy that the meeting between Marcie and Scott had not been more productive, she sought for some activity. She went out to the kitchen, put up a kettle of water for tea. Call Linda, she decided – making a mental note to take care of Angie's phone bill this month.

She dialed Linda's number. Almost immediately Linda responded.

"Mom, we can't believe Frank's dead," Linda said in anguish. "David thought we ought to have flown out for his funeral. Oh God, how awful this must be for Marcie—"

"We wouldn't have been welcome at Frank's funeral," Kathy told her. "But we've got a great lawyer for Marcie." She tried for a note of optimism.

"Dad still doesn't know?" Linda asked.

"I won't be able to talk to him until late Monday night," Kathy reminded. *Why do I always get so uptight when Linda talks about Glenn?*

"It's going to be an awful shock to him," Linda said.

"It was an awful shock to me – and to Marcie," Kathy shot back. Glenn wouldn't be happy if the murder spilled over into the New York City newspapers. It would tarnish his image to be the father of a woman accused of murder.

"I keep thinking I should be there with you and Marcie, but David is afraid for me to fly when I'm this far along."

"David's right." Kathy was firm. "You have to take good care of my grandchild." She felt a surge of love for the baby Linda carried. "And Marcie understands."

"Dad will come right up," Linda predicted. "He'll want to talk to Marcie's lawyer and—"

"Dad will find some business deal that keeps him in New York," Kathy interrupted and immediately regretted her show of hostility. "He'll phone."

"Mom, you're doing it again!" Linda's voice was strident. "Won't you ever forget the divorce?"

"I'm tired, Linda. And upset. I don't tend to be diplomatic at such times." The tea kettle began to whistle. "My tea kettle's going berserk. I'll call you tomorrow, Linda."

She dreaded the possibility of coming face to face with Glenn again – with his young wife and his young second family. Of course Glenn would come up here, she conceded. Marcie *was* his daughter – though he so often appeared to forget this. All Linda remembered now – forgetting all the hurts and disappointments through the years – was that Glenn had put up much of the money for her big fancy wedding.

She'd been happy when Linda and David became engaged. They were so in love, so right for each other. And theirs would be a fine marriage, she'd promised herself. Her daughters would not make the mistake *she* had made.

Then Linda's wedding plans kind of exploded. The guest list grew larger each day. A reception after the synagogue ceremony would be inadequate, Linda proclaimed. A sit-down dinner for three hundred

50

– *'counting David's side'*. Linda talked to a wedding consultant to handle the myriad details of invitations, flowers, music, photographs. *'Mom, you don't have time for this. You're so busy with the shop.'*

She'd been horrified when the costs exploded well into five figures. She'd borrowed on the house to open the shop. She was just beginning to bring that loan down. How could she take on something like this? David's parents were giving him and Linda money towards a down payment on a house. They couldn't be expected to help. Linda had been distraught when she'd suggested a less expensive affair.

"Mom, all my life I've dreamt of a big wedding," Linda wailed. "With a flower girl and a ring-bearer and six bridesmaids and a maid of honor. It'll be the most important moment in my life!"

Hating herself for having to do this, she approached Glenn. He'd tried to wiggle out. She'd told him this would make up for all the misery he'd dished out to his daughters through the years. And he'd finally come through. He and Linda spent more time together in those weeks before the wedding than in Linda's whole life, she'd thought with an unnerving fear that she was losing her older daughter to her ex-husband.

It was Linda who suggested that her little half-brother and half-sister be part of the wedding party. All at once she'd felt herself an outsider, Kathy recalled with pain. The cost of the wedding soared – her $5000 contribution seemed minuscule. Now it was Glenn who was being consulted about everything. As maid of honor, Marcie kept her updated on such matters as the rehearsal dinner – to which the mother of the bride was not invited. The father and stepmother were present.

Through it all, Kathy remembered, she and Glenn had battled.

"Look, I'm paying through the nose for this bloody affair," he'd shouted only days before the wedding. "Ronnie's her stepmother – she should walk at least half-way to the *chupah* with me and Linda. You and I will go half-way," he said grudgingly. "Then you and Ronnie switch." It was traditional in a Jewish wedding for the mother and father of the bride to conduct her to the *chupah* – the improvized altar.

"This is crazy," Linda sobbed. "I'm not going to walk between two people who hate each other. Dad'll walk with me. Just Dad alone."

She'd been heartbroken. Utterly crushed. This was a renunciation of her role as mother. She was not to be a part of the wedding party

– on the occasion Linda considered the most important moment of her life.

Marcie had been furious. She'd refused to attend the wedding, abdicated her cherished role as maid of honor. To friends and family Marcie had 'come down with a virus'. She'd blessed Angie and Ellen for being in constant attendance for the forty-eight hours before the wedding. They understood what she was feeling.

Linda had looked beautiful and serene – though she was furious at Marcie's reaction. Glenn's parents had been their usual obnoxious selves. She'd willed herself to be polite because that was the way she had been raised, she told herself. But what had gone wrong in the way she'd raised Linda that her own daughter could be so insensitive?

Angie and Ellen had tried to smooth over the situation.

"Kathy, if it were a Protestant or Catholic wedding, the mother of the bride wouldn't walk her daughter to the altar," Ellen repeated Angie's reminder. "That doesn't lessen her role of mother." But tears of compassion had shone in Ellen's eyes.

"It's a Jewish wedding," Kathy said, "and it's the mother's place to be at her daughter's side."

The wedding was over, Kathy admonished herself. *Forget it.* But now Glenn's younger daughter was in need of help. He felt strong resentment towards Marcie – but under the circumstances he knew people would expect him to rally to her side. It was important to Glenn to look good in the eyes of his peers.

Like Marcie, she didn't want to come face to face with Glenn. She hadn't seen him since Linda's wedding. But there was a chance he might be needed to help with clearing Marcie. And while Scott was being so wonderful about his fees, he would expect payment in time. Jeffrey Stevens had talked about $150-an-hour investigators – and instinct warned her there would be many hours involved in tracking down Frank's murderer. *To prove Marcie's innocence, we have to unmask the real killer.*

Kathy was touched by the friends who came to Angie's house to express their support for Marcie. Their outpourings of affection for Marcie brought tears to her eyes at intervals. The good people in this town understood that Marcie couldn't be guilty.

On Sunday morning Joe made breakfast for the three of them, tried hard to pretend all was right with their world. He drew Kathy into a lengthy discussion about her cherished shop, her plans for its future.

How could she think about the future of the shop, she taunted herself, when Marcie's life hung in the balance?

"Oh, I invited Scott to have dinner with us tonight," Angie told Kathy. "Joe knows some of the guys in that stupid Madison Militia. I thought he and Scott ought to sit down and talk about it."

"Good." Kathy struggled for a show of optimism. "Thank God for Scott." So quickly he'd become an important part of her life.

Joe glanced at the kitchen clock, turned to Angie. "Honey, we ought to be leaving for church real soon."

"I'll throw the dishes in the dishwasher," Kathy said. "You two run along."

People in Madison were strong on church attendance, Kathy remembered. On Sundays there was a quiet air of serenity draped about the town. Glenn used to make cracks about the guys who rushed to church and a few hours later – after too many beers – 'beat the hell out of their wives'. Even as a little girl she was aware of the special Sunday atmosphere in town – where families went together to their respective churches. Sometimes she was sure the reason Angie and Joe remained close despite the major differences between them was because the church was such a strong influence in their lives.

She was often flooded with guilt because she never seriously recognized her Jewishness except on the High Holidays, Hanukkah and Passover. She was an American who happened to be Jewish. Still – in a special corner of her mind – she stored her father's tormented story of coming face to face with the horrors of Dachau – the concentration camp his company had liberated.

'Most of us had seen three years of fighting – we thought we were prepared for anything. But what we saw when we liberated Dachau was hell on earth. On the highway approaching the camp we saw railroad cars off to one side. A curious soldier opened one car. It was packed with dead bodies – naked, emaciated, beaten. The scent of death was everywhere. We marched into the huge camp – the size was staggering. We saw five-feet-high stacks of naked bodies. The central crematory with two large furnaces. Hordes of liberated prisoners – half-starved, lice-bitten, typhus-infected – rushed to us in hysterical gratitude. What we thought was the sound of wind we soon realized was that of cheering men – though where they got the strength to cheer we couldn't imagine. Thirty-two thousand still clinging to life.'

Julie Ellis

Memorial Day was always such a somber occasion when she was a little girl, Kathy remembered. Dad would talk about buddies who'd died in the war or who lived half-lives in veterans' hospitals. Mom remembered classmates, neighbors who'd given their lives for their country. Dad said that was the last war this country fought for real ideals. Sometimes he'd tease Mom about the only reason he wasn't going to fight with Israel was because of Mom and her. He said that seeing Dachau and knowing Israel's struggles to survive had taught him to realize his Jewish heritage. As a child she went to Sunday school at the synagogue – as had Marcie and Linda. It was time, she told herself, to become truly involved in synagogue activities. Bless Rabbi Ginsburg for offering to be responsible for Marcie's appearance if bail was granted. *Please God, let that happen.*

In the late afternoon Ellen called.

"I'll be working all weekend," Ellen said. "I'm actually ahead of schedule. I'll see you late Tuesday evening."

"How're the kids?" Kathy asked.

"Oh, so excited about their trips. I'm the one that's nervous. Claire's only twelve – it's scary to think of her chasing around Canada on a bus tour. But her best friend is going – and one of the teachers from her school is among the counselors."

"She'll have a ball," Kathy predicted. "And you'll be just a phone call away."

"Ted's the youngest in his group, but his two buddies will be with him. And he was so eager for this trip." Ellen sighed. "We try so hard to be modern mothers – but it's not always easy."

"I think it's great you can afford to give them these advantages," Kathy said. "Glenn's new set of kids will be going off to fancy camps – young as they are – for the month of August. Linda keeps me posted – not that I'm interested." Glenn had cried poverty when she'd pleaded with him to contribute to camp funds for Linda and Marcie when they were younger. Kathy hesitated. "How's Phil?"

"Out at Montauk. He'll be there until the kids return." Ellen's voice was strained. "I wish I could get us back on course – but it's not happening."

They talked for a few minutes longer, until Ellen ordered herself back to work. It disturbed Kathy that Ellen's marriage – the truly perfect marriage of the three of theirs – was rocky.

*   *   *

54

With the heat wave broken Kathy suggested that they have dinner on the screened-in porch Joe had added to the house two years ago. She sat there now under orders from Angie and Joe to relax while they focused on preparing a festive meal. She was startled by her anticipation of Scott's presence at dinner tonight. It was because he was so wonderful about stepping in as Marcie's attorney, she told herself. Ellen had recognized his name – '*Oh, sure, Scott Lazarus is top notch. I haven't heard about him for a while, but he's handled some major cases. Marcie's in good hands.*'

Scott wouldn't have much to report yet, she warned herself. He'd been on the case less than a week. The urgent matter of the moment was Marcie's release on bail. Plus tracking down the True Patriot membership – and the member who killed Frank.

Scott's car was pulling up into the driveway. She hurried out to greet him. All at once her heart was pounding. *Why am I feeling this way?*

"Hi." In a polo shirt and slacks – clutching a package – Scott strode towards her with a charismatic smile. "I brought a bottle to go with dinner. That's all right, isn't it?" All at once he seemed anxious – as though, she thought, he might seem crass.

"Of course." How sensitive he was. "We're eating on the screened porch since the weather's so lovely. The scent of Angie's roses just fills the area."

"Mine are gone." His smile was wry. "Dessert for the deer who come in from the woods behind the property."

Kathy was relieved that Angie and Joe immediately came out to greet Scott. She was unnerved by the unfamiliar emotions that surfaced in her in his presence. She was forty-six years old – two months short of becoming a grandmother. *Why am I feeling like twenty and on the verge of falling wildly in love? No room in my life for that.*

It seemed so natural, Kathy thought – the way the four of them congregated in the kitchen. The two men occupied with opening the wine, she and Angie transferring platters of food to the table on the porch. But they were together this way to delve into the existence of the True Patriots.

It was Joe who – midway through dinner – introduced the topic that had brought them together this evening.

"The guys in the Madison Militia are kind of uncomfortable talking about it these days," he told the others.

"But ever since the bombing in Oklahoma City," Scott picked up, "membership in paramilitary groups has soared, the newspapers tell us. It's a fine line between the ones who make a lot of noise and the lunatic fringe teetering on violence." He turned to Kathy. "Eric Matthews admits he was a member of the Madison Militia for a short time. He didn't stay with the group."

"People clam up when you talk about them because they're scared," Joe said. "But after a few beers guys open up. Let's see what I can come up with."

"What about Eric Matthews?" Kathy turned to Scott. "Have you talked with him yet?"

"I interviewed him and his wife." Scott seemed uncomfortable she thought. "His wife worships Marcie. She kept talking about how Marcie saved her friend's marriage. Matthews offered to tell the police he could have misunderstood Frank's reason for calling him to the house, but that would be construed as an effort to clear Marcie. He's upset at having introduced a motive. Lee Ramsey – that's the assistant DA – is sure to subpoena him. He won't be any help to us on the witness stand."

It came down to one way of clearing Marcie, Kathy conceded. They must find Frank's killer – and the odds of doing that were terrifying.

Eight

E llen was at her computer at eight a.m. this sultry Monday morning. She was determined to complete a full day's work before Phil and the children arrived from Montauk in mid-afternoon. Phil always said she was the most disciplined person he knew – but she wasn't sure whether that was approval or complaint. In his heart did he feel she put her work before him and the kids? *Never.*

At shortly past ten her agent – Donna Reeves – called, dramatically apologetic about not having alerted her to a book party the following Thursday afternoon.

"It was to be two weeks later, but you know what it's like in this town in July. Everybody in publishing is off to the Hamptons for long weekends." Montauk was part of the Hamptons, Ellen remembered in a corner of her mind – but Phil wasn't out there because it was the chic meeting place for writers. "Promise me you'll be there. We need bodies."

"I'll be there." She'd come back into town Thursday morning, Ellen plotted. She must be in Madison when Marcie came before the grand jury – even though Kathy said they wouldn't be admitted to the courtroom.

"I want you to be especially nice to a new client of mine. Michael Lambert. He's rather shy at social events, he warned me – you'd hardly expect that of a foreign correspondent. But he's written this marvelous book – and I have an auction scheduled for next week."

"Sure." Phil always refused to accompany her to professional cocktail parties or dinner meetings. He said he felt like an outsider. "When and where?" It seemed so disloyal, she thought in a corner of her mind, to be going to a party at a time like this.

By one forty-five p.m. Ellen realized she was famished and stopped to throw a veggie burger into the toaster oven, an English muffin into the toaster. It was difficult to focus on work – despite Phil's claims about her discipline – when she knew he and the kids would be arriving soon. And Claire and Ted would be dashing off again tomorrow and Phil would be heading back for Montauk.

Wistfully she visualized Mom's house, multi-glassed red cedar sitting on a slight hill with woods on three sides and the ocean on the other. Oh, she loved to go to sleep with the sound of the surf in her ears! But that would have to wait at least another three weeks. *Why is Phil erecting this awful wall between us?*

An hour later she heard a key in the apartment door, rushed from her office to open the second lock herself. Angie thought it was terrible to live in a city where two or three locks on an apartment door were normal. People in Madison never locked their doors except overnight.

"Oh, you're all sunburned," she scolded, kissing first Claire, then Ted. Now lifting her face to Phil's for his perfunctory kiss.

"Yeah, we're flirting with skin cancer," Ted drawled. "Grandma and Dad kept yelling at us to wear sunblock."

"We did!" Claire scowled at her brother.

"Oh, I missed you all so much." Subconsciously Ellen allowed her eyes to linger on Phil. Had *he* missed her? Every night – lying alone in their queen-sized bed – she was aware of his absence.

"We missed you, too, Mom," Claire said exuberantly. "But we had a great time out there. I bought you a present at Claudia's Carriage House. I'll give it to you later."

Ellen's face glowed with tenderness. Claire adored spending an hour roaming about the fabulous Montauk gift shop, settling at last on some delightful small object to grace her mother's desk or dresser or night table.

Already Ted was at the refrigerator, inspecting both the lower area and the freezer. Claire joined him in this inspection tour. Their long-established routine.

"Have some fruit," Ellen ordered. "We'll go out for an early dinner." Involuntarily she glanced at Phil. Was he annoyed that she wasn't cooking dinner tonight? She was in no mood to cook – nor to settle for something 'sent in'. She wanted to sit down to a hot meal and be served, she told herself in veiled defiance.

She ignored Phil's lifted eyebrow when she announced her choice of an expensive restaurant. She was tired and uptight – and they could afford it. On their *joint* incomes, she told herself. She used the departure of Claire and Ted tomorrow to justify a special dinner this evening.

Only that evening – after a festive dinner that masked her own anxieties – did Ellen tell Claire and Ted about Frank's death and

Marcie's arrest. They stared in shock, mouths ajar in silent rejection of this news.

"Her lawyer will prove she's innocent, won't he – or she?" Claire was not too stunned to remember that women were lawyers, too.

"Hey, you read about people who're convicted and then found not guilty twenty years later," Ted said, as part of the ongoing sibling rivalry between himself and Claire.

"Don't even say it!" Ellen offered up a silent prayer. Marcie mustn't be convicted. Once – long ago – she and Kathy and Angie had set themselves out to make sure justice prevailed. Ignoring the law. Was this some backhanded retribution for their efforts? *No, don't be absurd.*

Earlier than normal Claire and Ted were fighting yawns.

"You're sleepy," Phil drawled. "Off to bed, both of you."

"Dad, it's just ten o'clock!" Claire protested.

"On a non-school night," Ted pointed out.

"You're sleepy," Ellen confirmed. "You spent the morning on the beach, three hours on the road in summer traffic. And you've got an important day tomorrow." Hope stirred in Ellen. Was Phil in a romantic mood after a week away from her? He'd been so bushed the last three weeks of school, he'd fallen asleep the minute his head hit the pillow. Often in these last months, he'd gone off to sleep before she even slid into bed. "We'll all call it a night."

After a mild effort at delay Claire and Ted ambled off to their respective rooms. Ellen watched for some sign from Phil that he would be joining her in the master bedroom.

"I want to catch a bit of the ten o'clock news." He reached for the TV remote.

"I'll have a cup of tea," she said after a moment.

"Decaffeinated – or you'll be awake half the night." His usual reminder when she had tea in the late evening.

"Would you like a cup?"

He shook his head without turning in her direction. He was engrossed in the news.

With tea in hand Ellen returned to the living-room, picked up the as yet unread current issue of *Publishers Weekly*. But tonight her mind wandered from the pages of the publishing bible. The happenings in Madison dominated her thoughts these last few days. Thus far Frank's murder hadn't been reported in Manhattan newspapers. Phil warned, though, that the story could hit the supermarket tabloids at any moment. If there was a lack of more lurid news, Frank and Marcie's names could be headlining those rags.

Ellen finished her tea, returned the mug to the kitchen and went to the master bedroom. Kathy was putting up a brave front, she told herself while she went through the nightly bedtime ritual – but it was clear she was terrified by the circumstantial evidence piling up against Marcie.

Phil was in bed, appeared to be asleep when she emerged from the bathroom. In earlier years this would be one of those nights when she'd lie with her head on his shoulder and talk about the anxieties that plagued her. And afterwards Phil would make love to her.

What's happening to us?

From the habit acquired when Claire and Ted were babies, Ellen awoke at seven a.m. sharp. Phil was asleep. The children would probably sleep late this morning. No rush. Claire was scheduled to meet her group at the designated spot at three p.m. At eight p.m. Ted's flight left JFK. In the silent apartment Ellen arose and prepared for the day, made herself a cup of Earl Grey – what Claire called 'the real thing' – and two pieces of rye toast. With breakfast in tow she walked to her office.

In the course of last evening her mind had managed to deal with a segment of the new book that she meant to revise. She could handle that before the others awoke. But this morning work was derailed at intervals by disturbing thoughts about the children's imminent tours.

On other summers – and school holidays – they'd gone on trips as a family. Neither Claire nor Ted had ever expressed any interest in 'sleepaway camps' – for which both she and Phil were grateful. They'd gone to Montauk to stay from school closing until Labor Day weekend. But this summer both had come up with these tours that included close friends. Like Phil said, the time came when you had to let go. And if there were any problems, all they had to do was pick up a phone and call. Collect.

A tender smile lit her face. She remembered consoling Kathy the summer Linda had gone off to camp for four weeks. Money had been tight in those years – she'd taken out a loan to cover camp fees. Glenn was still crying poverty – though they learned later that he and Ronnie had gone to Acapulco that summer. But Linda cried that three of her friends were going to this camp. *'Mom, I'll just die if I can't go, too.'* Marcie had never wanted to go to camp – she liked being close to home.

With gratifying speed Ellen finished the work she'd scheduled for the morning. The apartment was an oasis of silence now. She left the computer and went out to the living-room. Usually she enjoyed these periods of quiet when the children and Phil slept late. These were small parcels of time that belonged to her alone. But this morning she was restless. Call Madison, she ordered herself – see if there has been any new developments.

Angie picked up on the second ring. Mondays and Wednesdays were her days off from the office.

"Nothing new to report," Angie told her. "Just that what we hear of the assistant district attorney isn't filling us with delight."

"What's the problem?"

"Rumors say she's hot to run for political office. She's hell bent for conviction. Scott admits she'll probably put up a fight against bail."

"That doesn't mean she'll win." It was important that Marcie be granted bail – but that was a small issue. *How was Scott Lazarus going to fight the line-up of evidence the district attorney's office had as ammunition?* "How's Kathy?"

"Hanging in there." Angie sighed. "I keep telling myself Marcie's innocent until proven guilty – but in some people's minds she's already convicted."

"The evidence is all circumstantial."

"The testimony of those two nasty women next door who'll testify Marcie and Frank were having blistering fights for two days doesn't come under the heading of circumstantial evidence," Ellen said unhappily. "And Scott says the man who found Marcie leaning over Frank's body will testify he was there to discuss divorce. The life insurance policy is fact. It doesn't help that Marcie didn't know about it – they'll insist she lied. This is going to be one bitch of a summer! Scott hopes the case doesn't come to trial until at least well into September. He'll fight for that. He needs the time."

"I'll be up late tonight. No need for you and Joe to wait up. Kathy'll let me in. And Scott's going to clear Marcie – don't let yourself believe anything else."

Kathy paced about the small living-room. Angie and Joe had retired over an hour ago. Except for the spill of light from a lamp beside the sofa, the house was bathed in darkness. Tonight the post-bedtime silence seemed menacing. But she was grateful for the drop in temperature. A comforting breeze filtered through the windows, along with the sweet scent of summer flowers.

With a sigh of impatience she paused beside the phone table. Twice she'd tried to reach Glenn. She'd left no message on his answering machine. How could she reduce what she had to say to him to thirty seconds' worth of words? His plane was scheduled to arrive over two hours ago. At the same time that Ellen and Phil were at JFK to see Ted off for his camp in Madrid.

Damn, why wasn't Glenn home? How long would it take for them to collect their luggage, go through customs, and find a cab to drive them into Manhattan? Yet even as she was impatient to talk to Glenn, she dreaded this encounter. Talking with Glenn brought back so much that was ugly. Linda scolded her at intervals for not 'being civilized about the divorce'. A divorce was good for only one partner. The other partner and the children – if there were children – paid a heavy penalty.

She hadn't seen Glenn and his new family since Linda's wedding – yet the anguish of that last encounter was burnt into her memory. What should have been one of the happiest times of her life – the marriage of her daughter – had been a nightmare. *'For God's sake, Mom, bury your anger!'* Linda railed at intervals. Would she ever arrive at that state?

Even shopping for her gown – back when she'd expected to be a member of the wedding party – had been traumatic. Ronnie would be there, looking young and glamorous – and Ronnie could spend a fortune on a designer dress. She'd gone into New York to shop for the dress with Ellen. They'd traipsed through the evening wear departments at Bloomingdale's, Sak's, Bergdorf's, Lord & Taylor. They'd even gone down to the shops on the Lower East Side that offered 'mother of the bride' gowns. On their second day – touched by but rejecting Ellen's offer to pay for an exquisite Oscar de la Renta that ran into the low four figures – she'd settled on a lovely off-the-rack aquamarine chiffon that both Ellen and Marcie declared made her 'look like a movie star'. She hadn't worn the dress since – nasty memories spoiled it for her.

Try Glenn again. He had to be told. It wouldn't be right for him to learn about it in some tabloid. And he might just be needed if the ADA's objections pushed Marcie's bail into astronomical figures.

Gritting her teeth, feeling every muscle in her body growing tense, she reached for the phone and dialed Glenn's number.

"Hello." Ronnie's high-pitched, affected voice greeted her.

"Ronnie, this is Kathy. May I talk to Glenn, please?" Why – after all these years – did she react this way to Ronnie?

"Sure. Just a minute." Wariness slithered over the line to Kathy. She heard Ronnie tell Glenn that she was calling.

"What the hell does she want that couldn't wait till morning?" Kathy heard, and then Glenn was on the phone. "Yeah, Kathy – what's up?"

"Nothing pleasant," she said coldly. "Frank was murdered a week ago tonight." She heard his sharp intake of breath. "Wilma said she had no breakdown of your itinerary, so I couldn't call you." Wilma had an itinerary, she suspected – but that was only for important business associates.

"That's terrible!" Glenn was shocked. "But there was nothing I could have done about it. There was no point in cutting our trip short for the funeral."

"Marcie's family wasn't welcome at the funeral. Marcie is being held for his murder."

"What's the matter with that crazy kid?" Glenn yelled. "She always had that nutty streak!"

"Glenn, she didn't kill Frank!" How could he be so crass?

"I suppose you hired some local lawyer," he scoffed after a slight pause.

"Did you have some fancy Manhattan lawyer in mind?" All through their marriage he'd tried to tear her down. Whatever she did was always wrong. "Do you know what they charge?" She was deceptively calm.

"Who's defending her?" He was backtracking now.

"You may have heard of him. Scott Lazarus—"

"He's big-time. I haven't heard much about him lately, but he's handled a lot of high-profile cases." But Glenn sounded uneasy.

"I think I can get bank loans to handle his fees." Marcie would be pleased her father wasn't involved. "But after the grand jury hearing Scott will ask for bail and—"

"He figures the grand jury won't clear her?"

"Not a chance. He's sure she'll have to stand trial. But we've collected a lot of letters supporting her – and Rabbi Ginsburg will guarantee her appearance in court." *Why did Marcie's boss – Betty*

Julie Ellis

Williams – refuse to give us a letter? Marcie is great at her job.
Betty just said, 'We don't want to get involved.' "Marcie's bail will
be high, Scott said." If it's granted. "I'll need help in—"
"Look, I'm all tied up financially," he interrupted. "I—"
"I'll put up the house as collateral. If you'll put up your condo
and your house at Amagansett, we should—"
"I have huge mortgages on the condo and the house – I don't
have enough equity to do any good."
"Glenn, you're a rich man!" Her voice soared in rage. "This is
your daughter!"
"I'm rich on paper! I owe on everything! If you need bail money,
talk to your friend Ellen."
"She's already offered to help – and Angie, too." Marcie's father
might be a scumbag, but Ellen and Angie were there for her. "I *hope*
we can manage between us." But she'd clung to the belief that in an
emergency Glenn would be there with them.
"This guy Lazarus isn't just coming out of retirement, is he? I
mean, he's still sharp enough to handle this?"
"The first lawyer I spoke to – the best criminal lawyer in the
county, Angie said – figured his fee could run to a quarter of a
million dollars. But no, Scott hasn't come out of retirement. He's
been practicing locally for the past five years. He—"
"How the hell did Marcie land herself in a spot like this?" Glenn's
exasperation was seeping through.
"She was thrown into it! But she has strong suspicions about why
Frank was murdered and by whom. He was about to expose some
secret terrorist group in town. A bunch of fanatics who're arming
themselves with a small arsenal. She said—"
"Oh Lord, that's her wacky imagination running wild again!"
Glenn groaned. "Remember those stories she dreamt up when—"
"Stop it, Glenn! Frank told her about this group. They'd been
fighting about his getting involved – Marcie was terrified."
"Is her lawyer going to drag that out into the trial?" Now Glenn
exuded alarm. "Don't you understand what that would do? The
newspaper tabloids would descend on Madison in droves! The TV
tabloids would be after you for interviews. Look, Kathy, don't drag
my name into this mess! How could I ever explain it to the people
I do business with? The guilt by association thing would kill me!"
Kathy winced, willed herself not to lose her cool. All Glenn
ever thought about was himself. "You might tell them that your

64

son-in-law was murdered and your daughter wrongly accused – and that you're sure she'll be cleared."

"Does this lawyer think he can do that? Maybe he can cut a deal. You know – plead temporary insanity. Drag out that she was in and out of therapy as a kid."

"Are you out of your mind?" Kathy's voice was shrill. "Marcie didn't kill Frank. She loved him. And she was in therapy because she had trouble coping with our divorce." Tears of rage clouded her vision. "How can you talk like that?"

"I'm being realistic. But for God's sake, don't get involved with any newspaper journalists or TV people." Glenn cleared his throat. A gesture Kathy remembered – that always presaged his effort to avoid an unpleasant situation. "I'll try to get up there late in the week. I'll be in touch."

"Why bother?" she flared. "You've never been there when we needed you."

"Christ, don't start that shit again! Look, I have to run. Half of our luggage is still sitting out in the hall."

Kathy sat by the phone, staring into space without seeing. When had Glenn ever been there to help them? Thank God for Scott. On impulse she reached for the phone, dialed Scott's home number. He'd said, '*Call me at home if you need to talk to me after office hours.*'

"Hello . . ." Scott's voice came quickly. Sleepily.

"Oh Scott, I'm sorry! For the moment I forgot the hour."

"You need to talk," he guessed, and she felt an instant relief that he understood.

"I just got off the phone with Marcie's father. He's terrified of publicity that might reflect on him. I worry about bail money," she confessed. "I mean, if it should soar to some insane figure—"

"We'll fight for something you can handle," he soothed. She'd told him that she and Angie and Ellen would put up property as collateral. "I know the ADA who's handling the case is going to fight against bail, but I've been putting out feelers. I think we may swing it. And tomorrow morning I should get a release on the house – it'll be declassified as a 'crime scene' area. You and Marcie will be able to go home if – when," he corrected himself optimistically, "bail comes through. Or will it be too painful?" he asked in sudden solicitude.

"We'll close off the room where Frank was killed," Kathy said after a moment. "I think Marcie will want to go home. It's a house that's known a lot of living. It's been home to three generations."

"That must be a wonderful feeling. I lived in a small Alabama town – about the size of this – until I was ten. Then we moved to New York City. In the next eight years we lived in four different apartments – though my mother made sure we lived within a fine school district." He chuckled reminiscently. "Of course, this was a time when Manhattan had some great public schools. The worst sign of violence was a spitball fight."

He was talking to help her relax, she thought. What a wonderful, warm man. And again she was conscious of emotions she'd believed long dead. "You don't find it boring to live in a small town like this?"

"I've never felt more content, Kathy. I reached a point in my life as a Manhattan attorney when I dreaded waking up in the morning. I hated the pressures, the whole lifestyle. Here the pace is so different. It's a whole new world. I've made friends. I feel part of the town. I'm neither surprised nor upset when somebody calls me in the middle of the night to bail out a son or daughter or husband."

"What's sad," Kathy said, "is when families these days move out in different directions. Like my older daughter, Linda – she and her husband live out in Seattle. He's moving up fast in the computer field, and that's where he was offered the best job. I wish they'd settle for less and stay here."

"You said you plan to move back here and open another shop," Scott recalled.

"Once this madness is over, yes."

"I'm glad you've made that decision. I'm selfish – I want you here. I think you're a very special person, Kathy." The atmosphere was rich with implications.

"I think you're special, too," she whispered, caught up in this moment of truth.

"You know you won't be able to be present at the grand jury hearing tomorrow morning," he said, awkwardly puncturing the mood as though fearing they were moving too fast. "I think the verdict will come in fast. I'll ask for bail." Unexpectedly he chuckled. "Some people here in town pass me over for attorneys who play the politics game. They know that's not my *schtick*. But this time I *am* playing the game. I play chess with the judge – I'll push him a bit. As soon as I have any word at all, I'll call you." He hesitated. "Could we have dinner tomorrow night? We can discuss where we're heading with the case."

"I'd like that, Scott."

What was the matter with her? Didn't she understand that it was too late for her to become emotionally involved again? *That part of my life is over.*

Nine

The three women sat in the kitchen over second cups of strong, hot coffee. It was good being here with Ellen and Angie, Kathy thought. Ellen had arrived late last night. Angie was off from work today. A few minutes earlier Scott had called to say that the police had released the house to her – it was no longer a 'crime scene'.

At this moment he was headed for the grand jury hearing. Why couldn't she be there? But Marcie would know that wasn't allowed.

"Kathy, shouldn't we go over to the house and – and straighten up before Marcie comes home?" Ellen asked – intent, Kathy understood, on diverting her mind from the hearing. But they all knew bail might not be allowed – despite Scott's friendship with the judge.

"That won't be today," Kathy pointed out. "After the hearing, Scott applies for bail. Then Marcie must appear before the judge, who'll decide whether or not to grant it. She flinched in recall. "I feel sick each time I see Marcie in the detention hovel."

"Let's go over now." Angie was resolute. "It's my day off. Ellen has to go back to New York in the morning."

"Would you rather Angie and I handled it ourselves?" Ellen asked.

"I'll go with you." But a coldness closed in about Kathy at the prospect of walking into the house after what had happened. It would be like coming home from the hospital after Dad died – and then Mom. Even now she remembered the pain of opening the door and walking into the empty house. Dad, Mom, and now Frank. "We'll close off the den." The den – Frank's office at home – was where he'd been murdered.

"Call Scott's office and leave the phone number at the house," Ellen said. "Ask him to call you there."

The three women drove to the house in Angie's car. Kathy steeled herself for what lay ahead. Her heart pounded as Angie pulled up in the driveway. The telltale yellow tapes were gone. No signs barring entry. The lawn was parched, she thought subconsciously. She'd turn on the sprinkler later, water the flowers.

"That house is part of all our lives," Ellen said, caught up in nostalgia.

"I remember how wonderful your mother was to me when Vince died in Vietnam in early '67." Angie had adored her older brother. "My mother and father were devastated – they clung to each other. But your mother understood I was grieving, too."

"I remember how she covered for us when she realized we'd hitch-hiked to New York for that anti-war demonstration in New York," Ellen recalled. "We left her that weird note. Remember?"

They didn't know anyone who was going to take part in the anti-war demonstrations that were scheduled for August 6, 1966 – but they'd heard Ellen's father sound off against the Vietnam war with great eloquence. They knew about the anti-Vietnam teach-ins that were popping up on college campuses around the country. They'd all been warned about the dangers of hitch-hiking but were blissfully convinced that nothing horrible could happen to *them*.

On a sultry Saturday morning they caught a ride with an older couple who were full of talk about Luci Johnson's wedding today in Washington.

"Oh, it's so romantic," the seventy-ish wife murmured sentimentally. "She'll be the fifteenth White House bride and the seventh President's daughter to be married while living in the White House."

They smiled politely while the woman talked on about the wedding, the three of them wishing her husband would drive a little faster. The Times Square demonstration was supposed to start at twelve thirty – and they were eager to be there when it began.

"The wedding party is so large," the woman continued. "Forty-two people. One of the New York columnists – I forget which one – said Luci's wedding to Pat Nugent will be the most splendid of any Presidential daughter in American history."

"Pity Pat's brother can't be best man," her husband commented. "He won't be eating wedding banquet food – he'll be chomping on C rations over in South Vietnam."

At last they were dropped off at Riverside Drive and West 72nd Street in Manhattan. They were enthralled to discover that a group estimated at about 1,200 was preparing to march from here, across to

Julie Ellis

Broadway, then south to Times Square. They joined the procession, which was led by a contingent of young men playing funeral dirges on plastic horns and pounding on tin drums. Several dozen women garbed in funereal black followed – each carrying a placard that read 'We regret to inform you . . .'

At Times Square they converged with thousands of other demonstrators, marching from various areas of Manhattan. They filled the area from fortieth to forty-seventh Street for almost an hour before marching to the rally at forty-eighth Street and Park Avenue. A few stopped briefly to picket the Dow Chemical Company, the makers of napalm.

"Aren't you glad we came?" Angie whispered to Kathy and Ellen while they listened to the eighty-one-year-old pacifist Reverend A. J. Muste implore the United States to negotiate with the Vietcong. "Why is my brother fighting over there?"

Well before their eleven p.m. curfew they were back in Madison, Kathy remembered. While many kids their age were demanding – and getting – far more freedom, parents in Madison didn't respect the growing permissiveness. Madison boys – like Angie's brother Vincent – went to fight in Vietnam. The news media bemoaned the violence in high schools from coast to coast – but Madison saw little of it.

"Your mother read us the riot act," Ellen recalled tenderly. "But we knew she'd been scared to death your mother or mine, Angie, would call and ask to speak to us – even though we were supposed to be spending the day at your house and sleeping over."

"Everybody loved your mother, Kathy," Angie said.

"Remember *that* night – when your mother was visiting over in Greenville and her car broke down and she couldn't get back until two in the morning?" Ellen's voice suddenly thickened in pain.

"I try not to," Kathy whispered – but her mind, too, charged back thirty-one years. To that other murder that touched their lives – and bound them together forever.

"Come on." Angie punctured the mood. "We have a house to clean."

Kathy reached into her purse for the key, her mind taunting her with images of happier times – when Frank and Marcie were engrossed in settling into the house.

70

"Kathy, you go out to the kitchen and round up the vacuum cleaner and dust clothes and stuff," Angie ordered. Kathy intercepted the anxious exchange between her and Ellen. They wanted to close off the den before she approached it, she interpreted.

"Sure. Let's get this show on the road."

But part of her mind was noting that any minute now proceedings would start in the grand jury room – and Marcie would be indicted. *What is Scott doing about tracking down the slimy group that wanted Frank dead? Is his investigator on the ball?*

With the house reeking of lemon oil and lysol, they abandoned the house-cleaning at close to one thirty p.m. for lunch from the insulated bag Angie had brought along.

"When was the last time you vacuumed?" Angie teased Ellen while they brought the salad bowl and finger sandwiches Angie had prepared this morning to the dining table.

"Not for a lot of years," Ellen admitted. "Thank God for Pearl."

After several unhappy attempts at acquiring a nursemaid/house-cleaner Pearl had come into their lives – and peace reigned. Pearl had been with them since Ted was just past two and Claire a cherubic six weeks. She'd stayed all these years, only taking off summers to wield a firm hand over her own two children, each a year older than Ted and Claire.

At first Phil had been taken aback that she had hired help. But without Pearl she couldn't work – and if she didn't work they couldn't afford a spacious apartment and the car that allowed them weekend getaways from the city – both of which she and Phil cherished. Still, he never ceased to be upset that her income now far surpassed his own.

At just past two p.m. Scott called.

"Things went as we expected," he told Kathy. "Ramsey presented her case, and I presented mine. The grand jury's sitting. I expect they'll be back within an hour. I'll wait here in the courthouse." He hesitated. "Kathy, if the press or TV try to interview you, just say 'no comment' to whatever they ask." He sighed. "These days Madison tries too hard to imitate big city actions. They see all that hysteria on TV."

"How's Marcie?"

"She's anxious for bail. And she wants us to find Frank's murderer. She's searching her mind for clues."

"Which is more than the police department is doing," Kathy said tartly.

"*We're* working on it, Kathy. My investigator is out there on long shifts. And Joe's helping, too."

"Joe?" She was startled. Angie was instantly alert.

"He called me this morning. He thinks one of his construction crew will come up with a name. Let me get back to the grand jury room in case there's early action. I'll call later."

"Thanks, Scott."

"What's this about Joe?" Angie was uneasy.

"He called Scott to say he might have a name for him – from somebody on his crew. You know, about the True Patriots."

"I hope he's careful!" Angie managed a weak smile. "I know it's important to identify members of the group – but it scares me." As it had scared Marcie, Kathy thought. With good reason.

"Joe'll be careful," Ellen soothed. "Nobody'll suspect him of feeding information to Scott. He's 'one of the boys'."

Scott returned to the grand jury room. A pair of reporters – from the *Madison Daily News* and the new 'freebie' weekly that began publishing a few months ago – sat in a corner of the room discussing the case. They lowered their voices at his arrival. He didn't know the stand of the new weekly, but Marcie had told him that the *Daily News* had once identified Frank and her as 'local rabble-rousers' because of their ongoing fight against the Paradise Estates wetlands development.

The reporters knew – and he knew – that the grand jury would indict Marcie. The minute he'd walked into the room he was conscious of a super-charged atmosphere. But then murder involving middle-class residents was rare in Madison. When murder did occur, the perpetrator was a drug addict, gang member or pimp. He'd been immediately aware that this was a divided jury – probably half of them hostile towards Marcie, the other half almost a fan club. Kathy was right – Marcie had made a definite impact on this town.

Ramsey, the ADA, seemed sure of herself – but he read wariness in her eyes. He guessed she was familiar with his track record as a defense attorney. She'd be more wary if she knew he played chess regularly with Judge Harmon.

Normally he and Josh made a point of not discussing legal business. This time was different. Before the hearing he'd presented

Josh Harmon with an application for bail, submitted close to fifty letters praising Marcie's character, her track record as a social worker. He was betting on Josh's granting bail and in an amount that was manageable. *Don't let me be wrong.*

After only fifty minutes of deliberation the grand jury returned to the room with a verdict. Marcie was ordered held for trial. Judge Harmon scheduled the bail hearing for the following morning. Ramsey protested. She was overruled.

Scott strode from the grand jury room, sought out a public phone. Let him prepare Kathy for tomorrow's hearing. He was seeing her for dinner tonight, but why keep her on tenterhooks? And face it, he taunted himself, he wanted to hear her voice. It was unnerving, the way he got all revved up at the prospect of talking with her, seeing her. He was forty-eight years old, feeling emotions he'd thought long dead in him.

He dropped a coin in the slot, dialed. Kathy picked up on the second ring.

"Hello—" The warmth in her voice spliced with anxiety.

"It's Scott. We're on schedule." He couldn't bring himself to say, 'Marcie was indicted'. "Judge Harmon set the bail hearing for tomorrow morning. I was pushy," he admitted, "but he went along."

"What do we have to do?" she asked with that no-nonsense quality he admired in her.

"I want to pack our side of the courtroom with Marcie's supporters," he said. "Make sure Rabbi Ginsburg is there. If possible, some of Marcie's high school teachers."

"I'll get on it right away." Kathy exuded determination. He was sure she and Angie would bring out an impressive group.

"I'll see you for dinner," he reminded. "We'll talk more then."

He left the courthouse, walked back to the office. His mind warned him this would be a bitch of a case to win. Still, his gut reaction was that Marcie had not killed her husband. He had an instinct about such things that he trusted. Usually. But again, he asked himself if he was allowing his judgement about Marcie to be colored by his feelings for her mother . . .

Kathy felt a shaky satisfaction when at last she went to her room to dress for dinner with Scott. This had been a productive afternoon. At least thirty Marcie-supporters would be in court tomorrow morning. Scott would be pleased.

Angie had insisted she and Ellen would stay here with her until they knew the outcome of the bail hearing. Angie understood how painful it would be to go home without Marcie. She checked her watch. Time for a fast shower. She was grimy from the house-cleaning that preceded their phone marathon.

She walked into the tiny second bathroom that Joe had put in last year between the girls' bedrooms. Five minutes in the shower – no more, she ordered herself. Now her mind focused on Ellen's success of the afternoon. Ellen had gone to talk with Bill Collins, the young editor of the little 'freebie' weekly newspaper, the *Madison Guardian*. He'd agreed to run her profile of Marcie in the next issue.

Kathy positioned herself so that the vibrant hot spray pounded between her shoulder blades. Oh, that felt good! But instantly she felt guilty because Marcie sat in a six-by-eight cell with a wash basin, a toilet, a small bench, and a locker. When would Scott and his investigator come up with something that would clear Marcie? Scott said he would push off the trial date as long as possible. He'd been honest. *'The only way to clear Marcie is to trap the killer.'*

She stepped out of the shower, reached for a towel. Would Ellen's article affect possible jurors – as they prayed it would? The *Madison Daily News* was showing its bias now, she remembered with exasperation. They were making sweet, good Marcie appear a devious, conniving opportunist. Angie suspected it had something to do with the wetlands re-zoning situation. And again she asked herself, why did Marcie's boss refuse to give them a letter?

She opened the closet door. She'd brought so few clothes along. Over the weekend she'd drive to the apartment, pack up more things to bring back. She chose a Carole Little shift with a twenties air that would be cool and smart. How awful, she thought, to worry about her appearance at a time like this.

Right on time Scott arrived at the house. Never in the ten years of their marriage had Glenn ever appeared on schedule. She sensed that Scott was self-conscious in the presence of Ellen and Angie, made a pointed statement about briefing her on the private investigator's latest report. *All right, we both know this isn't a date.*

Driving to the restaurant Scott went over once again the routine of the bail hearing.

"Ramsey – the prosecuting attorney – will be opposed to granting bail. But don't be upset," he added. "I'm fairly certain the judge will be with us. He won't give his decision right away. He'll probably sit on it over the weekend. But I'm optimistic."

Not until they were seated in the restaurant, had ordered, and were alone did Kathy ask about the progress of Scott's investigator, brought to Madison from Poughkeepsie. In a corner of her mind she suspected the retainer she'd given Scott had been exhausted. She'd bring that up later.

"I've asked Jake to go back and double-check on Eric Matthews," Scott said. "I want to know everything I can about him."

Now she told Scott about the refusal of Betty Williams – Marcie's superior – to give her a character reference.

"I couldn't believe it. Marcie's a dedicated worker. Her clients consider her a treasure."

"I'll talk to Marcie about that," he said and scribbled in his notebook. "They may have some rule at the agency."

"Angie can't be at the hearing. She's so upset about that. But she has an appointment to show houses to a prospective buyer tomorrow morning."

"From what you tell me our side will be well represented," he comforted. He reached out to cover her hand with his. "We'll fight this through together."

Lee Ramsey pushed her chair back from her desk and reached into the large bottom drawer to draw out the sheaf of articles she'd cut from the *Madison Daily News* and the *Madison Evening Journal* – the evening edition of the newspaper – in the past few days. She felt a surge of satisfaction. The press had been most receptive to her – a situation she had plotted with care. She'd show them to Dad tonight. As cynical as he was, he still ought to be impressed. Damn it, when was he going to stop being so tight and come out to finance a political career for her?

"I finished the word-processing." Deirdre broke into her intro- spection with a martyred air. Deirdre resented spending one minute past five o'clock in the office. But this case was important to her – a pivotal point in her career. She'd instructed Deirdre to remain until the report was finished.

"Thank you, Deirdre." She contrived a grateful smile as she reached out a hand to take the folder. "Sorry to have kept you late."

She lingered at her desk for another few minutes to scan the

Julie Ellis

contents of the folder. No matter how much manipulation was necessary, she meant to win a conviction. No doubt in her mind – Marcie Loeb was guilty as hell.

Her father's words last night when she talked to him about her first homicide case echoed in her mind:

'*So you have a homicide – so what? Who's going to hear about it outside of this stinking small town?*'

There were ways to make sure people heard about it outside 'this stinking small town'. So they wouldn't be getting nationwide TV coverage. Millions of people read the supermarket tabloids. What was the name of that PR man down in New York who'd tried so hard to get her into bed? Chuck, she pinpointed – Chuck Jamison. He said he had great newspaper and TV contacts.

'*You ever get involved in a juicy murder case – you know, some great-looking broad to spread across the front pages – give me a buzz. I'll get you the kind of coverage that'll make you a national figure.*'

A smile lifted the corners of her mouth. Maybe – just maybe – the whole country would become involved in the Marcie Loeb murder trial.

Ten

Kathy and Scott lingered over coffee, both loathe to end the evening. She was reacting to Scott this way, she rebuked herself, out of anxiety over Marcie. Scott was the knight on the white charger who was going to rescue her baby. But she listened to Scott and thought, this is the man I should have met all those years ago.

At the Santini house Angie coaxed Scott to come in for a while.

"Joe's dying to talk with you," she said and called to Joe over her shoulder.

They settled themselves in the living-room, where a light breeze drifted through the windows.

"I thought I was on to something, Scott," Joe apologized. "You know how the guys talk over a few beers. A couple of them had plenty to say in support of the Madison Militia. The usual crap – 'Sure, we love out country – but the government stinks. It's all for the rich'. They made no secret about being members – none of the members do. But they want to distance themselves from the extremists – because of the Oklahoma bombing and the other craziness. When I asked, 'Hey, what's this True Patriot group I heard about,' I got zilch. Most of them don't know. But this one guy froze. I think Frank was on to something."

"Joe, don't go asking more questions." Angie was scared.

"What's his name, Joe?" Before Joe could reply, Scott turned to Angie. "He won't be involved, I promise you. I just want to put a tail on him, see where he leads us."

The phone rang. Angie went to pick it up.

"It's for you, Kathy. Glenn."

Automatically tensing, Kathy rose to her feet. "I'll take it out in the kitchen."

In the kitchen she reached for the phone, sat on one of the stools at the breakfast bar Joe had added last year.

"Hello." Glenn would offer some excuse about why he hadn't come up yet, she guessed.

"Kathy, I'm bogged down like crazy here. Working seventeen hours a day. I won't be able to get up this week. What's with Marcie?"

"She went before the grand jury this morning. She was indicted," Kathy said tiredly. "Tomorrow morning there's the bail hearing. Scott is hopeful she'll be granted bail."

"I don't see anything in the New York papers about the case," he said. Still, he was nervous. "Don't let any snoopy news people get to you."

"I don't intend to." She fought to keep exasperation out of her voice. Was that all Glenn had to say when his daughter was to be tried for murder?

"I'll try to get up some time next week." He was self-conscious now. "How's Linda taking this?"

"She's upset. What do you think?"

"That's not good for her this late in her pregnancy."

"Marcie isn't exactly having a party in jail!"

"Marcie was always the one you spoiled!" he shot back. "Look what it got her into!"

"Oh, go to hell, Glenn!" She slammed down the phone. Cold with rage, her heart pounding. Linda complained that she'd never learned to be 'civilized' about her divorce. What was 'civilized' about Glenn's behavior?

In the morning – after abject apologies for what she called her defection – Angie hurried off to the office to meet her prospective buyer. This had been a slow year – she was eager for a good commission. Kathy and Ellen headed to the courthouse for the bail hearing.

She wouldn't let herself be upset when the prosecutor from the District Attorney's office came out in opposition to bail for Marcie, Kathy vowed. Scott was hoping the masses of letters, Rabbi Ginsburg's offer to guarantee her presence in court, would be sufficient to convince Judge Harmon to grant bail. Still, it wasn't a prearranged deal.

The hearing room was already well-occupied when Kathy and Ellen walked inside. Kathy's face brightened at the sight of familiar faces – friends who refused to believe that Marcie could be guilty. Casey Norman – the ardent founder of the local environmental group – was here with two other members of the group. She saw Scott off in a corner talking earnestly with a smartly dressed, slim blonde, whose back was to her. Was that the prosecuting attorney? From a seat up front Rabbi Ginsburg waved, beckoned her and Ellen to join him.

"I prayed this morning for Marcie," he told Kathy as she and Ellen sat beside him. "She's a fine person. She couldn't have done this."

Then Marcie was brought into the room. Her face lighted at the sight of her mother. *Why must Marcie go through this awful ordeal?* Scott turned away from the blonde, saw her, lifted a hand in greeting.

The judge took his place. The hearing began. As defense attorney Scott presented his case first. Kathy leaned forward in her seat, determined not to miss a word that he said. He spoke with eloquence about Marcie's record as a social worker, quoted from several of the mass of letters attesting to her fine character, emphasized that Rabbi Ginsburg would guarantee her presence in the courtroom when the date of trial arrived.

"I'm impressed by the letters that have been presented," the judge acknowledged when Scott was finished. "At this moment I feel that granting of bail is indicated."

The prosecutor rose to voice her objection to bail. She sounded oddly familiar, Kathy thought, searching her mind for identification.

"Your Honor, I feel strongly that the defendant—" Lee Ramsey began but the remainder of her objection was lost on Kathy. She was dizzy with shock. She turned instinctively to Ellen.

"I don't believe it," Ellen whispered, her face drained of color.

"It's Leslie." She hadn't seen Leslie in thirty-one years. Leslie had been dark-haired then. Her face seemed vaguely altered now – but the voice was the same. It was as though the years had rolled away. She and Leslie and Ellen and Angie were fifteen—

"Don't say anything." Ellen's mouth formed the words – no sound emerged.

Kathy's hand reached out to Ellen's. The memory of that awful night rushed over her like a tidal wave . . .

The evening was unseasonably cold for April, the sky dark and forbidding, devoid of moon and stars. It was the kind of night when she wouldn't want to read a murder mystery in bed, Kathy thought while she and Ellen worked with sober intensity to coax a blaze from the birch logs they'd stacked in the fireplace. Angie was out in the kitchen making hot chocolate for them. The three of them engulfed in a heady sense of adulthood at being alone in the house. Tonight Kathy's mother had driven to nearby Greenville to visit a friend in the hospital.

Madison parents tended to keep a watchful eye on their teenagers in this era of young rebellion and promiscuity. In Madison – as in countless small towns throughout the country – parents read about teenage drinking and drug problems but were smug in the knowledge that little of that infected their own. Their major concerns were the startling climb upward of their daughters' skirts and the downward climb of their sons' hair.

"Your mom won't mind that we're having a fire, will she?" Ellen asked.

"She knows we'll be careful." Kathy thrust rolled-up newspaper underneath the grate. "Mom loves a fireplace, too. She says it's so romantic."

Now the logs erupted into orange-red flames, diverting heat into the room with a symphonic rumble like the overture to a Wagnerian opera. The two girls watched with pleasure.

"Angie, the fire's going great!" Kathy called out.

"It's getting warm. I'll take off my sweater," Ellen decided.

After Leslie, Ellen wore the prettiest clothes, Kathy decided. Leslie's mother bought her Villagers – blouses with little rounded collars, made of pure cotton with pastel flowers. Cable-stitched sweaters, slacks and Bermudas with fly fronts completed the costume. Villagers advertized that you had money, Mom said – and Leslie's mother always considered herself a bit above the rest of the town.

Angie came into the living room with three mugs of hot chocolate – whipped cream piled perilously high.

"This is the last hot chocolate I'll have for the rest of the year," she vowed. "If I gain another ounce my stomach will pop right out of my new Mary Quant." They knew it wasn't a Mary Quant original – just a JC Penny version. But they loved the look.

"I think Leslie's mom is a real creep to ground her because she wore eyeliner to school today." Ellen grimaced in distaste. "What was so awful about that?"

"She's a creep for other reasons," Kathy reminded. Of course, Leslie always had some excuse when she showed up with a black eye or huge bruises on her arm – but they all knew her mother got ugly when she was drunk. People talked about Mrs Hilton in whispers. Mom said it was terrible the way they gossiped.

"Shall we watch TV or listen to records?" Angie asked. "I brought over Bob Dylan's new album," she added in triumph. "*The Times They Are A-Changin'*."

"Records," Ellen decreed.

"Let's listen to his earlier album first." Kathy adored Dylan's *Blowin' in the Wind*. He sang about things that were important for their generation. What people were calling 'the Now generation'.

"Okay." Angie giggled. "My mom worries about the music we like. She says it teaches us to be disrespectful of our parents. But not in *my* family." Her eyes were eloquent. "Remember what happened when my dad said my minis made me look like a hooker? I had to let down all my skirts and was grounded for a month."

They sipped their hot chocolate down to the dregs while Bob Dylan's voice echoed through the small living room. Outdoors the wind was growing in velocity. Shutters were banging at the house across the road.

"Is that somebody at the door?" Ellen turned towards the foyer.

"It's the wind," Angie dismissed this, caught up in the power of Dylan's 'With God on Our Side' – his latest proselytising effort on behalf of pacifism.

"No, somebody's there." Kathy leapt to her feet.

"Ask before you open the door," Angie called after her as she hurried to respond.

"Who is it?" Kathy paused with one hand on the knob.

"Leslie." A terrified, high-pitched voice they all recognized. "Kathy, open up!"

Kathy pulled the door wide. Leslie darted inside – her face white and stricken. Blood was visible on the white blouse she wore beneath her open coat.

"You're hurt!"

"It's nothing . . ." Leslie was struggling to speak. Her eyes seemed to see some horrible image. "Not me—"

"You've cut your hand!" Angie rushed forward. "It's bleeding a lot!"

"You – you don't understand—" Leslie closed her eyes now, swayed.

"Make her sit down – I'll get bandages and Bacitracin." Kathy darted from the room.

"You've got to listen to me." Leslie's voice was shrill.

"We'll fix your hand," Ellen soothed.

"Maybe she should go to the emergency room – that cut may need stitches," Angie worried

"No," Leslie moaned.

Kathy returned with bandages, adhesive tape, and Bacitracin.

"Let me," Angie said. "I took that first aid course last semester. You have to keep pressure on the wound to stop the flow."

"You all don't understand," Leslie gasped while Angie worked to stem the flow of blood, manipulated bandage and tape. "It's not me – it's Mom." Her voice dropped to an anguished whisper. "I killed her!"

For an instant the other three froze in shock.

"Maybe she's just hurt. We'd better go see—"

"She was so mad." Leslie paused for a deep breath. "Dad was supposed to be home tonight, and he called this afternoon and said he would be delayed a couple of days. She started drinking the minute he was off the phone. Then a few minutes ago she came after me with a knife. I took it away from her – and I don't know how it happened – I stabbed her with it—"

"Maybe she's just hurt." Kathy exchanged anxious glances with the other two. "We'll go over to your house."

"Maybe we should call an ambulance," Ellen said.

"No!"

"You stay here," Angie soothed. "We'll go over. You stay right here, Leslie," she exhorted.

"You okay?" Ellen asked. "Do you want one of us to stay with you?"

"No," Leslie managed. "But she's dead. I know she is. Lying there on the kitchen floor."

"Can we get in the house?" Ellen asked. "Is a door open?"

"The kitchen door," Leslie said. "I ran out of the kitchen and straight here." The Hilton house was five blocks away, the nearest of the group in a more affluent neighborhood.

"Lock the door behind us." Kathy reached to take the phone off the hook. The other two were pulling on coats. Kathy went to the closet for hers, and the three girls hurried out into the dark night.

Too unnerved for speech they ran along the deserted streets in silence. Then the imposing Hilton colonial – lights blazing on the lower floor – rose before them. Was somebody already there? But they remembered Laura Hilton's penchant for keeping lights on in many rooms. They hesitated a moment, then skirted around to the rear.

"Leslie said the kitchen door was open," Ellen reminded, breathless from their race.

The kitchen door was slightly ajar. Kathy hesitated, pushed it wide. The three girls walked inside, fearful of what they would find.

"Over there," Kathy pointed after a moment, her heart pounding. In a far corner of the huge, super-modern kitchen Laura Hilton lay on the floor. The front of her delicate pink overblouse – popularized by Jackie Kennedy – was sodden with blood. Her eyes stared up at them without seeing.

"Oh my God, Leslie's right. She's dead!" Angie gasped.

"She went after Leslie with that knife." The large knife that lay on the floor. "Leslie's fingerprints are on it!" Kathy realized. "Angie, hand me that dish towel." Her one thought to protect Leslie – who'd suffered so much at her alcoholic mother's hands.

"Should we call the police?" Angie was ambivalent.

"No!" Ellen glanced about the room. "We have to make it look like an intruder came in. Her mother caught him – and he killed her."

While Kathy – gritting her teeth, trying not to look at Laura Hilton – wiped the knife clean, the other two smashed dishes and threw two chairs on their sides.

"The police will think it's funny there are no fingerprints on the knife," Angie reasoned. "We have to put in her hand."

"I can't do that." Kathy felt sick.

"I'll do it." Angie dropped to her haunches beside the body, hesitated, reached for a napkin that lay on the floor. Now with the napkin as a protective covering for herself, she maneuvered to place the knife in Laura Hilton's left hand, remembering that Leslie's mother was left-handed.

"Let's get out of here!" The house was on a corner, Kathy thought gratefully, the kitchen extending beyond the house next door so they could run out without being seen.

"Yeah—" Angie charged towards the door. "Come on."

They stopped dead as lightning flashed outdoors, then disappeared into the sky. While thunder rumbled through the night, they hurried from the house, down the empty streets to where Leslie waited for them.

Julie Ellis

"We'll say Leslie was with us all evening," Kathy said shakily as they approached her house. "She came over just minutes after Mom left. Nobody has to know that Leslie did it."

"I hope your mother hasn't come home yet." Angie was anxious. "Leslie'll blurt out everything."

There was no car in the driveway nor in the garage. Mom wasn't here yet, Kathy realized in relief. Nobody saw them leave or come back. Nobody was stirring on a night like this.

"What happens when Leslie has to go home?" Angie asked while they waited for Leslie to respond to the doorbell.

"You and I will go with her," Ellen plotted. "She wanted to show us her new outfit. It wouldn't make sense for you to go, too, Kathy. Angie and I both pass her house on our way home – that'll look natural. We'll find her mother – and call the police. If Leslie looks awfully upset, that's natural—"

"I hope Mom doesn't get here until we have Leslie out of the house." Kathy was anxious. "Nobody – not even Mom – can ever know about tonight."

"Nobody," Ellen said, and Angie reiterated this. "Let's take a solemn vow."

Leslie mustn't be accused of murder, Kathy told herself defensively. Her mother had gone after her with a knife. She'd just been protecting herself.

Without bothering to ask who was there, Leslie opened the door.

"You're going to be okay," Angie said firmly. "We've got a plan . . ."

Kathy produced a clean blouse for Leslie to wear. The bloodstained blouse was burnt in the fire. Leslie listened – numb and frightened – to their exhortations about how to carry this off.

"You've been with us all evening. Ellen and Angie will walk home with you. If anybody asks, you wanted to show them your new cardigan. What happened tonight is our secret. Nobody else will ever know. Not one person. The police will believe your mother was killed by an intruder."

Three weeks after Laura Hilton's death, her husband moved with Leslie to New York. For a little while they exchanged letters. Leslie was unhappy in New York – she suffered from nightmares. Her father was impatient with her, talked about sending her off to boarding school. Somehow they lost contact with Leslie. It was

84

an episode in their lives that the three girls were determined to obliterate.

"I don't believe this." Again, Ellen's mouth formed the words, but no sound emerged.

Kathy felt a tightness in her throat. Leslie couldn't know Marcie was her daughter. When she found out, it would make a difference – wouldn't it? How could Leslie prosecute *her* daughter? Something Scott said ricocheted in her brain now: *'Lee Ramsey doesn't have a heavy background – I understand this is her first homicide case. But she's sharp – and she's super-ambitious. She'll put up a rough fight.'*

Now she tried to focus on what Leslie – now calling herself Lee – was saying.

"I'll delay making my decision until Monday morning," the judge announced when at last Lee Ramsey concluded her objections.

But he'd said earlier he felt that bail was indicated, Kathy remembered. She clung to this. Instinct warned her not to approach Leslie – not at this moment. And they couldn't tell Scott about Leslie.

Let nothing go wrong. Let Marcie be granted bail on Monday morning.

Eleven

By twelve forty-five p.m. Ellen was headed for Manhattan again, mindful of the cocktail party in late afternoon. She wasn't in the mood for a party, she thought in distaste as she waited for the chance to merge into the highway traffic – but she'd promised Donna she'd be there. Like Kathy and Angie, she was still shaken by the discovery that the ADA prosecuting Marcie was Leslie Hilton. They were in agreement that Leslie – or Lee as she called herself now – had been unaware of their presence in the hearing room. What would be her reaction if she'd recognized them? What had brought her back to Madison? Had she checked around town and believed none of them lived here now? It took a certain amount of nerve to come back here after what happened.

The self-assured, smartly dressed prosecuting attorney was far from the insecure, wistful fifteen-year-old they remembered. Her mid-brown hair was now ash blonde. Cheekbones had emerged from baby fat. A skilled plastic surgeon had been at work on her nose and chin. But the voice was Leslie's voice. Right away she and Kathy had recognized it.

Would Leslie's role of prosecuting attorney work in Marcie's favor once Leslie knew Marcie was Kathy's daughter? Instinct told her – and Kathy and Angie, as well – that the woman up there protesting so vociferously against bail for Marcie was a stranger to the sweet, vulnerable fifteen-year-old they knew all those years ago.

'Kathy, put it out of your mind,' Angie had said. 'This is a cold, super-ambitious bitch.' That was what Scott had said about Lee Ramsey. 'None of us want it brought out, of course – but she'll deny that bizarre night ever happened. We won't gain a thing by confronting her.'

Now there was a break in the traffic. Ellen rushed into action, moved onto the highway. This merging with the stream of speeding cars was always the part of driving she loathed. But from here on the trip into Manhattan would be a snap.

Her mind returned to the hearing room and their first realization that Lee Ramsey was Leslie Hilton. She felt a flicker of apprehension. Was Kathy clutching at a hope that Leslie would be sympathetic to Marcie once she knew this was Kathy's daughter? Remembering how they had leapt to save her from a murder charge all those years ago, would she be compassionate? The woman they'd heard today had been almost vicious in her opposition to Marcie's being granted bail.

The three of them had agreed – Kathy couldn't tell Scott that they knew Lee Ramsey and under what conditions. In truth, she and Kathy and Angie had been accessories to Laura Hilton's murder – they'd hidden evidence. But they'd all been terrified for Leslie. Would a jury have convicted Leslie when they knew the truth? They'd been afraid to take that chance.

She was grateful that traffic moved smoothly. At two forty p.m. she was driving into their apartment building's garage. She didn't have to be at the party until five thirty. Donna had asked her to arrive early. *'I need you to shepherd Michael Lambert around – that way I can work the room.'* Plenty of time for a shower, a cup of tea, and what Phil called her 'meditation *schtick*'. So the others ribbed her about that – it helped her brush aside tension. When she encountered a block in plotting, she'd meditate and soon the block was gone. Maybe she could squeeze in an hour of work before she had to leave for the party. In truth, she was well ahead of schedule.

Inside the apartment she immediately switched on the living-room air-conditioner, then the one in the master bedroom. The weather was hot and sticky – an oppressive closeness permeated the apartment. But in a few minutes it would be comfortable. God bless the inventors of air-conditioning.

She debated about calling Phil in Montauk. Once she was home from the party, she'd want to settle down to three or four hours of uninterrupted work. No, she decided – she'd spoken to him yesterday. She didn't want to seem a nagging wife.

Other times when they were apart she'd made a point of phoning Phil nightly. She used to know his every thought. Now sometimes he seemed a stranger. At intervals through the years she'd felt uncomfortable at attending publishing parties without Phil. But not every husband or wife accompanied a writing partner, she'd convinced herself.

Yet once again she was conscious of discomfort at appearing without him – because of this new wall between them. At intervals men made passes. Part of her was amused by this, part of her was flattered. But since their marriage there'd been no other man in her life.

She followed her schedule as planned. She had showered, dressed, had a cup of tea, meditated. Now she sat down with her manuscript to give thought to the next batch of revisions. But her mind refused to co-operate. All right, leave it for later – when she wouldn't have to watch the clock.

Still, it was too early to leave. It was a ten-minute cab ride to the Turtle Bay address. See what was being reported on TV news. She flipped on the set, headed for her favourite chair, then paused in shock as the newscaster's voice filtered into the room. "From a quiet community of thirty thousand just two and a half hours from Manhattan comes the story of a sordid murder by a young bride . . ."

They'd conned themselves into believing the case wouldn't receive national attention. How distorted a news report could be! Marcie was being held for trial. What about 'innocent until proven guilty'?

". . . Big time criminal defense attorney Scott Lazarus has come out of retirement to handle the case . . ."

Scott wasn't in retirement, she remembered in exasperation. He'd just left his fancy law firm for a quieter existence – out of the limelight. Thank God he was there for Marcie. Was it because Scott was in the picture that the case was being dragged into the national news? Or was there a lack of tabloid news at the moment? With a grunt of impatience she rose to her feet and crossed to flip off the TV.

Change into other shoes, she ordered herself – more for something that required action than of necessity. If she was going to be standing around for an hour on her feet, she might as well be comfortable. Let the bright young publishing women walk around in three inch heels. Unwarily she remembered that Phil liked her to wear low heels – he said it made him feel protective. But now she seemed strong and independent – not in need of protection.

She took a final glance at herself in the full-length mirror on the master bathroom door. The part of her mind that functioned despite her anxieties approved of her reflection. The sea-green linen sheath – fashionably above the knees – was smart, right for a late June cocktail party where most of the women attendees would be arriving from their offices. The exquisite silver necklace and earrings – bought in a splurging moment after signing a $250,000 contract – hinted at a successful career.

She sighed. She was in no mood for a cocktail party this afternoon. Still, she'd promised Donna she'd be there. She enjoyed parties composed of small groups of people she knew well. She loathed the cocktail party scene of drifting from stranger to stranger uttering meaningless small talk. That had been Phil's excuse in those early years when she'd tried to coax him to go with her. He wouldn't go because he felt himself a failure in her world.

She reached for her Judith Leiber bag – another indication of her success – and headed down the hall to the door. The party was being held in the Turtle Bay town house of the publisher hosting the party. In the well-established custom it would be super-cooled out of respect for the men in jackets. She stopped short at the door, reached into the hall closet for one of her collection of scarves that could double as a stole if the air-conditioning was overwhelming.

A nostalgic smile touched her mouth as she draped the scarf about her shoulders. Last summer she'd driven into East Hampton with Claire to search for a birthday gift for Mom. They'd bought a purse at the discount-priced Coach shop there. She'd fallen in love with this scarf but hesitated about spending more money on herself. Claire had gone into East Hampton with Mom the next morning and bought it with her savings. *'An advance birthday present, Mom – since you love it so.'*

The taxi drew to a stop before an impressive Turtle Bay town house. She wouldn't have to stay long, she comforted herself. Other than Donna there'd be only three or four people present that she knew, and those only slightly. Exchange a little shop talk, then cut out.

She crossed the sidewalk to the ornate entrance. Masses of pansies rose exuberantly from the patch of earth before the house – protected from errant dogs by a two feet high wrought-iron fence. She touched the bell, heard chimes echo inside. Then a smiling doorman opened the door and ushered her into the foyer.

A few people stood in twos or threes about the sprawling, elegantly furnished living-room. Not one familiar face. In all these years she'd never learned to approach strangers with a casual 'Hi, I'm Ellen Courtney . . .' Then she spied Donna and felt relieved. Already Donna was charging towards her.

"Darling, thank God you could come. With this heat wave people are heading off for an early weekend. Come along and say something nice to my author. She's the world's worst bitch, but they expect her to sell like mad."

Ellen managed the perfunctory exchange and moved away. She saw Donna's eyes traveling towards the foyer where several people had just been admitted.

"There's Michael." Donna's smile was dazzling. She had high hopes for his book, Ellen remembered. "Be sweet to him. He hates coming, but he's got to learn to relax at these things. Michael!" she called, hurrying towards him. They exchanged a perfunctory kiss and Donna turned to her. "Ellen, this is Michael Lambert, who's written this marvelous book about the trouble in Kosovo. Michael, this is Ellen Courtney – she writes women's fiction. She's terrific."

Michael Lambert gave the appearance of being tall, though he was probably no more than five seven, Ellen thought subconsciously. It was the way he held himself. Probably about her age. Handsome, with sun-streaked brown hair and dark eyes. He'd do great at women's luncheons and book signings, she surmised.

"I'm surprised Donna didn't give me hell for not wearing a tie," he said with a chuckle when she'd dashed off. "Not even for a great book contract will I sink to wearing a tie."

"I think a mock turtleneck is acceptable these days." She brushed aside the memory of her London honeymoon, when Phil had been denied entry to fabulous Simpson's because he wasn't wearing a tie. In those days he'd been addicted to turtlenecks.

"I was out of the country for almost two years," he said wryly. "Then came back and holed up in a borrowed country house for eight months to write the book. The one Donna's handling. I have to get acclimatized again." His eyes told her – in a quiet fashion – that he found her attractive. "And I've never been big for the social scene."

"I grit my teeth and bear cocktail parties," Ellen confessed. "I hate making small talk with people I don't know – or know hardly at all."

"Everything is culture shock to me. For eight months I locked myself away and pecked at my Mac." He grinned reminiscently. "There were times in the Balkans when I was grateful for a manual Royal portable that I carried for no-electric emergencies. Emergencies became the norm."

Now he launched into some of the highlights of his time in the
Balkans. What a warm, compassionate man, she thought subconsciously. A woman Ellen recognized as the author of a current cult
novel came to join them, listened for a few moments to Michael's
impassioned report, then – with a bored smile – drifted away.
"I'm sorry. I'm monopolizing you." His smile was contrite. "You
probably want to circulate."

"Not at all. I told you. Cocktail talk bores me to death."

"Could we cut out and go somewhere to talk where we can have
some food? I'm starving – and cocktail bites aren't what I have in
mind." He chuckled. "I got into the habit of having dinner around six
o'clock up in the country. Then I'd settle down to a second writing
shift. I had so much I wanted to say – and I was impatient to get
it all down on paper while it was still fresh in my mind. I never
worked so hard in my life – but it was exhilarating and exciting."

"I know a deli on Third Avenue that's about a ten minute walk
from here," Ellen said after a moment's deliberation. "And I'm
hungry, too."

She was conscious of Donna's raised eyebrows as she and
Michael made their farewells. But she'd warned Donna she wouldn't
stay long.

"Oh, I'm glad to be out of that rarefied atmosphere." Michael
sniffed the warm night air with approval. "I was born and raised here
in Manhattan, but at every possible chance I run somewhere else."

"I like to get away regularly," Ellen conceded. "But I want to
know that I can come back here."

"Are you a native New Yorker?"

"No. I come from a small upstate town. After college graduation
I stayed here in the city."

Almost compulsively she talked about Madison as they walked
towards the Third Avenue deli. She told him about the trauma of
Frank's death and Marcie's being held on a charge of murder. She
felt warmed by his obvious sympathy.

At the deli they chose a quiet corner table. Few evening diners
had arrived as yet. They debated briefly over ordering, as though
to put this aside for further conversation. Over huge roast beef
sandwiches, then strawberry cheesecake and coffee they talked
about their careers, their working habits.

"Doing a book was a whole new ball game for me," Michael
said whimsically. "Talk about commitment! The longest I'd written

before that was a fifteen thousand word magazine article. It was a lonely business up there in that house near the Canadian border." No family, Ellen pinpointed in a corner of her mind. "I'm not a social animal, but sometimes I needed a voice besides National Public Radio."

"It can be lonely right in Manhattan. Except for summer vacations my family's out of the house by eight a.m. and start drifting in again at five p.m." She'd mentioned Phil and the children earlier. "I keep a network of friends that I talk with on the phone at intervals – you know, take a tea break somewhere along the line to resuscitate myself."

"I got such a high when I finished," he reminisced. "And then the horrible letdown. Was it any good? Would any publisher even bother to read it? I had crazy good luck – a guy I knew in Sarajevo hooked me up with Donna."

"Now it's on to the next book."

"I'm making notes already. But as soon as I know what's happening with the book, I'm heading for two or three months in Alaska. Recovery period."

"I hear Alaska is beautiful."

"Oh, honey, it's fabulous. I was there five years ago – just for a week – and I knew I'd have to go back again." He reached into his pocket for his wallet. "I carry a few photos with me."

No photos of wife or family, she noted as he flipped open his wallet to display shots of Alaskan scenery. A foreign correspondent would find that a difficult situation to handle.

Michael was lyrical about Alaska. "I tell you, I've traveled around most of the world in the last eighteen years, but there's nothing quite so mesmerizing as glacier-watching. I sat there in my boat, just drifting and listening to the sound of ancient ice crack and groan – and then a huge mass falls to become an iceberg on its way to the ocean. You sit there watching – and time stands still."

"Oh, God, it's late!" Ellen stared at her watch in disbelief. "I expected to be home and at my computer an hour ago."

"It's been great to talk shop with you. I have to hang around town for a while. Why don't we have dinner tomorrow night?"

"I'm so rushed with work," she demurred.

"You have to eat, Ellen. I discovered a terrific place down in the West Village. Good food, quiet, comfortable. Take off an hour or so for dinner – and you'll work better for the break." His smile was ingratiating. "Writers need to talk to writers – truck drivers with other truck drivers – small shop owners with other shop owners. Only there're a lot less of us."

"All right." Revisions were moving faster than she had anticipated. "Early, though," she exhorted. "I want to be home and at the computer by nine p.m."

"Nine p.m. sharp," he promised.

Scott was frustrated by his lack of progress in digging up substantive evidence in Marcie's favor. He sat at his desk on this late Friday afternoon and asked himself why Betty Williams – Marcie's boss at the social service agency – had refused to give Angie a character reference for her? *Is somebody putting pressure on her?*

Lee Ramsey would explore Marcie's work relationships. Betty Williams would be asked to testify at the trial. *Let me find out now just what the Williams woman might have to say on the witness stand.* He buzzed his secretary.

"Pam, will you get Betty Williams – she's the head of that agency Marcie worked for – on the phone for me, please?"

Twenty minutes later he was sitting in Betty Williams' office.

"I'm sorry to barge in on you late on a Friday afternoon," he said with ingratiating charm, "but I won't take up much of your time."

"That's quite all right." She was polite, but Scott sensed she was nervous. She'd expected this encounter and dreaded it.

"I'm trying to arrive at a real profile of my client. I know that a friend of Marcie's approached you for a letter attesting to her character. I understand you refused."

"It's not our policy to comment on our employees. At the time Marcie Loeb was on our staff."

"You never give out character references for employees?" He didn't buy this.

Betty Williams stared at a file on her desk.

"I didn't think I could do so in Marcie's case," she said after a moment.

"It's likely that you'll be asked to testify in court." His voice was soft but persuasive. "I'd like to know what your response would be under oath."

"I'm fond of Marcie – she's done some fine work for us. But there have been too many times when she's made decisions on her own. Rushing ahead on impulse to make decisions that weren't hers to make," Betty Williams emphasized. "She's a hard worker, yes –

but she's headstrong and determined to have her own way. And she allows her emotions to guide her. I debated for weeks – but I knew even before this came up that I would have to discharge her. She's no longer an employee of this agency."

Twelve

When she awoke on Saturday morning Kathy geared herself for a traumatic weekend. Even though Scott seemed certain Marcie would be granted bail, there was no guarantee.

A few minutes past nine a.m. Scott called.

"We need to talk," he said gently.

"When?" Instantly she was anxious.

"Would it be all right if I drive over now?"

"Of course." Joe was working today. Angie would leave for the office in a few minutes. "Would you like ice coffee or hot?"

"Hot, please." He chuckled. "I'm the old-fashioned type – morning's for hot coffee, even if it's a hundred degrees outside."

She put down the phone, sat immobile. What did Scott mean – '*We need to talk*'? He was unhappy about the evidence piled up against Marcie. Was he about to throw in the towel? She remembered what Joe had said. '*Scott never takes on a case unless he believes his client is innocent.*'

Ten minutes later Kathy heard Scott's car pull into the driveway. She rushed to the door. *Please God, don't let him walk out on Marcie!* Not just because he wasn't a greed-driven attorney like Jeffrey Stevens. Scott gave her hope, confidence when these were precious commodities. His strength reached out to embrace her, lift her up.

She pulled the screen door wide as Scott bounded up the path.

"Hi. Coffee's ready." She managed a wisp of a smile, her eyes striving to read his mind. She didn't want Scott to walk out on Marcie. She didn't want Scott to walk out of *her* life. Instantly she felt guilty. How could she think about herself when Marcie's life was on the line? Since the day Glenn walked out on them, she'd built her life around Marcie and Linda. There was no room for anybody else.

Scott sniffed appreciatively. "That's one of the world's most heavenly aromas." His answering smile was encouraging – but she mustn't assume everything was all right. *Why do we need to talk?*

95

"On weekends – for years now – I treat myself. Coffee from freshly ground beans. I started Angie and Joe on that several years ago. Right after I opened my shop." *Why am I rattling on this way?*

"Thank God, we're having a break in the weather." He walked with her into the house, down the hall to the kitchen.

Kathy poured coffee into two colorful mugs, brought them to the table in the small dining area, remembering that Scott – like herself – took his coffee straight.

"Why don't I fix breakfast for you?" she said belatedly. "It'll only take—"

"Oh no," Scott interrupted. "I had breakfast at half-past seven. This is coffee break time."

She sat down across from him, her throat tight with anxiety. Ellen kept telling her she ought to learn to meditate – but her mind had a traitorous way of wandering off when she tried. Maybe she'd try again.

"Is there a problem, Scott?" She fought to keep her voice even.

"Instinct tells me we may be on to something with this True Patriots group – but I could be wrong. Jake will have to put in a lot of hours for us to get answers. It'll be very expensive."

"Whatever it costs is OK. I'll work it out." She hesitated. "And you'll need something towards your own fee," she said awkwardly.

"Let's forget about that for now. Let's just focus on clearing Marcie." But his eyes were troubled, she thought with fresh apprehension while she waited for him to continue. "Late yesterday afternoon I spoke with the head of the social service agency where Marcie worked—"

"Betty Williams?" Kathy tensed.

Scott nodded, his expressive face telegraphing his dissatisfaction with that conversation.

"I couldn't understand why she wouldn't give us a character reference for the bail hearing." Kathy was bewildered. "What did she say to you?"

Scott was uncomfortable, apologetic. "She said that she had been gearing herself to fire Marcie."

Kathy gaped in shock. "How could Betty say something like that? Everybody at the agency loved Marcie. Her clients loved her."

Scott seemed to be forcing himself to continue. "She said Marcie had a way of going beyond boundaries, that sometimes she made rash decisions without consulting anybody else. She'd debated with herself about the situation, then decided Marcie would have to go. She'd planned on telling her at the end of the month."

"Scott, this is insane!" Her mind was in chaos. First, Eric Matthews lied about Frank's wanting a divorce. Now Betty lied about Marcie's standing at the agency.

"We'll go over this with Marcie," Scott soothed. "I don't know that Lee Ramsey will call Williams as a prosecution witness—"

"It would be damaging for Marcie if Betty is called, wouldn't it?" She felt sick, her mind cataloguing all that the prosecuting attorney would throw at the jury.

Should she go to Leslie, plead with her to help them? Could she make Leslie understand that Marcie was innocent? *Would Leslie care?* A 'super-ambitious ADA, vowing to win a conviction' – that was how Scott had summed her up. Could she reach past Lee Ramsey to Leslie Hilton?

"Marcie wasn't fantasizing about the True Patriots," Scott derailed her thoughts with this revelation. "Jake is sure there's some heavy military training going on at a farm about eight miles out of town. He tailed Joe's lead there. He says he's heard heavy gun fire out there at night – more than a couple of guys out hunting. So far we've found no link between Eric Matthews and the True Patriots," he cautioned. "He even walked away from the Madison Militia. But Marcie's convinced someone from the True Patriots wanted to silence Frank – and we have to run with that." Because they had nothing else, Kathy taunted herself.

"Why did Eric Matthews lie like that?" she persisted. "Why did Betty lie?"

"It could be some crazy misunderstanding." But he seemed frustrated.

Should she go to Leslie? Would Leslie just laugh at her? Dare her to bring out in the open what happened thirty-one years ago? Implicate herself, Angie, and Ellen? And it wouldn't help Marcie.

"Have you considered taking Marcie away from Madison until the trial?" Scott asked gently. "Provided, of course, that she is released on bail. As long as she doesn't leave the state, I don't think there would be a problem."

Kathy was startled. "I just assumed she'd want to come home." *Am I being insensitive?*

"You're probably right. I just thought it might be difficult for her here . . ." He hesitated. "The thinking in town is split right down the middle. A lot of people are supportive of Marcie. And there're a lot who – who aren't."

"Marcie and Frank were abrasive to a segment of local people." Kathy sought for the right words to express herself. "I used to tease the two of them about being 'holdovers from the sixties'. They felt deeply about people, wanted to give something back to the world."

"Urge Marcie not to talk to the press. The less she says the better."

"Do you know anything about Lee Ramsey's personal background?" Kathy asked, verbalizing the question that had tugged at her since she realized Lee Ramsey had been Leslie Hilton. She strived to be calm, but her heart was pounding.

"I explored that right off. She came late to the legal profession, moved here about eighteen months ago. She snared the ADA job almost immediately. She lives with her father – who's wheelchair-bound after a stroke – in a rather elegant house in Westwood Heights." The small, expensive development of custom houses at the edge of town. "I gather the old boy has money. She was married for several years, was divorced about nine years ago. She's charming, tough – but you realize that by now."

"Right."

Yes! I must talk with Leslie.

Lee Ramsey picked up the jacket of her Ellen Tracy pantsuit, dropped it over one arm, reached for her shoulder bag. She glanced at her watch. She'd be in Manhattan in time for her lunch date with no sweat. Then on to her appointment with her hairdresser.

She'd meet Chuck Jamison for lunch at Michael's – just across from his office and a four minute cab ride to her hairdresser. She'd made it clear to Chuck that this was a business luncheon – not a social encounter. She'd be back in Madison in time for dinner with Dad. He had this crazy thing about their sitting down to dinner together every night that she was free. Not that he gave a shit about her – it was part of the framework of his day.

She left her room, walked with quick, decisive steps down the carpeted hall and down the stairs. Her father sat in his wheelchair on the rear patio, where he spent much of his time birdwatching. A flicker of amusement brushed her perfectly made-up face. How often did those binoculars roam from the trees to neighboring windows? So he had the soul of a voyeur since his stroke, she shrugged. If people were too stupid to pull down their blinds or draw their drapes, let him enjoy the show.

"I'm going into the city," she said, standing beside his chair. "Shall I bring you anything?" A perfunctory statement that always brought a bitter reply.

"Sure," he drawled. "A new pair of legs to replace these."

"Stacy will be back from her grocery shopping soon – if you need something." Thank God for Stacy, she thought – not every housekeeper would put up with Dad's impatience.

She'd be running into summer weekend traffic, she warned herself at the first sign of a hold-up on the road. She slid a tape into the dashboard player and geared herself for stop-and-start traffic. Her mind focused on what she had to say to Chuck Jamison. This wasn't a routine PR campaign – her participation had to be kept under wraps. But this was an opportunity that must be utilized.

Sitting at a red light, she remembered her ex-husband's accusations at regular intervals during the course of their six-year marriage. *'Damn it, Lee! You spend your lifetime watching for opportunities to push yourself ahead! What about taking time out to live?'*

She'd been in advertising then – fighting to land a major account. Bert was a tax accountant who worked like a dog at intervals and wanted to play hard at intervals. She had no time for playing. He was bright and good-looking and passionate. Bright and good-looking were assets to the image she strived to create for herself. At first she'd enjoyed their lovemaking – though it wasn't the physical enjoyment of sex that she appreciated. She liked being held, being caressed, being told that she was beautiful and desirable. But that had palled after a while.

To the devil with Bert – he was part of the past. She'd waited to let him off the hook – though he'd been asking for a divorce over a year – until she decided to dump advertising and go to law school. She had to come home a winner.

She was forty-six years old – less than four years from fifty. A chill darted through her as she dwelt on this. What had she accomplished in her life? This was her last chance to become somebody. She needed to shove this case into the spotlight – make it a media circus. With her name splashed across the newspapers and on TV, she could leap-frog over the Town Council, promote herself into the State Assembly. Six years there – with the right promotion and a little luck – and she could move up into Congress.

She was furious when Dad first talked about returning to Madison, she recalled with sardonic humor – though she was sure nobody would remember them. She'd fought him like hell. Then she realized she'd be lost in a large Manhattan law firm. In Madison she could move into the political scene.

She'd hit the jackpot right off with the ADA role. So she was the token woman in the District Attorney's office. In the next forty-eight hours – if Chuck could deliver what he claimed – she'd be the prosecutor in a tabloid-touted murder case.

Ellen printed out her Saturday's output, stacked it away with the earlier revisions. For a few hours – buried in work – she'd been able to escape reality. She glanced at her watch. She'd be meeting Michael at the Village restaurant in an hour. It felt so odd to be having dinner with a strange man three nights in a row. But Michael was so eager to sit down and talk shop with another writer. And he made her laugh – the way Phil had in their early years.

She hadn't talked with Phil since Wednesday. He'd wait for her to call – he wouldn't want to run up Mom's phone bill. Tapping the Montauk number she was already growing tense. Without words, Phil had told her their marriage was in dire trouble – and she didn't know how to fix it.

"Hello—"

"Hi. Everything all right out there?"

"Great. I'm lying on the deck with the cordless phone here so I don't have to budge from the chaise. The sky's a gorgeous abstract in blue and white. The ocean's rough, making beautiful music." He paused. "Have you heard from the kids?"

"From both of them." Here was safe ground. "Ted's indignant because they don't sit down to dinner until ten p.m. You know – Madrid style. After all that talk from the sponsors about observing American meal times and American food. I gather he's a heavy customer at the snack bar in their dorm."

"He'll survive." Phil was casual. "Mom and I had a postcard from him, too – same complaints. And Claire called Thursday night – she said she tried you but just got your machine." She'd been at dinner with Michael, Ellen thought guiltily. "I think she's a little homesick. Her big gripe was that they have to be out of bed by seven a.m. each day. I gather she figured on sleeping late during vacation time. What's with Marcie?"

"We're keeping our fingers crossed that the judge will grant bail on Monday. Kathy's upset that there's little progress on clearing her." Phil was fond of Kathy and Marcie. They'd stayed close through the years, though they only got together three or four times each year. Thank God for telephones.

"It'll happen," Phil encouraged. "Little pieces will come together, and the answer will be there."

"It's frightening," Ellen said. What was happening between Phil and her was frightening. Here they were, talking like two casual friends – not husband and wife who'd been together for sixteen years.

"Here's Mom." Phil sounded relieved. "She wants to talk to you."

On Monday morning – despite Lee Ramsey's outraged objections – the judge granted Marcie bail. Kathy flinched when she heard the amount, though Scott had prepared her for an even higher figure. But preliminary negotiations had assured her that with Ellen and Angie putting up their residences as collateral – along with her own property – the bail could be met.

Rabbi Ginsburg had stood by his offer to be responsible for Marcie's appearance at the trial. Now he reached over to pat Kathy's hand.

"She's going to be all right," he whispered.

The judge reminded Marcie that she was being released in the rabbi's hands, that he must always be kept informed of her whereabouts. But it was understood that Marcie would be with her mother. Rabbi Ginsburg left the hearing room. Kathy remained with Scott to arrange for Marcie's bail. Anticipating this, Scott had seen to it that the papers had been processed. It wasn't necessary for Ellen and Angie to be here. Still, she and Scott had to wait around for almost an hour before Marcie was brought to them.

"Mom . . ." Marcie moved into her mother's arms, clung for poignant moments. "It's been so awful."

"We'll go home," Kathy said gently – trying not to remember that this could be only temporary respite. Scott was pushing now for a late October trial date. He said that the DA's office was going along with that.

"Let's go out the side entrance." Scott positioned himself beside Marcie. Kathy looked at him in question. Why the side entrance? "I noticed a couple of TV trucks when we came in."

But the side entrance was blocked because of workmen repairing a light fixture. They retraced their steps and headed for the front entrance.

"Oh my God!" Marcie gazed in panic at the horde of reporters and photographers pressing towards them. Camera lights flashed. A pair of TV vans sat at the curb. Not just locals, Kathy realized. They were facing national media.

"You're going to be all right, Marcie." A protective arm about her waist, Scott prodded her through the cluster of media people to his waiting car, Kathy at her other side. "No comments," he said brusquely in reply to the barrage of questions being shot at them. "No comments."

Scott helped Marcie and Kathy into the car, then slid behind the wheel.

"It's all right, Marcie. They won't bother us now," Kathy soothed. But she noted that Scott stared at intervals into his rearview mirror.

"We'll go to my house first," he told them.

"All right." Kathy was puzzled. Still, she'd been dreading Marcie's first encounter with the house since Frank's murder. Marcie sat with shoulders hunched – bracing herself for that moment, Kathy thought. Wishing to ease her pain.

"There's a TV van trailing us," Scott explained a few moments later. "When we refuse to talk to them, they'll leave – and they won't know where you'll be staying." He paused. "That is, we hope they won't."

Kathy was shaken. "I didn't expect anything like this."

"The tabloids are always on the prowl for a case they figure will promote a big following. This decade's expansion of the soap operas."

Kathy gazed out of the rear window. The TV van was right behind them. This was just a temporary stalling act, she warned herself. In a small town like this the media would soon track down the house. Would they hound Marcie until the trial? Ellen had said they could stay with her down in New York, she remembered in fresh gratitude. Perhaps they should.

"My house is just ahead," Scott said – with the TV van still tailgating. "The small white colonial." He took one hand from the wheel, reached into his pocket, pulled out a key case. "The first key is the house key." He gave the key case to Kathy. "You two make a fast run for the door. I'll fend off these characters."

Kathy unfastened her seat belt before Scott pulled to a stop, thrust open the door the instant the car came to a halt. She and Marcie ran up the flagstone path to the small, double-columned porch. She swore under her breath because the key didn't turn over immediately. Then the door was unlocked. She swung it wide. She and Marcie walked into the foyer. Scott was brushing off the two men who'd emerged from the van.

"This is a pretty room." Marcie gazed about at the charming traditional furniture. A lived-in room, Kathy thought, observing the books scattered about the coffee table. "Scott's a good man."

"The best."

Scott came into the house, paused at the living-room entrance.

"I'll put up coffee for us. And I'm sure there's something sweet in the freezer." His smile was almost shy. "In moments of stress I have a tendency to develop a yearning for cookies or cake."

"That's a national failing." Kathy picked up his effort at lightness.

"Let me make the coffee," Marcie said impulsively. "Please."

The three went out to Scott's large country kitchen, wallpapered in a cheerful ivy-covered trellis design with a sunlit background. An oak table with four captain's chairs sat at one side.

"The coffee's in the canister there—" Scott pointed. "And you can't miss the coffee maker." He crossed to the refrigerator, pulled out three aluminium foil-wrapped objects, popped them into the oven. "I hope you like hot cinnamon danish."

"Of course." Kathy felt awkward – the other two busy with tasks while she stood idly by.

"Kathy, sit down," Scott ordered, his voice tender.

"I should call Betty," Marcie began, and Kathy froze. "This time of year people are going off on vacation. The office is probably short-handed. And I need to get back to work—" She paused, turned to Scott. "Am I allowed to do that?"

"Of course, you're free to work—" He was disconcerted. His eyes sought Kathy's.

"Marcie, don't call Betty." Kathy was involuntarily sharp.

"Why not? Mom, I need to work. My clients need me." Marcie was puzzled.

"Betty is – well, not very friendly now." Kathy searched her mind for words. "When Angie went to her for a character reference – to present to the judge at your bail hearing – she refused it."

Marcie's face was drained of color. "I don't understand—"

"I went to Betty. I demanded to know why she wouldn't give us a letter," Scott explained, sighed. "She gave me some story about how she'd planned on firing you at the end of the month."

"That's weird!" Marcie blazed. "What's happening in this town? First, Eric Matthews lies about Frank wanting to divorce me – and now Betty lies about meaning to fire me. Why are they lying this way? Is it because they want me to be convicted for Frank's murder? *Why?*"

Thirteen

S cott paced about his office in simmering frustration. He *had* to believe in Marcie's innocence. Not just as her attorney but on a personal level. Kathy had come into his life, and now the whole world seemed brighter to him.

It happened so fast! But he knew that in the weeks ahead he meant to make Kathy understand he wished her to be a permanent part of his life. With her he felt reborn. Was he wrong in suspecting she was drawn to him – as more than Marcie's attorney? But if he failed to clear Marcie – if she was convicted – Kathy would be destroyed. There would be nothing for them.

The prosecutor would hammer hard at the insurance motive. Eric Matthews would be a hostile witness for the prosecution – but his statement was on the record and damaging. Betty Williams had been clearly upset at telling him she meant to discharge Marcie – but that was more damage he couldn't control.

Suppose Marcie was right – Betty Williams lied. Pursue that. See where that led. He reached for the Madison phone directory, flipped to the Ws. As expected, he saw at least a dozen listings under the name of 'Williams'. Williams, Agatha; Williams, Arnold; Williams, Betty. He paused. Betty Williams had her own line, but her address was the same as that for Arnold Williams. Her father? Her brother? Not her husband – she wasn't married, he recalled.

An affluent neighbourhood, he noted. What did her father – or brother – do for a living? Was there something here worth following up?

His mind charging ahead, Scott picked up his phone, dialled Angie's office.

"Jackson Real Estate." Her brisk but cordial business voice greeted him.

"Angie, can you talk?"

"Yeah, I'm alone for now—"

"What can you tell me about Arnold Williams? That's Betty's father or brother?"

"Her father. He owns a local plumbing supply company. He's been in business for at least twenty-five years, does real well." She chuckled. "He even stocks bidets – though there's not much call for them around here."

"What kind of a person is he?" Scott asked, running on instinct.

"He's sharp, active in local groups. Of course, that's part of being a good businessman."

"Is there any way we can link Arnold Williams to Frank?"

"No." She paused. "I mean, not really. I'm sure they know each other through the Rotarians or the Lions Club or the American Legion – some group in town."

"Nothing more direct than that?" Scott was disappointed.

"Wait, there *is* something else. You know how Frank and Marcie fought against the re-zoning of the wetlands. The hearing's been postponed until September," she reminded. "Arnie Williams desperately wants it to go through. He's Peter James's strongest supporter."

"He figures he can sell a lot of plumbing once those houses and condos go up," Scott interpreted. "There's a fortune in business there."

Angie was startled. "You don't think he killed Frank?"

"I'm not saying that. I want to get to the root of what Marcie has pointed out as lies. Remember how upset you were when Betty Williams wouldn't give you a letter about Marcie for her bail hearing? And then Betty firing her?"

"I was dumbfounded." There was an electric quality in Angie's voice now.

"I think Betty was worried that Marcie and Frank might ruin her father's chances at tying up a huge plumbing deal. With Marcie out of the way his chances were better, she'd assumed."

"What has that got to do with Frank's murder?"

"Possibly nothing – but I needed to know that Betty Williams was lying."

At five p.m. he had a meeting with Jake, who was running into dead ends on the True Patriots issue. They talked briefly, Scott gave him further instructions, and he left. Pam brought in papers Scott would need for a real estate closing in the morning.

"All clear?" she asked good-humoredly when he'd scanned the contents of the folder.

"All clear," he said, smiling. "Go home."

Ten minutes later Scott, too, prepared to leave the office. He debated about calling Kathy. Don't butt in, he ordered himself, though he longed to talk with her. This was Marcie's first night home – leave them be. In truth, he had no real news. Just strong doubts about Betty Williams' veracity. One less mark against Marcie.

The phone rang. He picked it up.

"Scott Lazarus—"

"Have you see the *Evening Journal*?" Angie sounded distraught.

"No, what's up?" His grasp on the phone tightened.

"They have a front page story that was supposedly 'leaked' to one of their reporters. They claim Lee Ramsey is going to ask for the death penalty – on the premise that Frank's murder was premeditated. Scott, can she do that?" Angie's voice was shrill with anxiety.

"Governor Pataki signed a death penalty bill," Scott reminded grimly. "Lee Ramsey's out to make headlines. She wants to be a superstar lawyer."

"I have to stay here at the office to interview a client who's looking for a house. This isn't something to tell Kathy over the phone. Could you go over and tell her? She has to know, Scott."

"I'm leaving right now." Lee Ramsey was out to build this case into a media circus.

He paused to call Kathy and say he was coming over.

"Just some things I want to go over with you," he soothed because immediately he'd heard alarm in her voice. "I'll be there in ten minutes."

Pulling into the driveway he saw drapes part slightly at a window of the house next door. The one belonging to the pair of women – Amelia and Edna Rogers – who'd reported hearing Marcie and Frank quarrel 'violently' for two days before his death. The Mitchells – on the other side – were still away on vacation. He hurried to the front door. Kathy stood there, pushing the screen door open.

"It's hot again," she said, making small talk to disguise her apprehension. "Tomorrow's supposed to be a scorcher. Thank God for air-conditioning."

"God and Dr John Gorrie down in Florida, who designed a system to make the air ice cool in his hospital back in the 1850s – and in 1902 Willis Carrier designed an electric system that's the father of today's air-conditioners. How did we survive before we had them?" He walked into the coolness of the foyer.

"We sweated." Kathy's smile was wry. "I remember how enthralled my mother and I were when my father installed our first air-conditioner. I was about ten. On really hot nights we'd camp out in the living-room in front of that wonderful machine. We ate, watched TV, slept there."

"And in big city tenements people slept on fire escapes – and some still do." Scott hesitated. "How's Marcie?"

"She's asleep in her room. Poor baby, she was just exhausted." Kathy's eyes were full of questions now. "I'll get us some ice tea. Ice coffee," she corrected herself. "You're a coffee drinker, like me. I have a pitcher of each in the refrigerator."

"Ice coffee will be great." He followed her out to the kitchen – gearing himself for what must be said. "Kathy, I don't want to upset you any more than you already are – but there's a nasty story in this evening's *Journal*." He fought against an urge to reach out to draw her into his arms. "A 'leak' to the effect that Lee Ramsey is going to ask for the death penalty." Kathy's face drained of color. "It doesn't change our approach – but I wanted to tell you about it before you saw it in a newspaper."

"Sometimes I tell myself I'm having a nightmare – this all can't be happening."

"There's another issue I've been trying to clarify in my mind. This business about Betty Williams—"

"She and Marcie always had such a good relationship." Kathy reached into the refrigerator for the pitcher of ice coffee. "I can't understand what's happened." She brought a pair of tall glasses from a cabinet. "To fire Marcie when she was always so pleased with her work!"

"I may have that figured out. I talked with Angie. She told me about Betty's father being in the plumbing field – and that the two of them had wanted the re-zoning for the wetlands to go through. They'd fought for it."

"You think Betty and her father want Marcie out of the way when the next public hearing comes up in September?"

"A huge amount of business is at stake."

Scott frowned at street sounds that suddenly disturbed the quiet outside. Cars were pulling to a stop. Excited voices filled the air. Kathy turned to him in consternation.

"What's happening?"

"The media discovered Marcie isn't staying at my house," he

interpreted. "That 'death penalty' rumor has brought out the vultures. Go upstairs to Marcie. I'll get rid of them."

"Get away from here! This is a decent neighborhood!" Scott identified the screeching voice as belonging to one of the Rogers sisters. "Go away or I'll call the police!"

Scott waited until he saw Kathy reach the top of the stairs, then went to answer the clamorous ringing of the doorbell. With a resolute smile, he opened the door and moved outside – closing the door behind him.

"What's Marcie's reaction to the death penalty?" a reporter called out.

Simultaneously variations on the same theme were shot at him from others. He blinked at the flash of a TV camera.

"Marcie Loeb – with the court's approval – is en route to New York City to stay with relatives of Rabbi Ginsburg until her court appearance." Scott was polite, calm, but determined to disperse the avid horde. "She'll give no interviews, no comments. I'm sorry – there's nothing else to be said."

Again, a rush of questions were tossed at him. He listened – unruffled – for a few moments, then held up both hands for silence.

"Marcie Loeb is not guilty of this heinous crime. She's devastated at the loss of her husband. There'll be no comments. We mean to prove her innocence in a court of law. That's all."

He reached behind him for the doorknob, for a moment fearful that he had locked himself out. No, the knob turned. The door opened. He went inside and locked it behind him. Outside there was much disappointed conversation, but they were beginning to move towards the cars at the curb. Most of them were outsiders, Scott guessed – not locals.

He dreaded walking into a supermarket in the next few days. He knew he'd see headlines about Marcie on the front pages of the tabloids. And there'd be colorful reports about his own return as a defense attorney. Did Scott Lazarus have the old stuff in him? Could he clear Marcie Loeb?

In an upstairs bedroom Kathy stood behind drapes closed except for a chink. She saw the media horde reluctantly depart.

"They've gone, Marcie," she said at last.

"All clear," Scott called on the stairs.

"Come on, honey," Kathy coaxed. "Let's go downstairs."

Julie Ellis

"I heard what they said." Marcie's voice was a shaken whisper. "But I don't care what they do to me. I just want to know who killed Frank. I want to see that monster punished."

"Marcie, I want that, too. We're trying very hard to find answers."

"It has to be somebody in the True Patriots! But nobody – except for a handful of people here in town – knows it exists!"

"I know it exists, Marcie," Scott told her. "Jake has tracked down their point of operations."

"Then shouldn't the FBI or the Bureau of Alcohol, Tobacco and Firearms be alerted?" Marcie demanded.

"We need more than Jake's report," Scott explained. "He's still chasing down evidence."

"Let's sit down and have dinner," Kathy cajoled. "People have been so kind – some of them," she amended. "They've brought roasts and casseroles and cookies."

Marcie closed her eyes for an instant. "I'm not hungry."

"Darling, you have to eat." Kathy turned beseechingly to Scott.

"Marcie, I'm going to need your help," he told her. "You can't do that if you fall apart."

"I won't fall apart." She lifted her head in defiance. "Frank wouldn't want that of me. Whatever you need me to do, just tell me."

"You two sit down and talk," Kathy ordered. "I'll throw together a fast dinner."

Over dinner and afterwards Scott asked Marcie a wide range of questions – and she responded with candor. Now the conversation zeroed in on the extremist paramilitary groups that seemed to be erupting all over the country.

"It's not a national movement," Scott pinpointed. "It appears they want to stay small, individual groups – but it still has ugly national overtones. And newspaper reports claim they're tightly knit. They have this idea that they have to protect themselves against the federal government. That they're in danger of losing their civil rights. And they're preparing to defend those rights with guns and automatic rifles and bombs. They come from all walks of life – ranchers who don't want to lose free grazing privileges, loggers who blame environmental regulations for the loss of their jobs, unemployed who blame the government for their situation. Then there are the neo-Nazis, who hate African-Americans, Catholics, and Jews."

110

"I should have listened to Frank," Marcie castigated herself. "If I had listened, I'd have known who was involved."

"We're working on pinning down membership. That's our main objective," Scott told her. "If anything Frank said pops belatedly into your mind, Marcie, tell me."

"Let me give an interview to the press," Marcie said zealously. "Let me tell them about the True Patriots. That's what Frank meant to do! He was going to expose them as soon as he had more facts to lay out! Nobody can tell us they don't exist," she challenged Scott. "Your investigator tracked down their training grounds!"

"We need more facts. It's too soon, Marcie." Scott hesitated. "And it could be dangerous." Meaning, Kathy thought in alarm, that they could come after Marcie. "Before we go public, let's know we have enough evidence against them to guarantee their arrests."

Scott left at shortly past ten. He felt Marcie was right about the True Patriots, Kathy thought. Suppose they were both wrong? What was there left to pursue?

"I'm so tired, Mom." Marcie intruded on her introspection. "I think I'll go up to bed. Okay?"

"You run along, darling. I'll be up soon, too. I want to call Jill and see what's doing with the shop."

Kathy spoke at length with Jill, then headed for the stairs. When the phone rang, she rushed back into the living-room to answer lest it awaken Marcie. The caller was Glenn.

"I just saw the ten o'clock news," Glenn said without preliminaries. "What the hell is going on up there? I haven't had a chance to get away yet, but—"

"You don't have to come up," Kathy interrupted. *Marcie doesn't want him here.* "The prosecutor hasn't come out officially yet, but the rumor is that she wants to ask for the death penalty."

"What's the matter with Marcie's lawyer? Can't he understand she ought to plead temporary insanity?"

"Glenn, she's not insane!"

"She's emotionally unstable – records will prove it!"

"Records will prove that she was very upset when her father walked out on her when she was five." Kathy struggled not to scream at him. "A common occurrence among young children in a divorce situation."

"A plea of insanity will get her off the hook!" he yelled.

"Glenn, she didn't kill Frank!"

"I understand she's out on bail—" A wariness in his voice now.

"Yes, we managed that." *Without him.* "Ellen and Angie and I."

"Where is Marcie? Not that she'll want to talk to me." An aggrieved quality replaced wariness.

"No, she doesn't want to talk to you. And Scott convinced the press that she'll be living in New York City until the trial. She—"

"They don't think she's here with *me*?" he interrupted in alarm.

"She's supposed to be staying with Rabbi Ginsburg's relatives. She's here with me. But sooner or later, Glenn, the media will ask questions about her father. I'll say nothing. Marcie will say nothing. But you can't hide in a closet."

"Marcie's always had a split personality. She's two people. The sweet, pretty little innocent – and the devious, controlling little bitch that we've both seen."

"I don't want to talk to you anymore. Goodnight, Glenn." She slammed down the phone in rage.

Tomorrow I'll call Leslie. We must talk.

Fourteen

Kathy went through the usual night routine. Check the back and front doors, turn off the downstairs lights. She saw the downstairs lamp in the Mitchells' house next door go off. In a couple of minutes their upstairs bedroom light would go on via the automatic timer. This was supposed to confuse possible robbers. A few years ago nobody in Madison worried about such things.

She wished that Tim and Grace were back from their vacation. Usually they spent three weeks every summer at their rustic cabin in the Adirondacks – what Tim called their 'escape from civilization'. 'No telephone, no TV, not even a radio,' Tim boasted. 'Just Grace and me and the fish.' But this summer, Kathy recalled tenderly, Grace had coaxed Tim into agreeing to a week's cruise to Nova Scotia before they went to the mountains.

Grace and Tim had bought their house just a year before Mom and Dad bought this one. They'd been so supportive when Dad – and then Mom – died. They'd been too polite to say anything, but she'd known right off that they hadn't liked Glenn. They adored Marcie and Linda.

Everything was all right, she told herself. Go on upstairs. She knew, of course, that tonight she'd again be plagued by insomnia. When was the last time she'd had a decent night's sleep? Not since that awful call from Marcie. Yet she recoiled from taking sleeping pills.

Arriving at the head of the stairs she saw no light from beneath Marcie's door. Hopefully she was asleep. She was so tired, so drained, poor baby.

She went into her own room – leaving the door half-open because she found it difficult to sleep with a closed bedroom door. Glenn used to hate that, she remembered. She always wanted the door open so she'd hear the kids if one of them woke up for some reason or other. The only time they'd closed their bedroom door was when they made love.

She'd just turned down the bed when the phone rang again. She hurried to pick up the bedroom extension.

"Am I calling too late?" Linda asked. A routine question when she called after ten.

"Darling, no." Didn't Linda know by now that no time was too late for her or Marcie to call? "Just let me close my door." She shut the door with a gentle movement that caused no noise, then returned to the phone. "How're you feeling?" She knew how each day dragged the final two months of pregnancy.

"Dad's so upset about Marcie's lawyer," Linda said. "He doesn't think the guy knows what he's doing."

"Scott is one of the best criminal lawyers in this country! Marcie and I have complete faith in him. We wouldn't dream of changing lawyers now—"

"What does Marcie know?" Linda grunted in exasperation. "Except to throw temper tantrums."

"Marcie doesn't throw temper tantrums," Kathy shot back. "She's very intense about things she feels are important!"

"Mom, you're always rushing to cover for Marcie. You'll never admit she can be wrong."

"That's not true." She was unnerved by this accusation. "You and Marcie are more important to me than anything else in this world." *But Linda believes I favored Marcie over her. Why was I never been aware of this? Linda was always self-sufficient – once the first year of the divorce was past. Marcie was the super-sensitive, vulnerable child.*

"Dad said the District Attorney is asking for the death penalty." Linda sounded distraught. That wasn't good for her, Kathy worried. "He thinks the lawyer should plead temporary insanity. If she's committed to a psychiatric hospital, she could be out in a year, Dad says."

"Linda, do you think Marcie killed Frank?"

"Dad says we have to be realistic. Think of the evidence they have against her," Linda hedged.

"This is your sister, Linda." Kathy struggled to keep her voice even. "You know Marcie. How could you – even for a moment – think that she killed Frank?"

"Dad says we have to—"

"I don't want to hear another word about what Dad says," Kathy broke in. "All he ever thinks about is himself. He wants the trial to be over fast so it'll disappear from the headlines. He's terrified of being identified as Marcie Loeb's father."

"Mom, can't you ever forget that you and Dad had an unhappy marriage? All I have to do is mention him, and you erupt into hostility."

"I'm sorry." Would she ever forget those awful years of trying to bring up her girls all alone? She'd gone out into the business world with so little experience, no skills. Each month she worried about the mortgage payment on the house. A trip to the dentist was a catastrophe. "How're you feeling?" She made a determined effort to divert the conversation. "Is this heat bothering you?"

They talked a few minutes longer – with Linda admitting yet again to being lonely because David spent such long hours working.

"He works two or three nights a week, goes in most weekends. But he's anxious about money – you know, with the baby coming and my not working." Linda wanted to stay home with the baby the first year, Kathy remembered – then resume a career in the computer field. "He worries about all our loans." The huge mortgage payments on their expensive eleven-room house, the two luxury cars acquired to provide the successful facade his firm expected. "He says he worked his butt off so long – college, then the years in grad school – and now he wants to enjoy the good things."

But what happened if an emergency arose, Kathy asked herself – and all their loans piled up unpaid? For how long could she see them through a crisis? And Glenn would never come through for either Marcie or Linda. The big wedding had been his final paternal act. He'd made that clear.

Listening to Linda pour out her fears, Kathy suppressed a sigh. Why couldn't David have accepted a job in this area? Why did he have to move with Linda to the other side of the country? In her mind she heard Linda's explanation. *'This was by far the best deal he was offered. He had to run with it.'* What happened to the time when families remained in their home towns instead of scattered over the face of the globe?

"I hear the car in the driveway." A lilt in Linda's voice now. "David's home."

Kathy sat at the edge of the bed. Her mind dwelled on the discovery that Linda believed Marcie was her favorite. How could she think that? She'd never doubted that Linda was hurt by Glenn's behavior from time to time – but Linda always dreamt up alibis for him to her friends. It was important to let them know she had a devoted father. Glenn was a devoted father, yes – to his second family.

She remembered how hurt Linda had been when Glenn had not showed up for her 'sweet sixteen' party. *'I'll get there before it's over – with your present. You'll be the prettiest "sweet sixteen" there – and I'll be so proud of you.'* She remembered Linda on the phone with her best friend the next day. *'It was awful! He was just twenty-two miles from here when some drunken idiot jumped lanes and smashed into him head-on. It's a miracle he's alive.'*

Scott would never have disappointed a child the way Glenn disappointed Linda and Marcie over and over again.

Marcie sat by the window and stared into the night. Scott was wrong, she told herself. He was listening to his legal mind, to reason. But her heart told her that to find Frank's killer she must make public accusations. Let all of Madison know what festered here in secret.

Scraps of what Frank had told her seeped into her mind now – though she had tried to tell herself she had heard nothing except his insistence that the group existed. *'They've been organized over a year – and nobody knows of their existence. They're a humongous bomb waiting to go off.'*

She couldn't do what Frank meant to do – but she could sound the alarm. Scott was wrong – they couldn't wait. She might be tried, convicted, and executed before the truth came out about the True Patriots.

Fired into action she left her bedroom, walked to her mother's door. Mom was asleep. She closed the door with stealth-like movements, then hurried with silent footsteps to the stairs, illuminated by the one wall sconce that remained on during the night.

She paused at the door to the den. Her heart was pounding. She wavered, fighting for the courage to walk into that room again. This was for Frank – to do what he wanted to do. She opened the door, reached for the light switch. Soft light bathed the room. The rug where Frank lay that awful afternoon had been removed.

All at once she was assaulted by dizziness. She reached out to steady herself. She didn't want to remember those horrendous moments when she'd hovered over Frank praying he wasn't dead. She didn't want to remember the ugly fighting those last two days.

With grim determination she crossed to the computer, sat down.

Best Friends

Close the door – Mom mustn't know I'm was down here. The door shut, she returned to the computer. Her mind was bursting with what she meant to say. An open letter to the residents of Madison – warning them of the extremists who trained in secret for the day when they would erupt into a destructive fighting force.

She knew there was no way the soft tapping of the computer keys could be heard beyond the room, yet at intervals she cast anxious glances towards the door. She wrote and revised – and revised again – until at last she was satisfied with what was said.

All right, run off one hundred copies on the copier. That wasn't much – but the word would spread like a California forest fire in August.

Clutching the copies in her hands she made her way out of the house and into the night. The only house light visible now was the lamp in the Mitchells' upstairs bedroom – which would go off at precisely one a.m. She'd plotted her area of distribution while she was at the copier. Half would be slid under homes in the nearby affluent section – the other half under the doors of blue collar families in the other direction.

She walked swiftly over the deserted streets – silent except for an occasional bark of a curious dog – willing herself to think only of her mission. When she was done, she'd creep back into the house and up to her bedroom. And in the morning, she surmised, all hell would break loose.

Fifteen

Before eight a.m. Kathy was in the kitchen, the coffee maker at work. She'd managed six hours of troubled sleep, courtesy of her allergy medication – but she'd been awake since sunrise. Her efforts to return to sleep had been futile. She was plagued by images of an imminent confrontation with Leslie. Don't think of her as Leslie, she exhorted herself. Lee. Lee Ramsey.

She glanced at the clock. Joe would have left for work already. Angie would still be at the house. She reached for the phone and dialed their number.

"Hello—"

"I'm building myself up to call Leslie this morning." Kathy sighed. "I'm a nervous wreck."

"Don't call her at the office," Angie said. "Call her at home this evening. She won't be able to talk at the office."

"Of course. God, I'm not thinking straight these days."

"Don't expect too much," Angie warned. "This is not the sweet little Leslie we used to know."

"What happened all those years ago has to mean something." Yet she, too, harbored misgivings. "Angie, I can't just stand by until something shows up in the newspapers, and she realizes I'm Marcie's mother."

"She'll still be the prosecuting attorney. But yes," Angie conceded, "knowing Marcie's your daughter should make her less the rampaging prosecutor."

"I want her to open her eyes and to listen to what Scott has to present. Even an over-ambitious prosecuting attorney shouldn't want to convict an innocent person." She heard the sound of her call waiting. "Angie, I have another call coming in. I'll get back to you later." She switched to the other caller. "Hello."

"You Marcie Loeb's mother?" a harsh male voice demanded.

"Yes . . ." She was instantly wary.

"Ain't it enough she killed her husband? Now she's tryin' to make this whole town look bad! You tell her to forget that shit

118

she's spreadin' around – or she won't be around to be convicted!"

"What are you talking about?" Kathy demanded, but she heard the phone slam down at the other end.

Unnerved, trying to assimilate what the caller had said, Kathy started as the phone rang again, sounding ominous. Oh, it was probably Angie, she rebuked herself, and picked up the receiver. "Hello—"

"We don't need people like you in this town!" The caller didn't bother to ask for any identification. "Get out before somebody burns your house down!"

"Who is this?" Kathy's voice soared in rage. But – again – the caller had hung up. *What are they talking about*?

Call Scott, her mind instructed – but before she could do this, the phone rang again. She hesitated – recoiling from another menacing, disembodied voice. The caller was insistent. She lifted the receiver, steeling herself for what would be said.

"Hello. Is this Marcie Loeb's residence?" A calm male voice.

"Yes . . ."

"I know this is awfully early to be phoning," he apologized, "but may I speak with her, please?"

"No, I'm sorry." Kathy was terse.

"Is this her mother?"

"Yes—" What was happening?

"This is Bill Cooper of the *Madison Guardian*. I'd like to interview her about the open letter I found under my door this morning."

"I'm sorry – I don't know what you're talking about." Trembling, she put down the phone, paused a moment, then took it off the hook. What did he mean, '*the open letter I found under my door this morning*'?

She poured herself a mug of coffee, sat at the table in the dining area. Phone noises were a raucous reminder that the receiver was off the hook. Then the phone was silent. Her mind was in chaos. In a few minutes, she promised herself, she'd call Scott. He'd understand what was happening. Thank God for Scott.

She was conscious of the unreal quietness of the house. Normally she would be listening to NPR news by now, watching for the weather report. But she was grateful that Marcie was sleeping – and in her own bed. She shuddered, envisioning the

Julie Ellis

tiny cell where Marcie had been confined for harrowing days and nights.

She stiffened at the sound of the doorbell. Terrified to respond. *Just sit here and be quiet. Maybe whoever is leaning on the bell will go away.* She glanced upward, hoping the loud intrusion wouldn't awaken Marcie.

The ringing stopped. Whoever it was had gone away, Kathy thought in relief. What was that craziness about an 'open letter'?

"Kathy!" She spun around to the sound of Scott's voice at the kitchen door. "Kathy, let me in!"

Kathy rushed to pull the door wide. "I was going to call you in a few minutes. I've had some weird phone calls. I don't know what's happening—"

"Where's Marcie?" He strode into the kitchen. "She has some explaining to do!"

"Mom?" Marcie's voice – defensive, defiant, scared – came to them from the stairs.

"Marcie, what the hell have you been up to?" Scott called to her in exasperation, then reached into a pocket for a sheet of paper. "Kathy, read what's floating around town!"

Kathy scanned the impassioned report of the presence of the so-called True Patriots in Madison – signed by Marcie. *Marcie's handwriting.*

"I don't understand." Kathy was bewildered – and alarmed. Scott was so angry. She'd never seen him like this. Was he about to drop Marcie's case?

Marcie walked into the kitchen.

"I did it in the middle of the night," she said quietly. "It was what Frank wanted to do – before they stopped him. I distributed just a hundred copies – but I knew the word would get around fast. It's true," she said passionately, her eyes defying Scott to refute her. "Your investigator knows it!"

"Yes, we know the group exists," Scott conceded. "But so far all we have is the location of their training center. Until they show themselves – until we have positive ID of the membership —we can't move. This takes time, Marcie—"

"I don't have time! We can't wait until I've been tried, convicted, maybe executed." Marcie ignored her mother's gasp of protest. "I have to expose the True Patriots. For Frank I have to do this!"

Scott took a deep breath, exhaled. Kathy's eyes clung to him.

"Marcie, this was not the time to do this. Don't you understand? You've put your life in jeopardy. I think it's urgent that we get you out of town."

"We can stay with Ellen in New York," Kathy told him. He was angry out of fear for Marcie's safety, she realized. "She said—"

"I won't run away," Marcie broke in. "I've told you. I must expose them – as Frank meant to do. I owe that to Frank. I can't leave now. I mustn't!"

Sixteen

Kathy and Marcie sat at the dining table and made reluctant stabs at their scrambled eggs while Scott argued at the telephone. "But I've told you what's been happening." Despite his efforts at calm, exasperation crept into his voice. "Marcie's being threatened. She and her mother need protection." He listened to the voice at the other end – his face reflecting his anger and frustration. "Yes, I understand your situation," he said. "I know you're short-staffed since the budget cuts."

He put down the phone, hesitated a moment, then bent to remove the phone line from the wall jack. Now he returned to his place at the table.

"They turned you down," Kathy said, struggling to mask her fear.

"I'll be all right," Marcie said with shaky bravado. "Mom, you go stay with Ellen."

"I'll stay with you," Kathy insisted.

"I think – at least for the next few days – I ought to arrange for private security." Scott paused. "It should be on a twenty-four hour basis."

"Whatever you think is necessary," Kathy told him. He was worried about the expenses. First the investigator, now the security guards. And she couldn't borrow on the house – it was collateral for Marcie's bail. She'd manage somehow. "And let's keep the security for as long as you feel we should have it."

"I'll go over to the phone company and arrange for another line. Unlisted," he emphasized and managed a whimsical smile. "I have some contacts over there – we'll have fast action." Now he turned to Marcie. His earlier anger had ebbed away. His face radiated compassion. "I'm not happy about what you've done," he said quietly. "But I can understand. But no more grandstanding," he warned. "If you want me on the case, you do as I say."

"I will." Her voice an apologetic whisper.

"I'll go over and talk to the security people right now." Scott pushed back his chair.

"Have your breakfast first," Kathy ordered. "And your coffee's probably cold. Let me give you a fresh mug."

"These security guards—" Marcie seemed to be searching for words. "Will they be armed? I hate guns. I was proud that Frank refused to hunt." In an area where most men hunted, kept guns in their homes.

"They have to be," Scott pointed out. "But they'll be on the outside at all times. I don't want you to leave the house," he stressed. "We're dealing with extremists." He sighed. "You won't reconsider leaving town?"

"I can't. That would be saying I lied. That I made up that story because I'm desperate to clear myself. And if they do come looking for me—" she lifted her head defiantly, "—won't that help us flush them out?"

"I'd have preferred to flush them out under other circumstances," Scott conceded. "But yes, that might bring them out into the open. We assume those nasty calls came from members, but they didn't identify themselves as such. They could be people just incensed at the suggestion that such extremists exist in Madison. And, as you said, there'll be those who'll insist this is your effort to implicate somebody else."

"But they exist!" Marcie insisted. "Your investigator tracked them down."

"We need to find the one member who killed Frank." Scott squinted in thought. "Marcie, I know how painful it'll be – but I want you to go back into your mind and try to remember that afternoon. I noticed cat hairs when I checked the area. You told me Frank was allergic to cats. How would you explain cat hair in the room?"

"It must have blown in through the open patio door," Kathy answered for her. "The women next door have two cats. At this time of year cats are shedding heavily."

"Did you notice anything unfamiliar when you walked into the room?" Scott pursued. "The scent of perfume? Cigar smoke? Did Frank smoke?"

"No. He was allergic to tobacco smoke," Marcie said, then stopped dead. "There was something." She clutched at the memory. "Cigarette smoke. Awfully heavy. Like Turkish cigarettes." Her eyes darted from Scott to her mother, back again to Scott. "Somebody had been in the room only moments before I came in! Someone who smoked Turkish cigarettes!"

"That's good, Marcie," Scott encouraged. "You keep thinking."

"That's all," she said after a moment – seeming exhausted now. "Nothing else."

"Somewhere along the line," Scott said reassuringly, "these little things will help us pin down the person we're looking for. The person who killed Frank." He reached for his mug, drained the contents. "Let me go over and talk with the security people. I'll have to spend some time at the office – seeing clients. I'll be back sometime in the afternoon. Keep the phone unplugged. Don't answer the door."

Twenty minutes after Scott left, Kathy and Marcie heard a car pull up in the driveway.

"Don't answer the door, Mom!" Marcie was fearful.

"Sssh," Kathy ordered and hurried to peer through a chink in the drapes. "It's all right," she said in relief. "It's Angie. She's heard about your open letter." Half the town had probably heard by now.

Shortly before three p.m. Scott returned to the house. He was accompanied by a pair of tall, muscular, armed security men. One was posted at the front of the house, the other at the rear. They'd be relieved at midnight by two other guards, Scott told Kathy and Marcie.

"I'll try again for police protection," he promised Kathy. He knew she was unnerved by the cost of private security in addition to all the other expenses, she realized. "I have an appointment in the morning to discuss it with the Police Commissioner."

"It's all right." Kathy forced a faint smile. "I'll handle it."

"Mom, I'm sorry—" Marcie was contrite. "Frank and I have a couple of thousand in our savings account. I – I can go to the bank and take it out." But Scott had said she was not to leave the house, Kathy remembered.

"If it's a joint account, the funds will be frozen for now," Scott explained. "It's part of Frank's estate."

"Marcie, you're not to worry," Kathy insisted. "I can handle this."

"I worry about what's being done to fight the re-zoning of the wetlands. Frank was the firebrand behind that. I feel awful about not seeing my clients," Marcie said. "I was thinking that maybe I'd write each of them, explain that they won't be neglected. Some are so fragile." She turned to Scott. "I can do that, can't I?"

"That would be the kind thing to do." His smile was reassuring. And it would be a distraction for Marcie, Kathy told herself. Something to fill what would be long, empty hours. "I have to get back to the office to sign some letters that Pam was getting out for me." He seemed to be debating now. "How would you feel about my coming back later to sit down and pick your brain?" he asked Kathy, a glint of wry humor in his eyes. "I'm on a fishing expedition – looking for something, I'm not sure what."

"That would be fine." She made a fast mental inventory of the refrigerator. "What about having an early dinner with Marcie and I?" She found strength in his presence. She was less afraid.

"I'll pick up dinner for us," he decided. "Anything special you'd like?" He gazed from Kathy to Marcie. "Or do you trust me?"

"We trust you." Kathy was unnerved by the emotions that welled in her.

Kathy and Marcie were starkly conscious of the pair of security guards that watched over the house. The two men had been briefed about who was to be admitted: other than Scott, only Angie and Joe – and Ellen when she came up from the city. They were aware of the telephone that sat unplugged. They were isolated from the world, Kathy thought – until the phone company brought in another line.

To fill the time until Scott returned, Kathy set the table in the dining area, ground beans for coffee. Marcie was poring over the telephone book in search of addresses for clients. She was frustrated that several were without phones.

Scott arrived a little past five carrying two huge bags.

"You bought enough for an army," Kathy protested while the two of them unloaded the bags. "Marcie, bring more plates."

They sat down to barbecued chicken, tossed salad, a bean salad, a variety of cheeses. Frozen yogurt had been stored in the freezer for the moment. A bowl of fruit salad sat at the center of the table. They were making a concerted effort to ignore the trauma that hung over their heads. Kathy coaxed Marcie to eat. Always slim, she seemed almost fragile now.

Scott tried to divert them with stories about his childhood in Georgia.

"I never saw the ocean until I was ten and we moved to New York. I saw the Atlantic, and I forgave my parents for dragging my brother and me away from everything we knew. It was love at first sight." For an instant his eyes lingered on her – and Kathy was disconcerted.

"Ellen's kids adore the ocean. Her mother-in-law has a house out at Montauk. They run out there every chance they get."

"I think I'll start on my letters." Marcie glanced from her mother to Scott with an air of apology. "I should get them out as soon as possible."

"Go ahead, darling," Kathy told her.

"I wonder what's happening with our campaign for the Senior Citizens Center?" Marcie was troubled. "Frank was so anxious for that to come through."

"I'll ask around," Scott promised.

Kathy waited until she heard the door to the den opened and closed before she spoke again.

"How could Betty Williams fire Marcie?" she demanded in exasperation. "Nobody could be more devoted to her clients. They love her. They bring her little gifts."

"The old greed deal." His eyes were somber. "Protecting her father's interests. A lot of money is at stake."

"Her grandfather ran a small grocery store here in Madison," Kathy said. "I remember my mother saying what a shame it was when the supermarkets came into town and he closed up."

"My grandfather ran a grocery store down in Georgia," Scott reminisced. "My father worked there on Saturdays from the time he was fourteen until he went away to college. He came out of the University of Georgia with a degree in journalism and went right into the army. He fought through the North African campaign. Sicily, Sardinia, Italy – the whole deal."

"My father fought in the Second World War." Kathy's face lighted. "He and my mother were married right after he got out of service. They bought this house under the GI bill. Sometimes I wonder what my father would think if he knew what the world was like these days," she mused. "Half the world erupting into small wars."

"When I was a little kid, I used to sneak out of my room at night to eavesdrop on my father and a couple of his friends while they sat around rehashing their war years."

"I've wondered sometimes if hearing our fathers talk about war – stripped of the glory supplied by Hollywood movies – caused the anti-Vietnam feeling of so many of our generation."

"Most of us were spoiled to death. Our parents had gone through the Depression and a war, and they wanted to see us spared that. And then they were shocked," he said humorously, "when we demonstrated against Vietnam and marched for civil rights and discarded their sexual mores. Most parents spoiled their kids," he reiterated. "My folks were strict – and sometimes I rebelled. But in the long run I've been grateful."

"Scott—" Kathy prodded herself back to the present. "Will Marcie's letter bring the True Patriots out into the open? That could work for us, couldn't it?"

"Kathy, we don't know that one of the so-called True Patriots killed Frank," Scott reminded. "That's one lead that we're pursuing. But I want to track down the person who came into that room smoking heavily and leaving a trail of cat hair. I have a gut feeling that he – or she – is Frank's killer."

Seventeen

Ellen printed out her day's work with a sense of elation. She'd wrap up the book in another week. But – as always these last days – she was conscious of an overwhelming depression when she emerged from work to reality. Frank was dead. Marcie was facing a murder trial. One moment life was beautiful – the next tragedy descended. And she was constantly haunted by the knowledge that her marriage was in trouble.

She checked her watch. A bit early to leave to meet Michael. It was ridiculous the way she kept meeting him for dinner night after night. But he was so uptight about the auction – and alone in New York. *'New York is a ghost city for me in summer – everybody I know has taken off.'* He was alternately pessimistic about the outcome of the auction and elated by his conviction that Donna would make a sensational deal for him. She'd known him for six days – but it seemed as though they'd known each other forever.

There was no reason for her to feel guilty about seeing Michael this way. They met at a restaurant, ate, talked shop, then he put her into a taxi to go off to her 'late shift'. He knew she was finishing her book, understood how she felt at this point. She enjoyed spending an hour and a half or two hours with Michael. He was warm, bright, witty – he made her laugh. The way Phil used to do.

Call Phil, her mind ordered. He and Mom ate at six – they'd have finished dinner by now. She reached for the phone. Phil picked up on the first ring. He was out on the deck with the cordless phone at his side, he explained. The weather was sensational.

"I'm having a real rest," he told her. "I lie on the deck and read or stare at the ocean. I walk on the beach before breakfast. Nobody on the beach that early, even though it's in season now. Just me and a town dog – usually a lab – out for a constitutional. And, of course, the gulls."

"Sounds heavenly." Ellen was brushed by nostalgia, remembering sunrises she'd watched with Phil at Montauk. Remembering that awesome moment when the orange ball slowly rose above the horizon.

"Sometimes Mom walks with me at sunset," Phil continued. "And you know she's stuffing me with great food."

"Mom's a terrific cook." All right, there were swatches of time when *she* didn't cook – but the Upper West Side was noted for its sensational take-out spots.

"What's with Marcie?" Phil was serious now.

She told him about Marcie's 'open letter' and the ugly phone calls Kathy had received at the house.

"It was the smart thing to do," he approved.

"I'm scared. All it takes is one crazy to pull off something awful. But they have two security men on duty around the clock." She clung to this knowledge.

"The letter will plant suspicion in some minds that one of that extremist group killed Frank. Remember, the jury will be picked from local people."

For a few minutes they discussed the kids. She'd commissioned Ted to bring her earrings from Madrid. Phil had given him money to buy a purse for Mom. Claire had promised to bring souvenirs from major points of interest.

She waited for Phil to say he missed her – but he said nothing of this. The inference was that he'd be back in town to meet Claire and Ted when they returned from their trips. She felt the same terrifying wall between them. *Nothing had changed.*

Phil put down the phone, sat at the edge of the chaise and stared out at the glistening ocean without seeing. Ellen didn't need him. On her own she was self-sufficient. Unflappable. Mom always called her a dynamo.

Ellen had created a world of her own that held no place for him. She loved living in Manhattan. She relished the contact with other writers, the availability of the city's great libraries, the theaters and museums. Still, she admitted the need to escape at regular intervals to the quiet of Montauk. Mom and Dad had bought this house his junior year in high school. They'd moved out full-time ten years ago. It had become his personal refuge. To him Manhattan was a symbol of his failure. Ellen belonged there. He didn't.

He heard the car pulling into the driveway. Mom had made a

Julie Ellis

quick trip down to the Ocean View Farmers' Market – which she called Montauk's version of Manhattan's Balducci's – to pick up one of their outrageously delicious cakes – meant to lift his spirits. She'd sensed over dinner that he was depressed. Damn, why was he so transparent?

"Phil—" Mom's voice drifted out to the deck a few minutes later. "Coffee's ready, and we have that luscious cappuccino mousse cake you like so much."

"I'll be right there." He tried to sound enthusiastic. Did Mom expect a special dessert to make him view the world in a different light? Immediately he felt guilty. Mom suspected his marriage was on shaky ground and was bewildered and upset.

"What a glorious day!" Mom smiled warmly as he walked into the dining area. She placed two mugs of steaming coffee on the table. "I wish Ellen had been able to come out this week."

"You know how she is when she's finishing up a book," he reminded. "Oh, she called while you were in town."

"How're things going with Marcie?"

"The trial is still weeks away. Ellen said Marcie's lawyer is hoping like hell to come up with the real murderer before Marcie goes to trial – but everything's iffy at this point."

"It'll work out," his mother soothed, bringing the cake to the table. "There's no way Marcie could have done it."

"Only in fiction does everything end happily." His smile was caustic.

"Sometimes we have to work for happy endings," she said after a moment.

"Mom, in four years I'll be fifty. And what have I done with my life?"

"You're a dedicated teacher – that's a gift to humanity."

"I teach in a fancy private school – because that's safe." Ellen had prodded him into this because she'd been frightened that he'd be assigned to a ghetto high school where teachers had to combat students with guns and knives and drug habits. "What's the challenge in teaching history to upper middle-class kids whose main worry is 'will I make it into an Ivy League school?'"

"Their lives are not all that idyllic," she rejected. "How many times have you tried to help students who're into drugs and alcohol and sexual promiscuity? Children, you've told me, who have no real family life because parents are off in pursuit of wealth and fame. Phil,

130

you do make a contribution. And what about your writing? That's a contribution, too."

"Half a dozen short stories in the past sixteen years?" he jeered.

"You have the summer off. Thank God, you didn't insist on teaching summer classes again. Why don't you use this summer to plot a new book? You always used to say you could work so well out here—"

"That was another time." He dug into his cake with vicious thrusts. "That's past history, Mom. Forget it."

Ellen left the apartment and cabbed up to Barnes & Noble – where Michael had suggested they meet. They'd have dinner somewhere in the neighborhood. These past evenings he'd taken her on an ethnic journey that had been such fun – that had made her feel young and adventurous.

She found him browsing at a collection of computer books.

"I just had a great idea," he greeted her. "What do you say to a picnic tonight? There's a gorgeous breeze out, and with the sun going down it's pleasant outdoors. And I know the perfect place."

"Where?" She picked up his convivial mood.

"On my terrace," he said triumphantly. All at once she was wary. She knew he was staying in a borrowed apartment in the West Seventies, but there'd never been talk of her going to his place or his coming to hers. "We'll see the sun set over the Hudson River, high above the city. And I need to talk to you about where I'm heading career-wise." He was serious now.

"Wouldn't Donna be better able to advise you than me?"

"Donna's shocked because I want to move into fiction for my next book. She thinks I'm crazy."

"No! You should do what your mind tells you." There was nothing romantic about this, she told herself in relief. Writers were a lonely crew – reaching out to one another.

"We'll talk about it at our picnic. Encourage me, Ellen." His smile was woeful. "I know so little about this business. Now, where around here do we shop for picnic makings?"

"Citarella," she told him. "What would please your fancy tonight? Are you in a seafood mood? Citarella has wonderful seafood hors d'oeuvres."

"Citarella's," he decided. "I'm in a seafood mood."

They headed south, paused twice to inspect the second-hand books offered for sale at the sidewalk tables that are part of the Upper West Side scene. The streets in the summer heat seemed devoid of the usual homeless wanderers – who were no doubt seeking comfort on nearby Riverside Drive.

They approached Citarella with an air of adventure, paused to admire the fish sculpture in the window, strolled into the immaculate premises that utilized every available inch of space to display an endless array of gourmet delights. Three walls of counter space plus a center island – served by perhaps a dozen smiling clerks.

"Gourmet heaven for upscale yuppies," Michael labelled Citarella's.

"Not just yuppies," Ellen scolded. "I've come here for a quarter-pound of nova – without nitrites, mind you – and I've splurged," she conceded, "after signing a contract that sounded great before taxes and agent's commissions, and had only small change left out of a hundred dollar bill."

"Okay, let's get cracking," Michael ordered in high good humor. "But none of the fancy fat-free items," he stipulated. "We'll live dangerously tonight. To hell with our arteries. And how do we know which smoked salmon – pardon me, nova to you native New Yorkers – to choose? They must have fifteen kinds here!"

They debated, settled on nitrite-free Norwegian nova – which Ellen confided she often took upstate to Kathy – asked for the seafood hors d'oeuvres, then bean salad.

"Vegetable lasagne," Michael decided. "It'll heat up in minutes."

"Bread," Ellen reminded. "Something exotic. Oh God, everything looks so tempting!"

"Focaccia," Michael decreed. "And for dessert tiramisu."

Their shopping completed, they headed for the luxury apartment building where Michael was staying. There was nothing romantic about this, Ellen told herself again. They were two writers who enjoyed each other's company – and he needed moral support. But sometimes their eyes met and she was shaken by the sudden emotions that invaded her.

The twentieth-floor corner apartment on loan to Michael offered the typical layout of Manhattan high rentals: dining area that blended into a fairly large living-room with one wall of windows, a kitchenette off the dining area, and what Ellen surmised was a master bedroom and bath. The furniture was modern, attractive, and expensive. The wraparound terrace – with a dining corner at one side and an array of charming patio furniture scattered about its lavish length – was spectacular, like the view.

"Oh, this is magnificent!" Ellen gazed about at the lush greenery, the troughs of multi-colored petunias, pink and red geraniums, a potted bush of red roses.

"Up here I feel isolated from the city," Michael said with supreme satisfaction. "But hey, let's get this show on the road. We've got picnic makings waiting to be dished."

They went into the kitchenette to unpack the Citarella offerings. Michael slid the two portions of vegetable lasagne into the toaster oven.

"This sure beats staying in a hotel." Michael chuckled. "I've spent time in a lot of them through the years – often under rotten conditions. Tehran in '80, Haiti in '86, Tel Aviv during the Gulf war. Belgrade in the current insanity—"

"Shall I put up coffee?" Ellen asked, glancing about the kitchenette.

"I'll do it. You bring out the plates and silver and set things up. And no snitching the hors d'oeuvres," he joshed. "We divide them up equally."

They sat in the comforting breeze on the terrace and watched the sun move lower in the sky while they ate. Not until they were digging into the tiramisu – a delectable custard concoction of mascarpone cheese and ladyfingers dipped in espresso – did Michael launch into talk about his new project.

"Do it," she urged when he finally paused for breath. "How can you deny that kind of enthusiasm?"

"Sometimes I think I'll be cheating – borrowing from my own life the way I'll be doing. It won't be a *roman à clef*," he said conscientiously. "But yes, a take-off on some of what has happened to me through the passing years." He was pensive. "I don't hate my wife any more. I've gone past that." Involuntarily Ellen thought of Kathy. Glenn still colored her life because of Marcie and Linda. At least Michael had no children. "We dragged it on for four years. I didn't know her any more. She was a stranger. It was after the divorce that I went the foreign correspondent route."

They talked about the years behind – delighted to discover that they'd shared so much. The high school and college years working with civil rights groups, the torment of the Vietnam years, the college

133

demonstrations. They felt themselves twenty-five years younger as they relived those young experiences.

"There were years when Dad was working all over the world. London, Paris, Melbourne, Tokyo. My mother and sister and I trailed along. Dad's retired now – he and Mom live in Sedona, Arizona. I'll stop off to see them on my way to Alaska."

"You've got plenty of material for a novel," she said softly. "Go for it."

"Let's face it. Most fiction mirrors life – not vice versa. Liz tried the marriage route two more times – and divorced again each time."

"Do you regret your divorce?" she asked in sudden curiosity. There was a sadness beneath his light mood that reached out to her.

"No. I regret not finding the woman I thought Liz was." His eyes clung to hers. Searching, making a disconcerting statement. Abruptly he rose to his feet. "I'll put up coffee. We'll have it with the sunset." He glanced at his watch. "Which will be in about twenty minutes. Possibly," he added because all at once clouds were hovering overhead, hiding the sun. "And I'd special-ordered a sunset."

Ellen sat alone on the terrace, struggling to deal with the unspoken exchange between them. *This wasn't supposed to happen.* They were two writers enjoying a brief friendship. Michael would soon be off to Alaska, and heaven only knew where after that. She'd probably never see him again – unless he happened to light in New York for a conference with Donna or his editor.

All at once raindrops began to fall. She hurried from the terrace into the living-room, stood at the slider and watched the drizzle gain momentum.

"The coffee's in work—" Michael came from the kitchenette. "My apologies for the lack of a sunset." He was deliberately casual as he walked to the thirty-five inch TV set. "I have a confession to make: I'm a news junkie. It's an occupational hazard." His smile was wry, his eyes tormented. "Would you mind if I flip on the news for a couple minutes?"

"Of course not." She contrived to match his casualness. They'd have coffee and she'd leave. He knew about her late shift at the computer. But she was conscious of the pounding of her heart.

Michael turned on the TV, began to channel-surf. All at once she snapped to attention.

"Michael, hold it there!" She dropped to the edge of a chair, leaned forward anxiously.

"Accused of murdering her husband, Marcie Loeb denounced a secret paramilitary group in Madison, New York . . ." Ellen clung to the newscaster's report. Earlier she'd talked with Kathy, had been briefed on this. It was frightening to think of Kathy and Marcie, holed up in the house with security guards on duty around the clock.

"Shall I turn it off now?" Michael asked gently when the newscaster moved on to a fresh item.

"Please."

"Your friend's daughter is courageous to come out with that story," Michael said.

"Why is this small town murder case of national interest?" Ellen demanded.

"Because Marcie and Frank Loeb could be any of the millions of listeners across the country," Michael explained. "It didn't happen in an urban slum. The two people involved are a middle-class, college-educated couple living the good life. Suddenly he's murdered and his wife is charged. That's high drama." He hesitated. "She has a good lawyer?"

"Scott's one of the best criminal lawyers in the country."

"Then it'll work out," he soothed. They heard the faint gush from the coffee maker. "The coffee's ready. I'll get it for us."

Ellen leaned back in her chair. Would it work out? Kathy was calling Leslie tonight. She'd always be 'Leslie' to them – 'Lee' was part of another, nightmarish era. Kathy said Scott was anxious to have the trial delayed another month or two. Leslie could help with that.

"You're still worried about the murder trial," Michael commiserated, approaching with two mugs of coffee.

"This is the daughter of one of my two best friends. I've known her all her life."

"She has a lawyer who you all feel is great," he comforted. "I know this is a grueling time, but it'll work out."

"Sometimes I just can't believe it's happening. It's unreal."

"That's now. Five years from now you'll use it as a plot for a novel," he jibed tenderly.

"Oh, Michael, no!" She recoiled from such a thought.

"Oh, not the way it happened. You could do it with a twist. There's this sweet, lovely young wife – but behind that charming facade is someone truly evil. She—"

"Michael, don't talk like that!" The way the prosecuting attorney talked! The way Frank's parents talked! "It wasn't like that at all!"

"Ellie, relax. I didn't mean to upset you."

"You make it sound so awful—" Her voice broke.

"I'm sorry I was so stupid," he apologized and reached to comfort her.

Suddenly she was in his arms. His mouth was on hers. Reason departed. Tumultuous emotions took over.

"Michael, this is insane—" But both knew there was no stopping.

At last they lay quiescent. Exhausted, exhilarated.

"I've been wanting to hold you this way since my first sight of you at that cocktail party," Michael confessed. "And each hour we were together my feelings for you intensified. We talked – and I knew you were the kindred soul I was sure I'd never find."

"Michael, we've known each other six days," she protested. *How could I let this happen*? Yet she felt a kind of rapture she had not experienced in years.

"It's a lifetime. We were together – mentally – through all the years – right up to today. I thought I'd never find you."

Reason struggled to the surface. "We mustn't see each other again. Michael, I'm not free for this." This was a tumultuous dream – not reality.

"You said you're ahead of schedule on the book," he reminded. "Come with me to Alaska. Just for a week or two. It'll be heaven on earth." His mouth was at her throat now, soft and persuasive.

In two weeks he'd be off to Alaska, Ellen told herself – and she'd never see him again. But for now he made her feel alive, desirable, loved. It had been so long since she felt this way . . .

Scott paced about his living-room, reviewing in his mind every aspect of Frank's murder. Jake had come up with so little, damn him! But he immediately felt guilty at this complaint. Jake was sticking his neck out on the True Patriot matter. Jake suspected military maneuvers were being carried out on that farm eight miles out of town. Two nights ago he'd parked his car, walked into the woods – despite all the 'No Trespassing' signs – and came face to face with six guys in camouflage and carrying assault rifles or 9mm semi-automatic pistols.

Scott broke out in a sudden sweat as he remembered Jake's report on the encounter. *'Hell, I thought my goose was cooked for sure. I never thought they'd believe I was out for deer – and that I believed they were ROTC on training maneuvers.'*

Jake had tracked down the owner of the farm, discovered it belonged to a Florida resident – who paid the taxes but rarely used the house. They could be way off track with the True Patriots in regard to Frank's murder – but even so, the organization ought to be unmasked. And his gut feeling was to go with Marcie's accusations.

Okay, Marcie had made a public accusation. Maybe he should run with it. He stopped pacing, reached for the copy of the *Evening Journal* that he'd picked up on his way home. He should have expected the scurrilous front page reaction of the *Journal* – which would be headlined again in the *Madison Daily News* tomorrow morning. The dastardly newspapers made Marcie appear devious, derided her story as an effort to divert attention from her own guilt. 'An evil woman stooping to malign this fine town with accusations of a non-existent terrorist group.'

The two local papers would fight for Marcie's conviction. That left the small weekly giveaway – the *Madison Guardian* – as their only mouthpiece. Now he remembered what Kathy had said about its editor – Bill Cooper – when he called this morning. *'He was polite – not nasty like the others. I gather he just wanted a story.'* Talk to him. Maybe Bill Cooper wanted something that would put his newspaper on the map. Like an exposé of the True Patriots.

Call Bill Cooper first thing tomorrow morning.

Eighteen

Kathy realized the urgency of contacting Leslie. Tonight for sure, she told herself when she awoke on Wednesday morning after another night of troubled sleep. Scott was sure the phone company would bring in the new line today. She couldn't bring herself to plug in their regular phone line again – she was sure that some wrathful caller would choose that minute to get through.

She was grateful that Marcie was asleep. She'd heard her prowling about the house during the night. Marcie might be out on bail, but living this way was like being under house arrest. Time dragged. Each hour seemed endless.

She went downstairs, put up coffee, searching her mind for some gourmet treat to prepare for Marcie's breakfast. Marcie ate only to please her, she thought tenderly. Scott had been so sweet with Marcie last night – trying to help her relax. How would they have survived this without him?

Marcie used to complain that there were not enough hours in the day for Frank and her – and now this wasteland of time stretched ahead. Angie was going to the library this morning to pick up some books for Marcie and her. But how could Marcie – or she – concentrate for any length of time on reading?

They'd give the house a thorough cleaning. She clutched at this diversion. She'd done nothing since the day Ellen and Angie had come over with her to put the house in order.

"Mom?" Marcie drifted into the kitchen. "Do you have stamps? I'll need a bunch for my letters."

"I always keep some on hand. We'll take care of it later." Kathy rose from the table. "I'll pour you some coffee. How about strawberry pancakes for breakfast?"

"Sure, Mom." She made a valiant attempt to appear casual.

Kathy talked about the weather – grey and unseasonably cool this morning – while she prepared the pancakes. Reminding Marcie how strawberry pancakes were a treat when she and Linda were small –

and their budget limited. *I'm rattling on again, the way I do when I'm nervous.*

"I wonder when Grace and Tim are due home?" she asked Marcie.

"Not for a week or so, I think." Marcie closed her eyes in anguish. "I don't suppose they know about Frank."

"Up there in their cabin they're out of touch with the rest of the world."

They heard voices outside, stiffened to attention.

"It's Scott," Kathy said in relief and hurried out of the kitchen and to the door, simultaneously anxious and hopeful. He probably just had news about the new phone line.

"Hi—" She was always conscious of a surge of comfort in Scott's presence. She wouldn't allow herself to think beyond that.

"We'll have rain by noon," he predicted. "Which means we won't have to worry about watering the plants this evening."

"I have a huge batch of strawberry pancakes in work. They'll be ready in a few minutes. Come out to the kitchen and help us finish them off." Her eyes were questioning, searching his.

"I'm afraid the new phone line won't be in until tomorrow," he apologized. "But they swear to me, tomorrow without fail."

"That'll be great." Unless the unlisted number leaked out.

"I've just come from the office of the *Guardian*," he said while they walked towards the kitchen. "Yesterday's *Evening Journal* ran a nasty story—" He paused as Kathy flinched. "Kathy, we expected that," he reminded gently. "But I have good news of sorts." He smiled encouragingly at Marcie in the dining area. "I had a long talk with Bill Cooper at the *Guardian* – and he's running a story on the presence of the True Patriots."

"That's wonderful!" Marcie was radiant. But the *Guardian* was a tiny newspaper, Kathy reminded herself – preparing to battle the influential Madison dailies.

"I gave him what Jake came up with – he'll quote Jake, word for word." A humorous glint in Scott's eyes. "Jake's a colorful man in his reports."

"That'll put Jake in a bad spot." Kathy was uneasy. But the support of the *Guardian* would be a confirmation of Marcie's accusations.

"Jake left town last night. He'll be identified as 'an anonymous source'. And Bill Cooper gave me some interesting facts. He said the two dailies are owned by Carson Fox."

"Fox bought the papers about eight years ago," Kathy recalled, bringing silverware and a mug of coffee for Scott to the table.

"The guy originally hailed from a small town in Alabama, where he had been active in the Ku Klux Klan—" Scott continued.

"First cousin to today's terrorist groups," Marcie pinned down.

"Everybody knows the two dailies are ultra-conservative," Kathy said. "But there's been no competition."

"The *Guardian* may be a giveaway weekly," Scott conceded, "but they've fought for the wetlands. They ran tough stories against Peter James and his Paradise Estates. They fought for bilingual teachers in our schools—"

"The *News* and the *Journal* squashed that," Marcie pointed out with revived frustration. "They said we were catering to a 'bad element'."

"When the *Guardian* comes out tomorrow, we'll see a lot of side-taking here in town," Scott warned. "Plenty of people are terrified of groups like the True Patriots. They haven't been happy about the Madison Militia – and this is a thousand times worse. But there'll be those who claim that the *Guardian* is just trying to be sensational. They'll swear no such group exists. But we'll get a hearing—"

"Scott, have your pancakes while they're hot," Kathy urged. Scott wasn't dragging his feet – as Glenn had scoffed. The battle was on to unmask the True Patriots.

With dusk settling about town, Kathy stood worriedly at the door with Marcie.

"I hate leaving you alone, Marcie—" But it was important to talk to Jill at the shop. And more importantly, she must talk with Leslie – away from the DA's office. Scott was trying to arrange a later trial date – but he predicted Lee would fight this. *'I can file just so many motions – I'm afraid they'll be dismissed.'*

"I'm not alone, Mom. Not with security guards fore and aft." Marcie brought her back to the moment. She tried so hard not to show her fears, Kathy told herself in pain. "Go on over to Angie's and call Jill."

Joe was waiting in the driveway to take her to his house. Scott insisted she not go out alone until the ugliness subsided. She walked the short distance to the car with the front-of-the-house security guard two steps behind. Joe opened the door and she slid inside. The guard closed the door, his eyes searching the area. Now he nodded in silence to Joe. This was weird, Kathy thought, light-headed from tension. Like a TV movie.

"I'll see you to the door and run," Joe said. "This is my bowling night." He sighed and Kathy chuckled.

"That's not the way to approach an evening of bowling."

"I'm not much in the mood for bowling, but Angie's practically throwing me out of the house. I'll be talking with the guys, and I'll be asking myself, 'Are any of you members of that son-of-a-bitching True Patriots gang?' A lot of us make cracks about the Madison Militia – but the Madison Militia guys don't hold secret military maneuvers, chase around in camouflage, and erupt into senseless killings. You just don't expect it in your own backyard," Joe said plaintively. "This has always been such a nice town."

Angie was at the door when they pulled into the driveway. Joe walked Kathy to the house.

"Except I know that Angie would kill me," he said, "I'd get myself a gun permit." Immediately he was stricken. "Kathy, I didn't mean to say that—"

"It's okay, Joe."

"Beat it," Angie ordered. "You're already late for your bowling."

The two women walked into the house, headed for the kitchen. The aroma of freshly brewed coffee drifted through the house.

"I figured you'd need coffee before you call Leslie."

"I hope she's home. She and her father will have had dinner by now – I wouldn't want to call while they were still at the table." Kathy was straining for calm. *This is a call I have to make.*

"Don't expect too much," Angie urged, reaching for the carafe of coffee. "This isn't the Leslie we knew thirty-one years ago."

"I just want her not to fight Scott's efforts to postpone the trial." *I want Leslie to push the police department into searching for the real murderer.* "Scott's anxious for a postponement. He says it's unrealistic to schedule the trial for late September. He needs more time." So far they had so little to work with. The cat hairs Scott noticed in the den – and Marcie's remembering the heavy scent of Turkish cigarette smoke when she came into the room, when neither she nor Frank smoked. And Marcie's conviction that the True Patriots killed him to avoid exposure.

"Sit down, Kathy. Give yourself a few minutes before you call."

Angie was remembering – as she was, Kathy guessed – that awful night when they'd taken justice into their fifteen-year-old hands. They'd been with Leslie at the funeral. The four of them had been terrified at what they'd pulled off – their distress was attributed to grief. And then – that same night – Leslie's father had whisked her away.

"No point in my stalling," Kathy said after a moment. She left her chair, reached for the cordless phone, brought it back to the table. "Pray I handle this right."

In silence Angie handed over the phone book. Kathy read the number underlined, dialed. Her heart pounding, she listened to the ringing.

"Hello. The Ramsey and Hilton residence." The housekeeper, Kathy surmised. According to facts Scott had dug up, Leslie's father still had money.

"May I speak to Lee Ramsey, please?" *Let her be there.*

"Who shall I say is calling?"

Kathy hesitated. "Tell her it's Kathy Marshall – who was Kathy Ross."

She waited, held up crossed fingers.

"She's home," Angie interpreted.

"I gather . . ."

"Kathy?" A note of incredulity in Leslie's voice.

"That's right." She struggled to keep her voice steady. "At first I didn't realize Lee Ramsey was Leslie Hilton—"

"I'd heard you'd moved away." Kathy sensed a wariness in her now.

"Yes. About seven years ago. But I plan on moving back." *She wonders why I'm calling. She doesn't know Marcie is my daughter.*

"And Ellen and Angie?" An impersonal quality in her voice now that put Kathy on guard.

"She's Ellen Courtney now. A successful novelist. Angie's a real estate broker. She married Joe Santini. He was a year ahead of us in high school. Leslie, I'm Marcie Loeb's mother," she blurted out.

"Oh my God!"

"Ellen and I were at Marcie's bail hearing—" She felt a rush of hope. "We didn't realize it was you until you began to speak."

"Kathy, I have a job to do." All at once a wall leapt up between them. "I'm the prosecuting attorney."

"Marcie's innocent! She and Frank were in love – they had a beautiful marriage. Marcie—"

"The evidence against her is strong," Lee interrupted. This was a district attorney speaking – not a woman who shared a terrible secret with her and Ellen and Angie. "But whatever, we shouldn't be discussing the case. It's—"

"Leslie, we're talking about my daughter!"

"Who has been indicted for murder." A pregnant silence hung between them. "If you're harboring thoughts of bringing up the past, *don't.*"

"That never entered our minds!"

"Because to do so," Lee proceeded with a menacing calm, "would bring out your own parts in that misadventure. Nor would anybody believe you after all these years." Yet a faint stridency was sneaking through – telegraphing her unease.

"We made a vow thirty-one years ago," Kathy said softly. "We never intend to violate it."

"What do you want of me, Kathy?"

"I want you not to fight Scott Lazarus when he asks for a postponement of the trial." Kathy took a laboured breath. "He'll ask for a December first date."

"And then what?" Lee demanded. A cold hostile stranger, Kathy thought. "What will you try next?"

"We won't try anything." *She regards us as 'the enemy'. Our helping her all those years ago means nothing.* "We're just asking for some time to prove Marcie didn't kill Frank. We know someone was in the room with him only moments before he was murdered. We need time to find that person."

Again, a pregnant silence. Then Lee responded.

"I won't fight the postponement. But don't push me further."

Kathy heard the hard thump of a receiver slammed down at the other end. The audience with the prosecuting attorney was over.

Lee sat immobile by the phone. She'd been convinced that no one in Madison would realize that Lee Ramsey had been Leslie Hilton. Hell, she'd left this town when she was fifteen. The face that stared back at her from her make-up mirror each morning had been subtly altered via the artistry of a top plastic surgeon. Her brown hair was now ash blonde.

What can happen? They won't dare go public with what they know

– they would incriminate themselves. They're guilty of obstruction of justice. But she was cold and shaken by this encounter. For a few agonized moments she was swept back into that other lifetime – which she'd thought was forever buried. The terror, the awful sickness that swamped her then was with her once more. She fought to pull herself out of this abyss. She'd come too far to be dragged down into the past.

Kathy's daughter was guilty as hell. That open letter people were talking about was grandstanding. She was a sharp little bitch trying to shift attention from herself. *She* could convince a jury of that, Lee told herself with towering confidence. Let Chuck get off his butt, use this case to make her a household name. *Nobody* – not even three ghosts from the past – would stand in her way.

Why hadn't Chuck pushed some of the TV tabloids into going after interviews? Maybe the lawyer who walked in and found Marcie Loeb hovering over the body. And Frank Loeb's parents. Yes! Her face was alight with triumph. They were greedy bastards, already trying to latch on to the insurance policy he'd taken out with his wife as beneficiary. They were vindictive – and here they'd have a chance to spill out all the nastiness in them to an avid audience.

She reached for the phone, dialed Chuck's number.

"Let's have some frozen yogurt." In tense moments Angie turned to food for comfort. "Low-fat," she emphasized.

"What other kind?" Kathy tried for a flippant note.

"You're worried that Marcie's alone at the house," Angie guessed.

"She's fine – nobody can get in with the security guards on duty. Anyhow, Scott said that most likely those were big-mouths making wild phone calls. They won't try anything weird."

"At least Leslie – Lee," Kathy corrected herself, "agreed not to fight Scott on a postponement." But Lee's voice echoed in her brain. *'The evidence against her is strong.'* Lee believed Marcie was guilty.

"Of course, we can't tell Scott—" Angie was bringing a pint of Ben & Jerry's Cherry Garcia from the refrigerator's freezer compartment.

"I know—" But he'd be so relieved when the word came through about the trial postponement.

The phone rang as Angie began to scoop frozen yogurt from the container. "Kathy, grab that call."

Kathy reached for the phone. "Hello."

"Kathy, what the hell goes on with the phone at the house?" Glenn demanded.

"It's unplugged. We had some nasty phone calls." What did Glenn want now?

"The *Post* ran some weird story in the late edition about an open letter Marcie gave out. Something about an extremist paramilitary group that wanted Frank dead? What's she trying to start up there in Madison?"

"She's trying to ferret out Frank's murderer." Glenn only called when he was worried about his own hide! The murder had spilled over into the national news – and he was scared he would become part of the scene.

"Does she have to make it a world event?" Glenn raged. "I'm in the middle of a major merger. I can't afford to be involved in this!"

"Marcie's not running around with a banner reading, 'Glenn Marshall of United Technology Inc. is my father'. The only way they'll find out is if you go on national television and announce it personally."

"Don't you have any influence with her?" Glenn demanded. "When is she going to learn not to say whatever nuttiness comes into her head?"

"Do you have a message for Marcie?" she asked, trying to hide her anger.

He cleared his throat. "Tell her I'll be up this weekend."

"There's no need for you to come up. I'll keep you informed of what's happening. Or keep reading the newspapers," she said. "This True Patriots controversy will cause some real fireworks."

But will it unmask Frank's murderer?

Nineteen

S cott awoke on Thursday morning after a night of uneasy sleep, with an instant realization that in a matter of hours this town would be divided into two camps. Marcie's open letter had created a flurry – but the front page of the *Guardian* would reach every soul in Madison. Ugly accusations would be hurled about – 'Marcie Loeb is defaming this town!' 'She's a liar, trying to turn folks against one another!' He would take any bet that the Madison Militia would distance itself fast from the True Patriots. They'd be scared shitless at being linked with a terrorist group.

The raucous shriek of his alarm clock was a jarring intrusion. He reached to turn it off, pulled himself into a semi-sitting position to contemplate the morning. Bill Cooper knew he was sticking his neck out – but it was the kind of action he relished. The *Guardian* had stuck its neck out before – though not as dangerously as this. Only twenty-seven, Bill was a sixties-style crusader – much like Marcie and Frank.

Was he exposing Marcie and Kathy to more danger with this tactic? But this was the only road to take. With a little luck on their side, some hothead in the True Patriots would explode, give them an opening to explore. Still, the situation could be hazardous.

This was Kathy's daughter – he must clear Marcie or Kathy would be destroyed. He sighed. This wasn't his normal mode of operation. How had be allowed himself to become so emotionally involved in this case? But he knew his life would be a wasteland without Kathy to share it. Here was the second chance he'd never expected to encounter.

The phone rang. Tense and wary, he picked up the receiver.

"Hello—"

"Scott, this is Bill Cooper." Bill's voice held an undercurrent of excitement. "The delivery crew is about to go out with this week's papers. I'm sending a boy over with a copy for you right now."

"Thanks, Bill. And thanks for jumping on the bandwagon with us."

"I'm not entirely unselfish." Bill chuckled. "This is the kind of story that moves a small paper into a new dimension." He hesitated. "Do you suppose Marcie would give us an interview to run in the next edition?"

"She can't do that. What about trying to dig up more background on Leonard Smith – the absentee owner of the farm where those creeps are training? The guy down in Florida." The real estate broker involved in the sale had been reluctant to talk about Smith.

"I'm working on that," Bill said. "I'm getting some weird feedback. The guy who owns the farm has a heavy investment in Paradise Estates."

Scott whistled softly. "He won't be happy if the wetland re-zoning doesn't go through."

"I couldn't dig up an address or a phone number for him. Just a post office box down in Miami. Does he *know* his farm is secret headquarters for the True Patriots?"

"Not necessarily," Scott admitted. "But all hell will break loose this morning when your crew starts making deliveries. Watch your back, Bill."

Twenty minutes later – when Scott had showered and dressed – one of the delivery crew arrived at his door with a copy of the *Guardian*. Scott stood in the foyer and read the front page feature story. The facts were laid out in simple but visual terms. The placid small town of Madison, New York was playing host to a secret terrorist group – and Marcie Loeb declared that one of its members had murdered her husband.

He'd take the *Guardian* over to Kathy and Marcie – but first, have breakfast at the diner and pick up some flak. Copies of the newspaper were kept in a pile beside the cash register. The breakfast crowd – mostly regulars – would have plenty to say.

The moment he walked into the diner Scott was conscious of a sudden hush at the counter. Most of those here knew he was Marcie's attorney. He'd represented two of them in court. His face impassive, he waved a hand in greeting, slid into his regular breakfast time booth. Gail – the ebullient waitress who usually served him – seemed subdued this morning.

"Two poached eggs, well done, whiskey down," she called to the short-order cook and went to the coffee maker.

"Hey, if we got creeps like that in this town I wanna know about it." A burly character at the counter broke the silence.

"The broad is nuts," somebody else scoffed. "She's tryin' to shove the Madison Militia into something they ain't – to get herself off the hook. She's guilty as sin." He cast a belligerent glance in Scott's direction. Scott pretended to be studying the menu.

Now there was a rush of excited conversation about the Loeb case and about the True Patriots.

"Look, the Madison Militia is not involved in extremist crap," someone rode over the clatter of voices. "Hell, I belong to the Militia. I'm pro-choice. I contribute to the community drives. I belong to the Lions Club. Sure – I believe we have to fight to protect our second Amendment rights. But the Madison Militia is out front – we don't plot violence."

As he'd expected, Scott thought; the Madison Militia was distancing itself from the terrorist group. But here and there a defiant undertone told him some knew the True Patriots were operating in this outwardly placid town.

Let one of them grow careless.

Lee had just walked into her office, was depositing her purse in a desk drawer, her briefcase at a corner of the desk when Bob Miller strode into the room.

"Have you seen this piece of shit?" He threw a copy of the *Guardian* on her desk – front page spread for reading.

She sat down, scanned the lead story. "They're really beating the drums." This would reach out to every one of the town's 30,000 residents. A few hundred saw or heard about Marcie Loeb's letter.

"Scott Lazarus had a nerve asking for police protection for her after she circulated that screwy letter." Miller grunted contemptuously. "And Bill Cooper's off the wall, running this bitchy story. Making this town look rotten!" A vein throbbed in his forehead. "Marcie Loeb won't get away with trying to shift the blame for her husband's death. I want a conviction."

"You'll get it," Lee said coolly. "But the *Guardian* might just be putting Madison in the limelight." She waited for this to penetrate his thinking. "It's the kind of story the national media will pick up and run with. And while they're doing it, let's get the message across that – though there's no such deal as the True Patriots – Madison is perfect second home territory. It'll be great publicity for real estate interests."

"Maybe," Miller conceded after a moment.

"Be realistic, Bob. Madison is not much over two hours from Manhattan. Forty minutes to great ski slopes, sprawling countryside for summer relaxation all around. Property values will soar." Bob Miller owned ten acres not far from town.

Their eyes met in mutual satisfaction.

"We'll be outraged at the *Guardian's* attack on our fine town," Miller drawled. "The *News* and the *Journal* will echo our sentiments. Paradise Estates will take advantage of all the hoopla and advertise in the real estate section of the *New York Times*. And like you said, the city will discover our potential as a mecca for second homes. But that doesn't change the Loeb case. I want a conviction, Lee."

They discussed the case for a few minutes longer. Then Miller left the office. Lee rose from her chair, crossed to close the door. She returned to her desk and reached for the phone, tapped in Chuck Jamison's number.

"Hello—" Chuck's voice came to her. His secretary didn't arrive until ten a.m.

"Chuck, Lee Ramsey. Have I got a story for you," Lee purred. "Spread the word around. Marcie Loeb insists that a terrorist group called the True Patriots is operating in Madison, New York. She claims *they* killed her husband."

"Did they?" Chuck demanded.

"No," Lee said impatiently. "But the involvement of a terrorist group makes it a national story. I'm faxing you a copy of the article. Chuck, get cracking!"

Angie spent the heat-record-breaking morning with a flaky client from Westchester County who had 'almost' settled on three different houses in the past three months. She returned to the office exhausted and disappointed. One more substantial commission and they'd pay off the mortgage on the house. Neither her parents nor Joe's had owned their own home. For Joe and her it was a source of deep pride to know they were property owners.

"I'm starving," Dottie greeted Angie. "Do you mind if I go out to lunch first? I'll just run across to Mulligan's. It's too hot to chase around today."

"Go ahead. Oh, will you bring me back a grilled cheese sandwich and ice coffee?" She rummaged in her purse for money. "I'll use my lunch hour to write the girls."

"Sure."

She knew the moment Dottie walked back into the office that something unpleasant had occurred.

"Have your grilled cheese while it's hot," Dottie said nervously. "And the ice coffee while it's cold."

"What's up?" Angie demanded. "You're stewing about something."

"I picked up a copy of the *Guardian* at the restaurant." She reached into her purse to pull out the folded-over weekly. "They ran an article about the True Patriots – and Marcie. Kathy told me about it."

"The restaurant was in uproar. People are furious that the *Guardian* could believe there's a terrorist organization here in Madison."

"It's here," Angie said flatly.

"How do you know? Just because it says so in the *Guardian*?"

"I believe Marcie. She says Frank had discovered the group's existence. They're paranoid – they talk about Soviet jets in middle America, just waiting to strike. They're sure the UN is out to overrun this country with armies determined to create a one-world government."

Dottie shuddered. "This all sounds like a bad movie script."

"But it's happening right here!"

Angie was restless for the rest of the afternoon. She worried that somewhere along the line Joe might have touched on a raw nerve when he was asking questions about the True Patriots. She left the office at the dot of five p.m., stopped off to shop cold cuts and salad for dinner. She was too uptight to cook tonight. Besides, it was hot again, she alibied herself. If she didn't heat up the kitchen, they might dispense with air-conditioning tonight.

Driving home she turned on the car radio. A local news program was interviewing Lee Ramsey. She spoke with cool deliberation.

"This so-called exposé was plotted to divert attention from the evidence against Marcie Loeb. But we've been given no proof that such a terrorist group exists."

How could Leslie – Lee, she corrected herself – be so vicious against Marcie? Knowing she was Kathy's daughter!

Arriving home, Angie was surprised to see Joe's car parked in the driveway. He always hung around a construction site beyond normal quitting time. Wanting everything to be up to scratch, right. So damned conscientious, she thought tenderly, in an era when it

Best Friends

seemed the norm to complain about workers in the construction
field. Why was he home early today?
She parked behind Joe's car, hurried into the house. The door
swung open as she approached.
"Hi." Joe smiled at her from the doorway.
"Hey, it's an occasion when you beat me home." She struggled
for lightness.
"We hit a heat record today, did you know? I called it quits half
an hour early – and I played truant, came right home." He reached to
take the supermarket bag from her. "Cold cuts and salad," he guessed
and grinned. "I'm not complaining – it's that kind of day."
"Did you see the *Guardian*?"
His smile was rueful. "Yeah. One of the guys brought it along.
A lotta talk about it, Angie—"
"They believe it?"
"Mostly not," Joe admitted. "A couple of guys – ones I know are
in the Madison Militia – talked loud and clear again about their not
being a terrorist group."
"The one you said froze when you asked about the True Patriots,"
Angie began with studied casualness, "was he on the job with you
today?"
"He doesn't work with me – he bowls with us." Joe cleared his
throat. He was reading her mind. "There's no way he can know I
fingered him for Scott's investigator."
"It's scary, Joe—"
"Relax, baby." He slid his free hand about her waist. "Let's
dump this stuff in the fridge, and you give me one of your fancy
massages." On occasion – when his back ached from long hours
on the job – Angie would use her amateur skill as a masseuse to
bring him relief.
In the master bedroom Joe stretched across the bed on his stomach
and waited for Angie.
"Okay, show me how good you are," he coaxed.
He was uptight, she realized while her hands kneaded the tense
muscles in his back. He was worried. He shouldn't have given Scott
the name of that man! He could be in bad trouble. Yet how could
they not help Marcie?
"That's great," Joe said after a few minutes and swung over on
his back. "You've got magic hands."
"Hungry now?" It was early for dinner.

151

"That can wait." His arms reached to pull her down to him. "Stop worrying about that creep – we'll be okay." It was incredible, she thought, the way he read her mind.

"I don't like what's happening."

"I'm interested in what's happening now . . ." He was manipulating her onto her back.

"Joe, it's broad daylight—" But she was responding.

"Close your eyes and pretend it's night."

She was never one of those women who just pretended to enjoy sex. For her – as with Joe – it was the ultimate pleasure on this earth. Never, she told herself with pride, had she denied herself to Joe.

"You're pretty good for an old broad," Joe joshed.

She clung to him, rejoicing in their mutual pleasure. In a corner of her mind she remembered overhearing a candid moment between Joe and Phil several years ago – when Ellen and Phil were here for a weekend. *'Look, I know Angie is sharper than me – she's got a kind of sophistication I'll never have. But I know how to make her happy.'*

Maybe Scott shouldn't have huddled with Bill Cooper on that story in the *Guardian*. She'd want to die if anything bad happened to Joe. She'd never forgive herself for encouraging him to help Scott uncover the True Patriots.

Twenty

After a steamy day, the evening was unexpectedly cool. Ellen enjoyed the warmth of Michael's body as they lay entwined together on a chaise on the terrace of his apartment-on-loan. A faint haze over the moon lent a silver cast to the sky. Traffic muted at this lofty height. Bach's Brandenburg Concerto drifted to them from the living-room's CD player. She and Michael encased in a post-lovemaking euphoria.

She felt as though they were isolated from the world, Ellen mused – yet even now guilt infiltrated her that she allowed the relationship with Michael to continue. It was almost as though she had no will.

"I must get home, Michael." She forced herself to be realistic. "I still have editing to do before I go to bed."

"I wish you could stay all night." His mouth brushed her cheek. "All the days and nights of our lives . . ."

"It's been a wonderful evening."

"Think about going with me to Alaska for two weeks," he coaxed, rising to his feet. "You're finishing up the final draft of the book."

"Michael, I wish—" Her smile was wistful. "I'm grateful for this."

They left the building, began to look for a taxi for Ellen. At a corner Michael – an admitted 'news junkie' – paused at the newsstand to pick up the late newspapers. Ellen read the headline of the *Daily News* and froze. 'Marcie Declares Terrorist Group Murdered Husband.'

"Michael, let me read this!" Her hands were trembling as she grasped the paper. In lurid terms the newspaper reported the uproar that had hit the normally serene town of Madison, New York. *I knew the story was to break this morning in the Guardian. I didn't expect it to hit the front pages of a Manhattan tabloid.*

"That's your friend's daughter?" Michael was instantly alert.

Ellen nodded. "I'll drive up tomorrow morning. I don't know that I can do anything—"

"Let me drive up with you." Michael's voice was electric.

153

"Maybe I can help. Thirteen years ago I worked to unmask a white supremacist group in Alabama. Four years later I was part of a team that busted up a neo-Nazi organization in Idaho. It's imperative we expose these groups."

"It's all so insane!" She wavered for a moment, then clutched at reality. "No, it would be wrong for me to arrive in Madison with you."

"I'm a journalist friend who wants to help," he pursued. "With my background that's understandable."

"I'll go up early in the morning, come back the following night," Ellen plotted. "Mainly to offer moral support. I'll stay with Kathy."

"I'll register at a local hotel. We'll leave around six thirty a.m., stop on the road for a quick breakfast. We'll be in Madison by – nine thirty a.m.? We'll be driving against traffic," he reminded.

"Michael, it's crazy," she protested. Yet Michael *was* an experienced journalist. Perhaps he could be helpful. Marcie needed all the help she could get. "All right," she capitulated. "We'll be in my car by six thirty a.m." No will, she chastised herself – she had no will in Michael's presence.

Back in her apartment Ellen called Phil, let him know where she was – even though they seemed to be living separate lives.

"Hello—" Mom's voice, sounding anxious. She'd forgotten – late phone calls always alarmed Mom.

"Mom, it's Ellen," she said quickly. "I just wanted to tell Phil I'll be going up to Madison in the morning."

"How's the new book coming?" Mom was one of her most devoted fans. "I'm dying to read it."

"Right on schedule." Ahead of schedule – allowing two weeks for play before the kids returned, her mind taunted. "I'll bring you a photocopy as soon as it's finished."

"What's happening in Madison?" Mom was solicitous. "About the trial?"

"It's been postponed until the first Monday in December. But there's—"

"Ellie, hold on. Here's Phil."

"Sure, Mom."

"What's this uproar about a terrorist group in Madison?" Phil asked. "We just heard something about it on the ten o'clock news."

Best Friends

"Suddenly the case is national news." Ellen grunted in disgust. "It made the front page of the late edition of the *Daily News*. This is the group I told you about. I'm driving up in the morning to be with Kathy and Marcie. I'll drive home the following night."

"Is it going to mess up your work schedule?"

"I'll manage." She hadn't meant to sound sharp. "I hope Marcie and Kathy aren't making themselves a target for violence."

"They're going through a rough time." He paused. "Ellie, be careful."

They talked for a few minutes about Ted's recent letters from Madrid. 'I can't believe these tiny cells they put us in! I thought Jesse and I would be roommates. There's space in each room for just a cot and a tiny chest. And dinner's still served at ten p.m. – but we've got a snack bar that saves us from starvation.'

Ellen said goodnight and focused on preparing for bed. Set the alarm for five forty-five, she told herself. Michael would meet her at the garage at six thirty sharp. Oh, and call Kathy to say she and Michael would be up in the morning.

Sitting on the living-room sofa with Seymour Shubin's latest suspense novel open across her lap – but as yet unread – Kathy started at the sound of the phone, then reached for the cordless that lay on the coffee table.

"Hello—" Relieved that the new line had been connected, yet wary.

"I know it's late to be calling," Scott apologized.

"No, Scott," Kathy said. "I'm so grateful that we have the new line now." Being a local small town lawyer provided perks. She'd never have gotten the new line so fast on her own.

"I've been working – and so has Bill Cooper – to come up with some background on the owner of that farm. I called in some favors. Presumably this Leonard Smith bought it as an investment two years ago. But he took ownership in the name of a corporation. Some dummy corporation, it appears."

"Why?" Kathy was mystified.

"Apparently he – or the corporation – is using it as a tax dodge. Or there's some angle that keeps eluding us."

"But that farm is being used now," Kathy pinpointed. "Jake has

155

proof of that. Shouldn't the police investigate? I mean, if they're trespassing."

"The cops won't go in there to check unless there's a complaint from the owner."

"But a terrorist group is operating out of that farm!" Waves of frustration assaulted her. "Why can't it be checked out?"

"The police have nothing to run with – yet," he emphasized.

All at once the night quiet was punctured. Shots were being fired. Glass shattered. Upstairs – in the front, Kathy pinpointed.

"Scott, somebody's shooting at the house!" Marcie was in an upstairs bedroom – at the rear.

"Get down," he ordered. "The guards will handle it. I'll be there in a few minutes!"

The shooting had stopped. She heard a loud exchange between the two security guards.

"Mom?" Marcie's voice – harsh with alarm – called from upstairs. "Are you all right?"

"I'm fine." Kathy fought for calm. "You OK?"

"Yes—" Marcie was hurrying down the stairs.

"I'll talk to the guards." Kathy darted towards the front door, pulled it open.

"We've got the license number of the car," one guard told her while the other returned to his post at the rear. "I'm trying to get a call through to Mr Lazarus."

"He's on his way over. We were talking on the phone when it happened."

"What's going on out there?" Amelia Rogers leaned out from the front door of her house. "This used to be a decent neighborhood!"

"It's all over, ma'am," the guard soothed. "Just some crazy drunk on a shooting spree. Nothing to worry about."

"We'll never feel safe until *she's* out of there!" Amelia Rogers shrieked. "I hope she gets the death penalty!"

"Maybe you'd better go back inside," the guard said gently as Kathy and Marcie huddled in the doorway. "But they won't be coming back. I'll bet on that."

By nine twenty a.m. Ellen was turning off the road that led into Madison. She felt uneasy now about arriving with Michael – and yet she was grateful for his presence. No questions about him from Angie, she realized with relief. She wouldn't be seeing Angie and

Joe on this trip – they were leaving this morning for Lake George
to visit the girls.

"You don't have a wide choice of hotels here in town," she said
with a contrived air of casualness. "A total of three plus the motel
at the edge of town."

"So it won't match the Ritz in Paris or the Dorchester in London,"
Michael drawled. "I'll survive."

The town seemed unusually busy this morning, Ellen thought as
she turned onto Main Street and headed for the Madison Plaza –
the most centrally located of the three hotels. She was surprised to
discover no space available at the hotel parking area.

"So we'll have to walk a block," Michael jibed.

They located a place to leave the car, walked back to the hotel.
In the ornate hotel lobby – his weekender in one hand – Michael
approached the registration desk.

"I'd like a single, please, for—"

"I'm sorry, sir," the clerk cut him short. "We have no vacancies
at the moment."

"Oh?" Michael lifted an eyebrow in astonishment, went to rejoin
Ellen. "No vacancies. Is there a convention in town?"

"There's never a convention in Madison." But she was puzzled.

"You suppose the clerk just didn't like my looks?" Michael
joshed.

Out in the street again, Ellen glanced about curiously. "It looks
far busier than usual."

"Where do we try next?" Michael asked.

"The Willows. It's only three blocks down – let's leave the car
where it is and walk there."

They walked briskly down Main Street. Already Ellen was
questioning herself about the wisdom of bringing Michael here.
But they'd be returning to the city tomorrow evening. And in
another week or ten days – with his book auction over – Michael
would be leaving town. She didn't want to think about that.

People were milling about the lobby of The Willows. Several
prospective guests stood waiting to register. With Ellen at his side
Michael joined the line.

"I'm sorry, sir. We have nothing available at the moment," the
registration clerk was telling a young man weighed down with
camera equipment. "You might try later to see if there's been a
cancellation."

Exchanging a perplexed glance, Ellen and Michael abandoned the line.

"What's going on here?" Unsettling vibes were reaching through to Ellen. Could this be a media blitz?

"You said three hotels and a motel," Michael recalled. "Where do we go from here?"

"The Drake, just around the corner," Ellen began but stopped dead at pressure from Michael's hand at her arm.

"That's a TV network crew from New York—" He pointed to a truck cruising along Main Street. "And the man ahead of us at the registration desk was a photographer."

"Michael, what's happening?" She didn't want to believe what her mind proclaimed.

"The news media is moving into Madison."

"Let's go over to the Drake." Ellen was grim. "There has to be one hotel room available in town."

Michael reached for her hand. "I'd prefer not to pitch a tent on the village green."

"This is becoming a circus, Michael!"

"We'll find me a room somewhere," he soothed. "How many newspaper reporters, photographers, and TV people can be pouring into town?"

"Obviously dozens." Ellen flinched at the vision of what lay ahead. "It's the 'murder case of the month'."

"What the hell—" Michael stopped dead, swiveled about to inspect an occupant of a chauffeur-driven black Rolls Royce waiting for a red light to change.

"What is it?"

"Let's keep going." He was brusque. "That's not a character I'd care to meet just now."

"Who is he?"

"A Colombian drug lord named Juan Torres. Slippery as a firehouse pole and sharp enough to outwit the best police brains in half a dozen South American countries. The word is that he slipped out of Colombia a few weeks ago one step ahead of an assassination squad. Probably with millions in cash." Michael chuckled. "All in small bills. That's the way the drug traffic operates. And Torres had no time for laundering."

"How does anybody carry out millions in small bills?" Ellen was amused by the image.

"It isn't easy," Michael confirmed. "And laundering in Miami – where he took up residence – is rough now. But what's he doing in Madison, New York?"

"His being here couldn't have anything to do with Frank's murder," Ellen began and paused. "Could it, Michael?"

"It doesn't seem likely – but where Juan Torres surfaces, something ugly is transpiring." He paused, squinting in thought. "Is there anything in Frank's background that would be a link to a drug lord?"

"Nothing!" For an instant Ellen was angry.

"Cool it," Michael scolded. "I'm just asking myself why a high-up drug lord from Colombia surfaces in a small, upstate New York community."

"Maybe he's why the media is pouring in town."

"I doubt that anybody – except for me – is even aware he's here. I ran into him four years ago in Bogota. It wasn't a pleasant occasion. I'm sorry, honey. The media circus beginning a run in Madison, New York revolves around the Loeb case – and Marcie's accusation that an extremist group is operating here. Not around Juan Torres."

Twenty-One

E llen waited by the entrance in the small, shabby lobby of the Drake while Michael talked with the desk clerk. She couldn't hear their conversation, but finally the clerk handed Michael a pen. Thank God, they had a room for him. It was unbelievable that something like this could be happening in Madison.

Michael turned away from the desk, was pantomiming to her. He was going up to his room to drop off his weekender, she interpreted. Then they'd drive to Kathy's house. *How had the case escalated into national headlines?*

The least popular of the three hotels, the Drake was seeing a lot of traffic this morning. No doubt the hotels and the restaurants were glad for the business. But this wouldn't set well with the locals, she surmised. How had an extremist organization come to exist here? But wherever one popped up, the townspeople were astonished.

A few minutes later Michael emerged from the elevator, strode to her side.

"It's not a room," he said, prodding her towards the door. "It's a linen closet furnished with a single bed. But it'll do for one night." He grinned. "I've slept in worse."

They hurried back to the car and headed for the house.

"I keep asking myself what Juan Torres is doing here." Michael shook his head in bewilderment. "I'll bet you don't see many Rolls Royces in this town."

"This is more station wagon and pick-up truck country." A wisp of a smile lighted her face. "Ted's dying for the day when he can get a driver's license. He fantasizes about driving a pick-up truck. That's the macho scene in towns like Madison and Montauk."

"I keep wondering if there's some weird connection between Torres and these True Patriots characters – but I can't see any. Torres is big time. These extremists play up the 'small cell' scene. That's regarded as keeping them undetected – less likely to be infiltrated. It's what's known as 'leaderless resistance'. It was the strategy of a Grand Dragon of the Texas Ku Klux Klan some years ago – and seems to be the strategy of a neo-Nazi group called the Aryan Nations that operates out in Idaho."

Ellen shuddered. "It scares me. I read articles in the *Times* and in the news magazines – and it all seems unreal."

"It's real enough," Michael said grimly. "And the situation has to be dealt with before it grows stronger."

Approaching the house, Ellen became aware of a uniformed man pacing across the front.

"That's one of the guards," she guessed.

She pulled up before the curb. The guard was checking the license number of the car. Kathy had alerted them to her arrival. They knew that Michael was coming with her – and the rationale for this.

"We're expected," she told the guard, and he nodded.

Already the door had swung open. Kathy stood there. Afraid to run out to greet them, Ellen thought compassionately.

"I'm so glad you're here—" Kathy reached to embrace her. "We had a drive-by shooting last night."

"Oh my God! You didn't mention it when I called. Are you both all right?"

"We're fine," Kathy said. "Shaky but unhurt. I gather it was just meant to scare us. It happened right after you called—"

"Ellen?" Marcie's light, musical voice drifted towards them.

"Marcie, yes." Ellen's face lighted. "Darling, it's so wonderful to see you—" She moved forward with outstretched arms.

"You must be Michael," Kathy said.

"Right." Michael smiled warmly. "And you're Kathy."

Ellen swung around in dismay. "How rude of me! I was just so shocked to hear about the drive-by shooting – and then I saw Marcie."

"You're forgiven," Kathy said indulgently. "Come into the living room and let's get comfortable. We have coffee up, and Marcie baked this morning. You know she's the culinary expert in this family."

"You all sit down," Marcie ordered. "I'll bring in the coffee and my chocolate babka." She was trying so hard to be casual, Ellen thought.

"I talked to Scott earlier," Kathy said. "He should be over any minute. He's anxious to talk with you, Michael."

"There's not a lot I can offer." Michael was all at once serious. "But I thought I might just come up with something from my own encounters with terrorist groups that would be helpful."

"Michael's just back from the Balkans," Ellen said. "He has a book on his experiences there that's up for auction."

"What's this about a drive-by shooting last night?" Michael asked.

Ellen grew cold with shock as Kathy related what had happened. "The police moved fast," Kathy acknowledged. "They found the car. It had been reported stolen an hour earlier."

"It was a scare tactic," Michael surmised.

Kathy nodded. "That's what Scott said. Though the message isn't clear."

"It could be just creeps angry that you've 'besmirched their town'," Michael said drily. "Or it could be the terrorist group you've exposed telling you to recant."

Ten minutes later Scott arrived. Kathy introduced him to Michael.

"I hope you don't think I'm intruding—" For a moment Michael seemed uncomfortable. "But terrorist organizations are a pet hate of mine."

"We need all the help we can get," Scott assured him.

"I don't see any direct connection – but Ellen and I spotted someone when we drove into town who set off warning signals in my head. A guy in a chauffeur-driven black Rolls Royce."

"Nobody in Madison owns a Rolls." Scott was immediately alert.

"I recognized him from an ugly encounter down in Colombia four years ago. He's Juan Torres, a South American drug kingpin on the lam. I understood he was hanging out in Miami recently. But what's he doing in a town like this?"

"We have the usual drug problems," Scott conceded. "But too small an operation to interest a man like that."

"Could there be some money laundering deal in the works?" Michael fished. "Miami's gotten overheated with laundering – and you can be damn sure Torres brought a bundle out of South America. Is there something going on here that could involve millions of dollars? Triple-digit millions," he emphasized.

Scott leaned forward in excitement. "Torres hopes to launder money through Paradise Estates!" he guessed. "It's a major development here that's being held up because of re-zoning requirements. Peter James paid a fortune for the land – it was part of an estate that was being settled. He's handed over a lot of money for lumber that's being held for him because he was afraid of a wild upsurge in lumber prices. Then he ran into the re-zoning problem. It's causing a hell of a lot of contention here. But I don't see how this would involve Frank's murder – or the True Patriots."

"Let's back up," Michael said slowly. "Start from the beginning and fill me in."

Michael listened to Scott's report, interrupting at intervals to ask questions.

"So you know for sure that a terrorist organization is operating here?"

"They've gone undercover. I suspect running into Jake that way shook them up. We trailed the guy who we know is a member – he led us to the farm." Scott sighed. "He's leading an exemplary life now. He goes to work, comes home, spends his evenings with his wife and kids. I've driven around that farm area for hours late at night. No gunfire. Nothing."

"Have you alerted the Bureau of Alcohol, Tobacco and Firearms?" Michael asked.

"They're unable to move in without concrete evidence. You know the situation today. They lean over backwards not to create tensions." Scott gestured his frustration. "Marcie *knows* that Frank was about to expose the True Patriots. Now we've got Torres in town – possibly in a money laundering deal with Paradise Estates. But how does that tie in with Frank's murder?"

"Let's put that on a back burner for now," Michael said. "You figure your best lead is to track down the True Patriots?"

"Right. But how do we do that when they've gone into hiding this way?" Scott challenged. "What would you do?"

"Look for small giveaways. Who in town has been receiving large numbers of packages? They could be guns, assault rifles. Check with the garden supply stores to discover who's been buying huge amounts of ammonium nitrate. A great fertilizer for farmers. But mixed with oil – by a person with a basic knowledge of chemistry – it becomes a powerful bomb. The kind that Oklahoma City will never forget. And never lose sight of the one guy you know *is* a member of the True Patriots. Somewhere along the way he's going to slip up."

Scott remained until Pam called to remind him that he had a real estate closing immediately after lunch.

"How long will you be here?" he asked Michael.

"Until late tomorrow," Michael said. "Shall we do some reconnoitering tonight?"

"Good thought," Scott approved. Ellen was uneasy. With a man like Torres around, could it be dangerous? "Let's cruise around the countryside."

"Come over for dinner, Scott," Kathy said. "You two can make your plans then."

In the mid-afternoon Scott called to say that he had finally received word from the police chief.

"After last night's shooting, the Chief agrees to have a police car with two officers on duty from nine p.m. until six a.m., starting tonight. I don't know how long they'll keep up this schedule, but meanwhile you'll save some money." He was worried, Kathy realized, about her financial situation. It was nineteen days since Marcie was arrested – and Glenn had done nothing to help her. *His own child.*

"There's one more thing I should tell you," Scott began – and his voice warned her this would not be pleasant.

She tensed in alarm. "What is it?"

"Frank's parents are to be interviewed on a network TV tabloid program."

Kathy felt sick. She could envision the untruths, the nastiness they would spew to millions of watchers. They'd play up the insurance policy Frank had never told Marcie about – and how they were convinced she'd 'seduced' Frank into marrying her. "When?"

"Monday night. Don't watch it, Kathy. I'll be there at the house to make sure you don't," he joshed.

"Scott, we'd never survive this without you." Her theme song these days.

"I want to be there for you always. I know this is not the time to talk – but when this nightmare is over I have so much I want to tell you."

"Let it be over soon." Her heart was pounding. Scott wanted to be a permanent part of her life. "I pray every night for an end to this."

"I'm working on it."

"You won't do anything dangerous tonight – when you're driving out there with Michael?" They would be stalking the farm, she surmised. "Be careful, please!"

"We won't take chances. But if we should hear what sounds like maneuvers again, then I'll fight to have the ATF make inquiries. Michael's willing to testify along with me." He managed a wry chuckled. "It's strange, isn't it, to be hoping they're holding maneuvers tonight."

Off the phone, Kathy joined Ellen and Marcie in the kitchen. The two were planning the dinner menu – as though this was a normal occasion. Ellen had said that Michael was a writer friend who was a client, also, of her agent. Michael was more than that, she thought uneasily. Each time their eyes met, they made silent love. It was beautiful – and frightening.

Ellen admitted her marriage was rocky. But she and Phil had been together for sixteen years – they had two precious children. Please God, don't let Ted and Claire suffer as Marcie and Linda suffered when Glenn walked out on them! She and Angie had always said that Ellen had the perfect marriage. *What happened to Ellen and Phil?*

At ten forty p.m. Scott and Michael left the house in Ellen's car, with Scott at the wheel. At this hour most of Madison's residents who were not already in bed for the night were preparing for that destination.

"Shall we head right out for the farm?" Scott asked, churning for action.

"Let's cut through the main section of town first," Michael suggested. "I'd like to know where Juan Torres is right now. The hairs on the back of my neck tell me he bears watching."

"The one thing that could have brought him to Madison would be Paradise Estates," Scott said. "And I keep asking myself – how is Frank's murder connected with that?"

They drove through town – a panorama of silence except for the one bar where jazz erupted onto the street.

"This is Friday night," Scott reminded. "The only places open and swinging will be the few bars in the area." He pondered for a moment. "If Torres is registered at one of the hotels, his car will be in its parking area."

"Okay, let's check that out," Michael agreed.

But no black Rolls Royce was on any of the hotel parking lots. And there was no indoor parking in Madison. Now the two men headed out of town.

"The farm where Jake heard gunfire belongs to some guy in

Florida," Scott told Michael. "Probably bought as an investment. The deed is in the name of an obscure corporation – some tax dodge. The guy lives in Miami."

"Where Juan Torres hangs out now," Michael pinpointed. "Maybe – just maybe – there's some link between Juan Torres and the True Patriots."

"There's no doubt in my mind," Scott admitted, "that somebody from the True Patriots murdered Frank. And that drive-by shooting is the kind of warning that Torres could be expected to deliver."

"But why would a Colombian drug lord be working with a small town extremist organization?" Michael voiced the question that hurtled through Scott's mind now.

"That's the piece of information that could bring this whole puzzle into place."

They drove along the night-empty roads with their senses on high alert. Moonlight lent an almost eerie brightness to the area. Houses were far apart now. Only the occasional sounds of an animal scampering in the woods disturbed the stillness.

"The farm is just ahead," Scott told Michael. "I've driven around on three different nights – just the perimeter. But not a peep came out of there."

Now they saw the 'No Trespassing' signs that were posted at regular intervals. But again, only silence where they'd hoped to hear the sounds of semi-automatic pistols, assault rifles. They circled the farm acreage twice, then reluctantly agreed this was futile.

"Where the hell is Juan Torres?" Scott wondered aloud. "Or has he left town already?"

"Could he be staying with some big wheel from Paradise Estates?" Michael projected.

"That would be Peter James," Scott said. "James leases the closest thing to a mansion existing in this town. He's been there almost two years – that's how long he's been fighting to put Paradise Estates into action."

"What do you know about this James character?"

Scott searched his mind. "Not much. He's made it clear he represents a lot of money. He built an office at the edge of the wetlands area. He keeps a small staff there. He's from New York City. His father was in the construction business – he took over when the old man died." All at once his hands tightened on the wheel.

166

Signals going off in his head. "His mother was South American. An old, wealthy family – very powerful."

"That's the connection between him and Juan Torres!"

Scott felt a rush of adrenalin. "Let's drive over to Peter James' house. I know – we're just fishing. But we might come up with some answers."

The lower floor of the huge Georgian mansion that was Peter James's residence was brilliantly lighted. Sitting in the circular driveway of the house was a black Rolls Royce.

"Okay, Juan Torres is staying with Peter James," Michael said as they drove past the house.

"Let's circle around and drive by again," Scott said. Peter James drove a white Cadillac, his wife a powder blue Lincoln Continental – both probably in their four-car garage. Who owned the grey Dodge Spirit that sat behind the Rolls?

Scott made a right onto a deserted side road, swung around and back to the road they'd just left.

"Slow down," Michael said. "Somebody's coming out of the house."

Scott dropped to twenty-five miles an hour – slow enough to identify the three men who emerged onto the columned veranda.

"I recognized Torres," Michael said when they were past the house. "Who were the other three men?"

"Peter James," Scott said, his mind in high gear. "Eric Matthews – and Dan Reagan, president of Madison Central Bank." *What are Eric Matthews and Dan Reagan doing at a late night conference with Peter James and Juan Torres?*

Twenty-Two

Kathy took a deep breath of relief when she saw Scott turning into the driveway. She called to Marcie and Ellen.

"They're back."

The two men came into the house, settled in the living-room to report their findings.

"What's Eric Matthews doing with Peter James?" Marcie was puzzled. "And Dan Reagan."

"Eric's handling their money laundering operation," Scott surmised, "and that's going through Dan Reagan's bank."

"I don't understand this whole money laundering operation." Marcie gazed from Scott to Michael.

"It's drug money we're talking about," Michael began. "These drug lords collect millions of dollars each week in small bills. They hire squads of couriers to run to small banks all around the country to turn cash into money orders or cashier's checks with no payee named."

"I'd take any odds that Eric Matthews is handling the courier operation for Torres," Scott picked up. "He—"

"Fiona says he's out of town a lot," Marcie broke in. "Quick business trips, she called them."

"He runs around with valises full of cash and comes back with the money orders or cashier's checks. These are deposited into Paradise Estate accounts here in Madison and probably in other cities. Torres will show up as a major stockholder in Paradise Estates – and his money is clean." Scott gestured eloquently. "Of course, this is a tricky business for banks. Any deposit over $10,000 has to be reported to the government."

"But these deposits are small," Kathy interpreted, "so there's no reporting to the government."

"The government gets very interested, however, when too much of a bank's outstanding deposits are in cashier's checks. And these are checks that earn no interest," Michael pointed out. "Very profitable for the banks."

"Dan Reagan is involved in covering up the Paradise Estates deposits," Scott pursued. "For a fancy fee."

"James hired a local lawyer," Michael pinpointed, "who knew all the inside wheeler-dealing that goes on in town. Eric Matthews worked out the deal with Reagan."

"And Eric knows who's on what side in this re-zoning situation," Scott added. "Without re-zoning on the wetlands James can't proceed with Paradise Estates."

"Eric sat in on our emergency meetings to fight against re-zoning," Marcie recalled. "We just assumed he was on our side!"

Michael turned to Scott. "You said somebody named Smith bought the farm where this extremist group carries on its activities. A guy who lives in Miami?"

"That's right—" Kathy pounced, feeling a surge of excitement. "Like Torres!"

"Let's see if there's a link between them." Michael rose to his feet. "I'm calling a newspaper editor down in Miami that I've known forever. He was a foreign correspondent before he took over a newspaper there." Michael glanced at his watch, frowned. "It's late – I'll buzz him in the morning. He owes me a favor."

"You said you're staying at the Drake. That's one step above a fleapit," Scott told Michael. "Why don't you pick up your gear and stay at my place? I have a guest room that's dying to be used."

"Great." Michael's face lighted in approval. "Shall we hit the road?"

"Don't sit up all night talking," Ellen warned good-humoredly. "You have an important phone call to make in the morning."

"I'd like to bring in Jake again for a couple of days," Scott told Kathy, and she nodded in agreement. The bills were staggering – but she'd worry about them later. "As Michael suggested, we ought to keep a tail on the one person we know belongs to the True Patriots. Even though he seems to be leading an exemplary life at this point."

Scott and Michael had sat up talking until dawn. From habit Scott had awakened early. Now he was impatient for Michael to emerge from the guest room. The Miami editor Michael knew might come up with something important on Torres – and on Leonard Smith. Was there some connection between Torres and Smith?

He was putting up coffee in his large country kitchen when

Michael emerged – unruly dark hair still wet from the shower.

"A cup of coffee and I'll phone Don down in Miami," he promised.

"Coming up in minutes." Scott gazed out of the bay window at the sun-parched grass. "I was hoping we'd see some rain. We keep expecting but not getting." Clusters of grey clouds moved across the sky. "At least it isn't so hot this morning."

A swooshing sound from the coffee maker told Scott the coffee was ready. He poured, brought two mugs to the round pine table at one corner of the kitchen. Michael took the cordless phone from its wall receptacle and sat in a captain's chair at the table to call Miami. He frowned when there was not an immediate response.

"It's early," Scott reminded.

"This character lives in his office," Michael began, then shifted. "Don, how're you doing?"

The two men exchanged banter for a few moments, then Michael announced his reason for calling.

"Don, a friend of mine – Scott Lazarus – needs some information." He paused. "Yeah, that's right, the defense attorney." Michael shot Scott the traditional victory signal. "Look, this is damned important to me. Help him all you can, old boy."

Scott listened intently while Michael explained the information required. Then Michael nodded approval of Don's reaction. "Yeah, call Scott as soon as you come up with answers. I'll give you his office number and his home number. And Don, get on it fast, will you? An innocent defendant needs clearing."

The two men discussed the situation in depth while Scott made breakfast for them. God, he was grateful for Michael's presence in town! This might be the break they needed. After breakfast – while they waited for word from Miami – he and Michael would make the rounds of garden-supply houses, as plotted at dawn.

At the first garden-supply store where they checked – with a conjured-up research report they were supposedly doing – they learned that Paradise Estates had ordered heavily of fertilizer. The next six garden-supply houses reported the same.

"Mr James – he plans on having the finest landscaping in the county," the last salesman declared. Or had Peter James been furnishing the True Patriots with material for bombs?

"Let's go back to the house," Michael said when they left the garden-supply store. "Tell the women what we've learned."

Kathy greeted them with news that Pam had been trying to reach Scott. "She said she had some information from Miami that sounded important."

Exchanging an elated glance with Michael, Scott rushed to phone his office, gestured to Kathy to pick up on the cordless.

"Pam, what's up?"

"Some man named Don said to tell you that the Leonard Smith you mentioned is really a South American named Gonzales. His daughter – who spends a lot of time in Miami – is married to some American real estate developer. Guess who?"

"Peter James."

"You got it. This Don person said if you need any further information, buzz him."

"Pam, that's great! I'll be back in about an hour." Scott put down the phone, repeated what Pam had told him.

Michael whistled softly. "So the farm that's True Patriot headquarters belongs to James's father-in-law. James is laundering money for Torres. And Eric Matthews and Dan Reagan are involved in the whole scheme."

"Eric lied because he wanted me convicted for Frank's murder!" Marcie blazed. "He didn't know how much Frank had told me about the True Patriots! He wanted me out of the way, too!"

"James and his clique were getting frantic about the re-zoning. He set up the True Patriots to take care of anybody who got in the way of the re-zoning appeal," Michael reasoned. "These extremists are paranoid about what's happening in this country. They misread every government action. James knew he could build up their hysteria to a point where they would be useful to him. He'd promised them great jobs – and now the government threatens to kill the development. Because of people like Frank and Marcie Loeb. Now, how do we prove this?"

Ellen and Michael left Madison in early afternoon. Michael had been helpful, she thought with pleasure. His friend in Miami had come forth with useful information.

"Traffic's light for a Saturday," Michael said.

"Maybe because of the weather." A light drizzle had begun to fall as they left Madison and was becoming a full-scale rain.

Julie Ellis

"I love driving in weather like this." Michael allowed one hand to leave the wheel and reach for hers for a moment.

Now lightning zigzagged across the sky. There was a sudden chill in the air. All at once rain was pounding on the roof of the car. Michael closed the windows. He leaned forward over the wheel to peer ahead – the downpour limited visibility.

"There's something passionate about a rainstorm."

"I know," Ellen whispered.

Michael focused on driving. Cars moved slowly ahead. "You know what I want to do right this minute?" A sudden intensity deepened Michael's voice. "I want to make love to you."

"In the middle of a rainstorm, in a moving car?" Yet she understood his feelings – and was conscious of arousal in herself.

"In a room with drapes closed against the world," he said softly. "In that motel just ahead." A neon sign flashed at the edge of the road.

"Michael, we can't—"

"Why can't we?" he challenged, already changing lanes. "Moments like this are precious. We shouldn't let them escape."

The motel was not the glitzy kind to which she – and most Americans today – was accustomed, Ellen thought while she waited in the car and Michael went into the office to register. An anachronism from another era. A row of tiny white-trimmed red cottages set in a semi-circle, with a larger cottage serving as office and – probably – home for the owners.

Michael darted through the rain back to the car – key in hand.

"It's the closest unit," he said, opening the door. "Let's run for it."

The room was small, with a wide picture window – drapes discreetly drawn. A queen-sized bed, a dresser, a night table, two lamps, and a chair comprised the nondescript yet not displeasing furniture. A collection of Utrillo prints adorned the walls. The room lay in semi-darkness. Michael made no move to switch on a lamp.

"Not even a TV set. That's supplied on request."

"We don't request," Ellen said while Michael reached to draw her close.

"Let's get out of these wet clothes." But Michael was reluctant to release her. "We'll change into dry things later—"

"Michael, I can't get out of them if you don't let me go," she said with shaky laughter.

172

Michael stripped quickly, flung back the clean but much-washed bedspread, brought the two pillows together into one mound while Ellen undressed.

"You're beautiful." He reached for her again. "You light up my life."

"Oh, Michael—"

"I love you, Ellen. I want you with me forever."

After they'd made love, they lay entangled together beneath the covers – the room remaining in darkness. Reveling in the afterglow of passion.

"Ellen, go with me to Alaska for two weeks," he coaxed yet again. "We'll fly to Seattle, then go by ship to Prince William Sound—"

"Michael, how can I?" But she yearned to be persuaded.

"You pack a bag, and we go together to the airport. It's a ticket to heaven. I'd like it to be forever—" His voice was a silken caress. "But I'll settle for crumbs. The two of us at Prince William Sound. Silent except for the ebb and flow of the tides, the music of the waterfall nearby, an eagle or hawk flying across the sky. We'll sit on the beach at Harrison Lagoon and watch sea otters cavort on a raft. In the distance the snow-covered Chugach Mountains – and most exciting of all, we'll watch the glaciers."

"Michael, I wish I dared," she whispered.

"You dare," he insisted. "For two weeks that'll endure for a lifetime. Monday's the auction. We can be bound for Alaska on Tuesday. Rationalize it," he ordered in a surge of high spirits. "Set a segment of your next book in Alaska. And share a chunk of heaven with me for two weeks."

"I'm scared." But she remembered Marcie and Frank. *Happiness is so fleeting. Why not grasp at it when it came along – for as long as it could be held?*

"You have a right to take two weeks out of a lifetime for yourself." It was as though Michael read her thoughts. "We'll go to Alaska. I'd like it to be forever," he said again, "but I'll be grateful for two weeks."

Phil gazed at the rough sea, crashing against the shore and creating miniature cliffs along the beach. A sight he loved. The rain was letting up, he realized. He left the wide expanse of glass across the front of the house and walked back to the kitchen, where his mother was preparing fresh bread to go into the oven. She baked, he told himself guiltily, when she was upset. She couldn't understand why he was staying up in Montauk all this time when Ellen was down in the city.

"Mom, I'm going to take a run into town," he said. He made these brief sorties to cure his restlessness. "You told me you wanted seafood for dinner. I'll pop into Ocean View and shop."

"No lobster," she warned wryly. "I can't bring myself to cook them anymore. Not since Claire got so upset when she saw the routine."

"I'll check on what looks most exotic," he joshed. "But no lobster."

He left the house and went to the car. The rain dissipated to a drizzle. The ocean was already changing from the murky gunmetal grey of stormy occasions to a lighter grey reflecting the sky. There might even be a real sunset.

Traffic was light for a summer weekend, for which Phil was grateful. The rain was keeping people at home, he surmised. He found a place to park almost in front of Ocean View, went inside to shop. He settled for salmon steaks, bought the last of the Ben & Jerry's Cherry Garcia – which Mom adored. In a slightly improved state of mind, he returned to the car.

He turned onto Old Montauk Highway. This was the glorious scenic view that Ellen always loved. Maybe he should be down in the city with Ellen while she finished up the new book. He always felt guilty that she worked so hard, brought in the major portion of their income. Could they ever get back to those early days that were so wonderful?

All of a sudden he saw the deer charging across the road, swerved to avoid hitting it. His last conscious thought before smashing into a pole and losing consciousness was that the deer had made it to safety.

By the time Ellen and Michael arrived in Manhattan, the rain had given way to wan sunlight. They left the car in the garage, walked to Dock's on Broadway for an early seafood dinner. Michael was so sweet, so understanding, Ellen thought. He knew how important it was for her to finish the book. By tomorrow night it would be wrapped up. On Monday she'd call Sentinel Copy to pick up the manuscript – and in the established fashion they'd deliver four perfect copies to Donna's office. And on Tuesday she and Michael would board a plane for Seattle.

Ellen was pleased that they were arriving ahead of the usual Saturday night hordes. Over dinner Michael talked about his anxiety at switching to fiction for his next book. She realized he was seeking her encouragement.

"The auction on Monday is sure to give you financial security," she pointed out. "You can afford to do what you want – take that chance."

"I'll do it." He glowed with fresh confidence. "You're so good for me, Ellen."

Michael didn't press her to linger over dinner. He walked her to her building knowing he was not to accompany her up to her apartment, that the presence of the doorman ruled out a goodnight kiss.

"I'll talk to you tomorrow. Not too early," he promised. "Because you may work late tonight. I'll dream of you. I'll dream of us at Prince William Sound."

Ellen walked into the lobby, waited for an elevator to descend. She felt wrapped in unreality. For a brief period she was living a strange, wonderful, exciting life. But nobody would be hurt. Not the kids – not Phil. To Phil she was the enemy these days. This time with Michael was a precious gift, she told herself defensively.

She'd phone Phil tomorrow night and tell him, then catch up with Claire and tell her. She'd call Ted in Madrid and let him know that she was going to Alaska. She'd write him from Prince William Sound, but she wouldn't be home to receive his letters. For two weeks the family would exist without her. *The trip is research for my next novel.*

She'd check in with Kathy while she was away. She wasn't walking out on Kathy and Marcie by disappearing for two weeks. There was nothing she could do by staying here. The trial was many weeks away.

Marcie must be cleared, she thought with fresh anguish. Kathy was sure Leslie believed Marcie was guilty. She and Kathy and Angie had believed what Leslie told them. Why couldn't Leslie – Lee Ramsey – believe Kathy? Why wouldn't she help in finding the real murderer? She was in the District Attorney's office – she could do things! Scott kept saying that the only way to clear Marcie was to find the person who killed Frank.

* * *

175

Kathy glanced at the clock. It was past midnight. Where was Scott? She'd asked him to come over when he and Jake were done with their surveillance – no matter how late. Exhausted from the trauma of these last days, Marcie was asleep in her bedroom. The house was eerily quiet.

She tensed into alertness. A car was pulling up at the curb. She hurried to the door. It was Scott.

"You had a long night—" Her voice was uneven in her anxiety.

"Nothing at the farm," he said, walking into the house. "We know they're lying low. But there was a poker game at Peter James's house. Juan Torres was there, Dan Reagan, and Eric Matthews – their cars out front."

"But poker was just a diversion," Kathy surmised.

"We managed to drive by again when the game broke up. There was somebody else there – I know him only by sight. He's an officer at Madison Central Bank."

"Part of the money laundering operation," Kathy pounced.

"We couldn't get close enough to hear anything – there were security guards around the place. Torres must be growing nervous."

"I put up coffee a little while ago – decaf." Kathy fought against disappointment. "It's ready now."

They settled themselves in the dining area with mugs of freshly-brewed decaf.

"Peter James is calling for an earlier date for the re-zoning appeal," Kathy said. "But you saw it in the *Madison News*."

"A lot of people are still for it," Scott reminded. "You know – all the extra jobs, extra revenue coming into town."

"And the business about the True Patriots – that's all being swept under the rug."

"By the two dailies, yes. I bumped into Bill Collins in the course of the evening. He says that the drive-by shooting Thursday night didn't set well with some folks here in town. He's running a front page story again in the *Guardian*. And Jake's on the tail of the guy Joe pinpointed – hoping he'll lead us to something important."

"This is all unreal. Who would believe that a town like this could harbor a terrorist group?" All at once Kathy felt drained.

"We read about them existing – in towns like this," Scott reminded. "Articles in *Time* and *Newsweek* and *US News & World Report*. And now we have Juan Torres and his money laundering set-up. No place – large or small – is immune these days."

Ellen came awake reluctantly. She'd stayed at the computer until almost three a.m. But the ringing of the phone was insistent. Her eyes grazing the clock on her night table, she reached out and brought the receiver to her ear. It was already past ten.

"Hello—"

"Oh, honey, I woke you up." Mom was contrite. "You were working late last night."

"That's all right, Mom. I should be up early." Mom scolded her – but with affection – for working on weekends and holidays. *'Ellie, you have to take out time to live.'* And that's what she was about to do.

"Phil didn't want me to tell you – but I knew you'd want to know—" Mom was stumbling over her words, the way she did when she was upset.

"Mom, what's happened?" Alarm shot through her. "Are the kids all right?"

"The kids are fine," Mom soothed. "We talked to Claire yesterday afternoon, and there was a letter from Ted on Friday. But Phil had a little accident last night. He's okay now – though the doctor at the hospital told him to take it easy for the next seventy-two hours—"

"What kind of accident?" Terrifying images assaulted her.

"He was driving on Old Montauk Highway – and you know how the deer jump out on the road this time of year. He managed not to hit the deer, but the front of the car got bashed in when he swerved off the road and hit a pole. He suffered a slight concussion and some bruises – though he's all right. But the accident brought some things into focus for him – he's so upset that he came out here and left you working in New York. He's planning on driving into the city late this evening – when he figures the traffic will have subsided. He—"

"He mustn't drive yet!" Ellen broke in. "I'll be out there in three or four hours. He's so awful about taking care of himself."

"I told him just to lie on a chaise on the deck and do nothing more strenuous than gaze at the ocean for the next seventy-two hours."

Off the phone Ellen sat motionless, her mind in turmoil. How had she thought she could run off to Alaska for two weeks with Michael? That was fantasy land. Phil and the kids and Mom were reality. Gearing herself for what she must say to Michael, she reached again for the phone.

Within an hour Ellen was driving out of the Queens Midtown Tunnel en route to Montauk. The morning was grey, a chill in the air. Thank God, she wouldn't run into heavy beach-bound traffic! Mom had jolted her out of a fairytale world into reality. She was impatient to see Phil, to know he was all right. He was never one to coddle himself. But the doctor had ordered him to take it easy for seventy-two hours.

How had she and Phil allowed this wall to come up between them? They must work together to tear it down. Now Kathy's exhortation charged across her brain – '*Ellie, fight to keep your marriage together. You have a major investment in it. The most important investment of your lifetime.*'

How could she have considered going off to Alaska with Michael? *Perhaps* no one would ever know – but how could she take such a gamble? She had thought only of herself – but she should have been thinking of her family. Now her mind darted back through the years – to crucial moments in their lives. For everybody in this world life was an obstacle course. You learned to handle the hurdles. She and Phil must make it over this latest hurdle.

She was making good time on the LIE, she comforted herself – though she suspected there'd be a slowdown on Route 27 from Southampton to Montauk. Sunday summer traffic could be bumper-to-bumper in spots. She wanted to see for herself that Phil was all right. Why did it take this accident to wake her up?

At Exit 70 she left the LIE. Approaching Southampton she always felt herself almost at the house. But today – though the traffic was light – each mile dragged. It wasn't a good beach day. People stayed home or shopped at the malls.

In Bridgehampton there was a flurry of activity in the shops and again in East Hampton. Today, she admitted to herself as she drove past the Amagansett shops, she wished they had a car phone. She wanted to hear Phil's voice. To know he was all right.

The barrier between Phil and herself must come down. Their way of life – the children's way of life – was at stake. She must make him understand that they were a *family*.

Please God, don't let it be too late.

Twenty-Three

Kathy scolded herself at intervals for being afraid to leave the house unless Scott was beside her. She'd convinced herself that the drive-by shooting had been a scare tactic. Neither she nor Marcie was meant to be harmed. Ditto the hate mail. She ignored Scott's grim reminder that she and Marcie could have been killed.

Pouring herself a mug of freshly-brewed coffee, she glanced at the kitchen clock. It was almost noon. Scott would be over shortly with the Sunday newspapers and what he called a Sunday brunch 'care package'. She was eager for his arrival. He'd become such an important part of her life. For a little while – when her mother was dying and perhaps a year beyond – she'd felt that way about Glenn. But so quickly she'd realized she couldn't lean on Glenn for support. Glenn was always looking for a crutch – at least in the years of their marriage. Scott was a different breed. His strength was a bottomless well.

He was driving the twenty miles to the fancy new mall where hot bagels and nitrite-free smoked salmon were available. The three of them would have brunch when he arrived. When she opened the new shop, she told herself in a rush of unwary expectations – *if* she opened her new shop – here in Madison, she'd stock the refrigerator units with all the nitrite-free foods that Marcie liked.

She listened for sounds from the upper floor. Only silence. Thank God, Marcie was sleeping late this morning. Poor baby, she was exhausted from so many sleepless nights and the tensions of virtual house arrest. But Scott was confident they were close to a breakthrough. '*Just a few tiny pieces*,' he kept saying, '*and the puzzle will be complete.*' But when would that happen?

Eric had deliberately incriminated Marcie with that story about Frank's wanting a divorce. Scott was sure it had something to do with Frank and Marcie's fighting the re-zoning appeal by Paradise Estates. And he was convinced that Juan Torres was financing Paradise Estates with money he'd managed to bring out of Colombia. Yet the familiar question taunted her. How was this connected with Frank's murder?

She started at the sharp intrusion of the phone. The new line. She was wary each time it rang even though it was an unlisted number.

On the seventh ring – steeling herself for more ugliness – Kathy picked up the receiver.

"Hello—"

"Hi, Grandma!" David's ebullient voice greeted her.

For an instant Kathy froze in shock. "Linda had the baby?" About four weeks early, her mind tabulated.

"Your granddaughter is about four hours old," David reported. "She's the image of you."

"Linda's all right?" Kathy was simultaneously euphoric, in awe, and alarmed. "The baby wasn't due for another four weeks."

"Linda's fine. She just drifted off to sleep. She'll call you later. And the baby weighs six pounds three ounces. She has all the requisite equipment. It all happened so fast – Linda didn't even have time to call and tell you she was in labor."

"I'm dying to fly out—" Kathy was torn now. How could she leave Marcie?

"Mom, it's okay," David soothed. "Linda understands you need to be there for Marcie. And Glenn's flying out this afternoon." She was 'Mom' – Linda's father was 'Glenn'.

"Oh, great," she said perfunctorily. But all at once she was cold. Linda had called her *father*. She'd drifted off to sleep before calling her mother.

"He's only staying until tomorrow afternoon," David said. "He has some big deal on in New York on Tuesday."

"Glenn always has some big deal on," Kathy said and silently berated herself. This wasn't a day to display her anger at her ex-husband.

But Linda had called Glenn before calling her. That would hurt for a long time.

She and David talked for another few minutes, then he said goodbye.

"I've got to get over to the nursery and see your granddaughter. I don't have to tell you – she's the most beautiful baby of the lot."

Kathy sat staring into space – her mind beset by questions she hadn't thought to ask David. Caught up in recall of the births of

Best Friends

Linda and Marcie. Oh yes! She longed to fly out to Seattle to be with Linda and to see this first grandchild. A precious gift in the midst of her anguish.

Now she heard sounds on the upper floor. Marcie was awake. She hurried to the hall, called upstairs.

"Marcie! Linda's had the baby!"

A moment later Marcie was hurrying down the stairs.

"Girl or boy?" Marcie demanded, charging into the kitchen. "Not that it matters – so long as it's healthy."

"It's a little girl. And David says she's the image of us!" Everybody always said Marcie looked just like her. Linda resembled her maternal grandmother.

"You'll want to fly out there." Marcie's smile was tender.

"No, I'll stay here. Linda will call us later, and we'll talk."

"Mom, you don't have to stay here with me."

"I *want* to stay here with you."

"I wish Frank and I had had a baby." Marcie was wistful. "We were planning on it, you know."

"I know, darling." Tears filled Kathy's eyes. "We'll both love Linda's baby." She couldn't bring herself to say that Marcie was young – there could be children in her future. This was not the time. "She was early," Kathy acknowledged. "But in the regular nursery, David said – not with the preemies."

They heard the sound of a car turning into the driveway. Scott, Kathy surmised. The guard wouldn't allow anybody else into the driveway.

"Scott went over to that new mall to bring us hot bagels and smoked salmon. The kind without the nitrites," Kathy joshed lovingly.

"Scott's a sweet guy." Kathy was conscious of questions in Marcie's eyes. Were she and Scott giving themselves away? But there was no space in her life now for anyone but her girls.

For a little while, Kathy thought, the house seemed to reverberate with a pleasant excitement. She and Scott settled themselves about the table in the dining alcove – talking only about Linda and David and the baby while Marcie brought out plates and silverware, poured coffee. Angie and Joe were at Lake George – she'd tell them about the baby when they got home tonight. She'd tried to reach Ellie – but the answering machine was off.

That meant she was out of town. She'd probably run out to Montauk.

"Oh, you can't eat bagels and smoked salmon without cream cheese and onion," Marcie announced in rare high spirits and strode to the refrigerator to bring out these items.

For a little while they were engrossed in an enjoyable breakfast. Kathy talked about the new shop she planned to open in Madison. The three shut out the ugliness that hovered over them.

After a second round of coffee, Marcie pushed back her chair and rose to her feet. "Do you mind if I read the papers now?" Marcie glanced from her mother to Scott. "There should be some reports on the fundraiser for the Senior Citizens Center." She was anxious about this. "Eric was co-chairman, along with Frank. They're not going to drop the whole deal now, are they?"

"Go ahead and read," Kathy said gently. "I'll clear away here."

Marcie retreated to the living-room with the Sunday papers. Scott helped Kathy with the minor clean-up from breakfast.

"There should be some way to flush out the True Patriots," Kathy said impatiently. "You believe Juan Torres is mixed up in it?"

"I'm sure of that." Scott was somber. "It's an operation he understands. I wouldn't be surprised to discover he's the one who armed them."

"For what reason?" Kathy probed.

"To be there if Peter James decides he needs rough action to get his re-zoning across," Scott said bluntly. "They won't even realize they're being used. Remember, Paradise Estates is a multi-million dollar deal."

"I don't believe this!" Marcie returned to the dining area. "Not one word in the papers about the fundraiser for the Senior Citizens Center! Frank worked so hard on it."

"What kind of fundraiser?" Scott asked.

"A formal dinner at the country club and a concert afterwards. Everybody was so excited about it. Madison *needs* a Senior Citizens Center." Marcie hesitated. "Mom, I can't talk to Eric – not after all his lies. Could you ask Fiona about the fundraiser? She knows everything about it – she sat in on the meetings to take notes. If they don't go ahead immediately with the plans, the whole campaign will fall apart."

"Marcie, I'm sorry," Scott apologized. "I was supposed to check on that for you."

Best Friends

"I'll talk to Fiona," Kathy promised. "I'll go over tomorrow morning." Meaning when Fiona was alone at the house.

"I'll go with you," Scott said. "I don't want you running around this town alone."

The town seethed with ugly undercurrents, Kathy thought uneasily. To walk about the streets of Madison was to feel the tension on every side. Strange faces, out-of-town license plates on the cars, an air of threatening invasion had permeated Madison in the last three days. Hotels enjoyed full occupancy, lines waited for tables at restaurants.

And tomorrow night, Kathy remembered with anguish, Frank's parents would appear on a TV tabloid to scream for vengeance for their son's death – convinced Marcie had killed him.

By the time Ellen approached Montauk, the sun had broken through the clouds. The ocean was a vivid blue, reflecting the sky. The air sweet and clean. Why had she waited so long to fight for what was most important in her life? Work – the exhilaration of acquiring security – had gotten in the way. But what would financial security mean if she destroyed the family in reaching for that?

Mom had tried to put her on warning. Mom had seen what she had not. Let it not be too late to save what was most precious to her in this world. No more long silences between Phil and her. Let them talk through their problems.

Her heart began to pound as she turned off the highway and headed for the house – set just above the dunes and facing the sea, with huge expanses of glass that brought the outdoors inside. All at once she braked. A pair of very young deer were ambling along the road. Phil loved all animals – as she herself did. So he'd swerved and hit a pole. She was suddenly cold as ice. *He could have been killed.*

She swung off the road into the driveway. The garage at the back of the house – its doors open – told her that Mom was off to one of her volunteer luncheons. She parked, darted from the car and up the long flight of stairs that led to the deck.

On the segment of the deck shaded by an awning, Phil was sprawled on a chaise. He hadn't heard the car, hadn't heard her come up the stairs. Was he asleep?

"Phil?" she said softly – for a poignant instant fearful. But he was stirring.

"Ellen—" He pulled himself upright. "What are you doing here?"

183

"Mom called this morning." She walked towards him – managing a tremulous smile. "She told me about the accident—" Fate taking a hand.

"Mom shouldn't have bothered you with that." He grunted in rebuke. "It was nothing."

"That's what she said." Ellen sat at the edge of a brightly-cushioned chair beside the chaise, restraining her impulse to lean forward to kiss him. "But I had to see for myself that you were all right."

"You should have called. There was no need to take you away from your work."

"I've finished the book. Ahead of schedule," she said with an effort at lightness. But there was that wall between them again! "It's all ready to go to Sentinel for copying. I was so frightened, Phil—" She took a deep breath, searched for words to express what needed to be said. "We have to talk. What's been happening to us scares me."

"You're doing fine." His voice was brusque, his eyes guarded. "What's there to be scared about?"

"You keep shutting me out. We always used to be able to talk." But they hadn't talked, her mind taunted – not for a long time.

"You don't need me, Ellen. Your work consumes you." He managed a philosophical air – but it was suspect.

"I don't neglect you or the kids!" The image that leapt into her mind was unnerving. Was that how Phil saw her? "You won't ever go with me to parties or conventions," she reminded defensively. "I've asked you – over and over again. Other husbands go."

"It's not my world." He turned away, focused on a sailboat on the water.

"It *is* your world. You turned away from it—"

"I couldn't afford to be part of it. I had to earn a living. I couldn't sit around a year or two or more and wait to come up with another 'big book'."

"You share whatever success I have. I couldn't have moved into writing if it wasn't for you." She leaned forward, her mind in high gear. "Phil, you have a sabbatical due." Which he consistently dismissed. "You could take it this year. Give yourself a year of freedom to write. It's important for all of us."

Best Friends

"And if I come up with nothing?" he challenged. But she saw a gleam of shaky hope in his eyes.

"There'd be nothing lost." She forced herself to sound matter-of-fact. "You can always go back to the school. You're a fine teacher, Phil – they're happy to have you. But give yourself that year. Give *us* that year—" Let them learn to talk out their problems. To compromise.

"It sounds crazy—" Again, he was wary.

"Let me back into your life. The way we used to be. Because without you, Phil, I'm lost."

The atmosphere was suddenly electric. "I was so sure you didn't need me." But uncertainty infiltrated his voice. "I was just a hanger-on, an appendage from another life. You were the successful writer, the mother who managed her kids so well."

"The kids need a mother and a father. Parents who can communicate. Let's be a real family again."

"I thought I'd save the sabbatical for later – for some emergency that might arise." But he was wavering.

"The emergency is *now*. Take the year off and write. I know how many books you've started and discarded because there was never enough time to move ahead."

"I don't know if I have another book in me."

"Give yourself a chance to find out. Give *us* another chance, Phil."

"I've missed you so much," he whispered. "I thought – I felt so useless—"

"Oh Phil, no. No! And I've missed you so." She was conscious now of unexpected arousal, felt this mirrored in Phil. She reached out a hand with the need to touch. "Where's Mom?"

"She went to some luncheon." He cleared his throat in that remembered manner that meant he was passionate. "Then she has some meeting afterwards—"

"She won't be back for hours." Ellen rose to her feet – her face radiant. "Phil, let's go into the house and make love."

"I'm not sure I know how anymore." But already he was on his feet, pulling her close.

"It's like riding a bike." She reached for his hand. "Once learned, you never forget."

A stray deer had saved her making a tragic mistake, Ellen told herself. She'd been lost – but she'd found her way again.

*   *   *

185

Monday morning began hot and humid. By eight a.m. a dreary drizzle that did little to alleviate the heat began to fall. At ten a.m. – when they were confident Eric Matthews would be at his office – Kathy and Scott headed for the Matthews home to talk with Fiona. In this weather Fiona would be home with her young children.

"Do you suppose we should have called first?" Kathy asked, all at once uncomfortable as Scott pulled up before the small Matthews house.

"No. This is just a casual visit to please Marcie." He reached out to squeeze her hand for a moment, his smile quietly reassuring.

Yet Kathy sensed that Scott was glad to have an excuse to visit Eric Matthews's home. He, too, was ever conscious that Eric Matthews had deliberately lied to the police.

They left the car and ran beneath a single umbrella to the entrance to the house. They heard the ingratiating sound of a man's voice – and in the background the music from *Peter and the Wolf*.

Scott touched the doorbell. Chimes tinkled, then they heard footsteps coming towards the door. The door swung wide. Fiona appeared, startled but happy to see them.

"Mrs Marshall, please come in—" Her smile included Scott.

"Fiona, do you know Scott Lazarus?" Kathy asked.

"Not personally," she admitted shyly. "But I know he's Marcie's lawyer." Now her eyes were troubled. "My friends and I all feel so awful about what's happened. We all know she couldn't have done it."

"Marcie asked us to talk to you," Kathy explained, walking with Fiona into the tiny foyer. "She's so worried about the fundraiser that was being planned for the Senior Citizens Center."

"Eric was working with Frank on that when – when Frank was killed. But Eric hasn't said anything about it since. I mean, everybody's been so upset and all—" Fiona crossed to lower the TV volume. Her small son moved closer to the screen. Her toddler daughter – oblivious to the storyteller – played with a stuffed animal in her play-pen. "But let me get you some coffee."

"You don't need to do that, Fiona," Kathy said quickly.

"Please." Fiona's smile was ingratiating. "And you tell Marcie we're all praying for her." Not all, Kathy thought. Not Fiona's husband. "She's got a lot of friends in this town."

"I'll tell her," Kathy said.

"You make yourselves comfortable – I'll be right back." Fiona headed for the kitchen.

Kathy was aware of the pungent scent of stale cigarette smoke. Her gaze followed Scott's to the end table beside a lounge chair. A pack of Turkish cigarettes lay there. A cigarette butt in the ashtray.

"Meow—" A huge, grey Persian cat slinked into the room, crossed over to Kathy. "Meow—" He lay at Kathy's feet with an expectant air.

"Oh, you're a beautiful boy," she crooned.

She stroked his back – her mind in high gear, her heart pounding. Suspecting her hand would come away with a swathe of grey fur. Remembering Marcie's conviction that someone had been with Frank before she walked into the den. '*Someone who smoked Turkish cigarettes.*' And Scott had found grey cat fur in the room – though Marcie and Frank had no cats.

Her eyes sought Scott's. But Scott was inspecting the books on a pair of wall-bracketed book shelves. He turned, beckoned to her, pointed to a book that rested between a pair of paperback romance novels. The book was *The Turner Diaries*. Scott had told her about this novel by a man named William Pierce.

'*It's a novel about the fertilizer-bombing of a government building. It's been the bible for paramilitary groups since 1978.*'

Twenty-Four

S cott's eyes met Kathy's with an admonition for silence. The tension was almost unbearable. But they must have coffee with Fiona, Kathy exhorted herself. Pretend not to have made a staggering discovery. The man who had been in the den with Frank before Marcie came in had been Eric Matthews. *Eric killed Frank.*

Kathy forced herself to focus on Fiona's tiny daughter, pulling herself to her feet to offer a stuffed purple dinosaur to the two strangers in her living-room.

"Is that Barney?" Kathy asked, lowering herself to toddler level.

"Yes!" The cherubic smile brought a touch of pain to Kathy. So sweet and innocent. How would her father's crime color her life? A crime they must prove, Kathy warned herself.

She contrived to carry on making small talk with the beguiling toddler while Scott moved about the living-room, searching – she understood – for more evidence against Eric. But they *knew* Eric killed Frank.

Fiona returned with coffee. Kathy avoided meeting Scott's eyes lest she betray her excitement, contrived casual conversation until Scott made a polite excuse about needing to get back to his office. They escaped in guilty haste.

Sliding into the car beside Scott, Kathy felt giddy with relief. *They knew who killed Frank.* But not until they were out of the driveway and on the street did Kathy allow herself to speak.

"It had to be Eric!" She was conscious of dizzying triumph.

"It's all coming together." Scott nodded in satisfaction. "Eric killed Frank because he was going to expose the True Patriots – and that might implicate Paradise Estates. Frank thought Eric was on his side, called him over to the house to tell him what he'd discovered. Eric killed Frank, heard Marcie approaching, sneaked out the den slider onto the patio and around to the front of the house."

"Most people here still don't bother locking their front doors in the daytime," Kathy picked up. "He heard Marcie scream, hurried back into the house to find Marcie hovering over Frank's body. Providing himself with a perfect alibi!"

"Kathy, this is all supposition," Scott pointed out.

"But it's so obvious! The Turkish cigarettes, the grey cat fur. That book. Eric was in the den with Frank before Marcie came in. Take this to Lee Ramsey!"

"We can't go to her without more concrete evidence," Scott warned. "We'll dig into Eric's every move. We'll—"

"Can't you talk to the District Attorney? Not Lee Ramsey – she's just an assistant DA. Bob Miller, her boss."

"I can't go over Lee Ramsey's head without strong supporting evidence. She's convinced she has an airtight case. We need strong evidence to tear that down. I'll drive you home – then I'm calling Jake. We'll nail Eric Matthews."

"Will we see you later?" Kathy asked.

"Sure." His eyes left the road for an instant to rest on her. "I cherish our time together."

"I need you near me," she whispered. "You keep me from falling apart."

"Hang in there, Kathy. Soon there'll be a time for us."

"Tonight Marcie's in-laws go on that TV show." She recoiled from the vision of this. "Marcie has some wild idea that we should watch."

"No way," Scott rejected. "We'll be having dinner together. I'll bring over Chinese take-out." He paused – in some inner debate – then continued. "I've refused to talk to them – but Pam's received several calls from New York TV programs wanting to discuss my being interviewed."

Kathy stiffened in shock. "Scott, you wouldn't?"

"No, I wouldn't. You know that."

"Angie said she read some gossip columnist who reported that the TV program was paying Frank's parents fifty thousand dollars." She shuddered. "That's so sick."

"We'll convince Marcie not to watch. That would be masochistic. Why don't you call Angie – invite her and Joe over for dinner with us? They're back from Lake George, aren't they?"

"They came back last night."

"It'll be good for Marcie to see other people. Call Angie and Joe," Scott said. "Dinner about seven?"

"That'll be great. I'll tell Angie."

Angie understood that something precious was developing between Scott and her – and reveled in it. Did Marcie see it, too? Sometimes she was sure – and knew that Marcie approved. It seemed so unreal – yet so wonderful.

She felt reborn, blessed with a second chance. Something she had never anticipated. She wasn't cheating Marcie and Linda to love Scott. Yet she knew, too, that this love could go nowhere unless Marcie was cleared.

Kathy found Marcie at the door when she returned to the house.

"Did you talk to Fiona?" Marcie asked anxiously. "What's happening about the Senior Citizens Center?"

"Nothing's happening now, but—"

"Talk to Bill Collins about it," Marcie urged. "He knows how important the Center is to this town. Ask him about running—"

"Later," Kathy soothed. "But I have good news. Some guardian angel sent us to talk with Fiona – to get inside their house." Her face was radiant. "Marcie, we *know* that Eric killed Frank."

Marcie listened with rapt attention while Kathy reported what they had discovered at the Matthews house.

"That 'paramilitary bible' links him to the True Patriots," Kathy pointed out. Yet she was ambivalent about Marcie's jubilation. "But we need more to persuade the District Attorney's office to go after Eric. This is what we've pieced together," she cautioned.

"Poor Fiona. She'll be so crushed," Marcie sighed. "She worships him—"

"Darling, we're not out of the woods yet," Kathy cautioned.

"But I know someone was there before I came into the den—"

"We'll have to prove that in court." Fear moved in to erode her earlier elation. "Scott will check into every move Eric makes. He's sure Eric will trip himself up somewhere along the line."

"Suppose he doesn't? The prosecutor will say I made up the bit about the Turkish cigarettes. She'll say Scott was lying about the grey cat fur."

"Scott will clear you." Kathy fought for confidence. "Either before the trial or at the trial."

Marcie was very still. What could she do to help her? Kathy agonized. She felt so helpless – when Marcie needed her most.

"I'm going to write a letter to Bill Collins pointing out the need for the Senior Citizens Center," Marcie decided. "I want Bill to make a strong case for the Center. It's so important, Mom. In a way, it'll be a memorial to Frank."

Kathy spent the early afternoon cleaning the living-room and dining area in preparation for what she'd described to Marcie as 'our little dinner party' – though both areas were immaculate. She was conscious of a compulsion to keep busy. She'd had a long talk with Jill at the shop. Everything was going smoothly there. *But what are we doing to clear Marcie?*

Her mind warned her not to expect overnight miracles. Her heart ached to put an end to this nightmare they were living. To Scott and her everything was so clear now. *Why can't we go to Lee? Or her boss?*

When the phone rang at shortly past three, she approached with a mixture of eagerness and caution. Was it Scott or another ugly phone call? The new number was already public knowledge. Without looking up the stairs, she was sure Marcie was hovering there in trepidation. Each phone call elicited alarm.

"Hello—"

"Hi, it's me." Pam's ebullient voice came to her. "Is Scott there?"

"No, he isn't," Kathy told her. "Though he will be around seven. If you don't catch up with him, shall I give him a message?"

"Yeah, please. I'll be closing up at five sharp today – I'm running to a dental appointment. Tell Scott that his friend down in Miami called back. You know, the newspaper editor. He said he'd be in his office another couple of hours – but just in case they missed connections, he wanted Scott to know he's come up with new info on Juan Torres."

"Did he tell you what it was?" Kathy gripped the phone with a sense of urgency.

"He sure did," Pam bubbled. "The Miami police have a warrant out for his arrest. On charges of money laundering."

That's why Torres traveled in a car with Virginia license plates. He's on the run. Off the phone Kathy repeated Pam's message to Marcie.

"If Torres is apprehended, it could put a crimp in Peter James's plans for Paradise Estates." Marcie was suddenly hopeful.

"Juan Torres's arrest could implicate Peter James and Dan Reagan – and Eric Matthews."

"If Eric is part of the money laundering scene, that'll kill his credibility as a witness, won't it?"

"I should think so." Kathy struggled to sound optimistic. But there was still the insurance policy that Marcie never knew about – and what awful lies would Frank's parents unleash tonight on television?

Again there was the jarring intrusion of the phone. Kathy reached to pick up – hoping it was Scott.

"Hello—"

"Mom—" It was Linda. Her voice harsh with rage.

"Darling, are you all right?" They'd had a long talk last night. Linda had been euphoric.

"I'm fine." Linda was struggling for calm. "The baby's fine. David's fine. But I'm furious at Dad!"

Kathy was startled. "What did he do?"

"David told you Dad was coming out for what he called a 'quickie'. He said he had to be in New York late this afternoon. Mom, he's taping a TV interview! About Marcie!"

For a moment Kathy was shocked into silence. But only for a moment.

"That's despicable! After all his fears about being identified as Marcie's father?"

"He bragged about how he pushed his fee up by another ten thousand. I couldn't believe he could be so rotten!"

"I'm never surprised by what your father does." Kathy made no effort to conceal her contempt. But today Linda didn't accuse her of being 'hostile'.

"David's so angry," Linda continued. "I've thought sometimes that he was a little hard on Dad. But I was the one who was blind. You and David saw him for what he is."

"It's low even for him," Kathy said quietly. "But we'll survive it. Some new evidence has surfaced. Scott is convinced – as I am – that Eric Matthews killed Frank. Pray we can prove that to the District Attorney."

Kathy paced restlessly about the living-room. Marcie was in the den – revising for the third time her letter to Bill Collins about the urgency of a Senior Citizens Center. It was almost five o'clock – Pam would be leaving the office any minute. Had she heard from Scott? Did he know about the warrant for Juan Torres's arrest?

Call Pam, her mind ordered. Talk to her. She reached for the phone, tapped the number, waited for a response.

"Scott Lazarus's office—" A hurried quality in Pam's voice.

"Pam, it's Kathy. Have you heard from Scott?"

"Not a peep. I'm cutting out in a couple of minutes. I left a note on his desk. And if he doesn't come in, you'll be sure to tell him." It was a statement rather than a question.

"I'll tell him," Kathy promised. "You haven't heard anything further from Miami?"

"Just that one call," Pam confirmed.

Off the phone, Kathy paced in frustration. Why couldn't Scott run with what they knew? It was so clear – Eric Matthews killed Frank. She couldn't bear this waiting for something to happen.

She stopped pacing, her mind in high gear. *I can make it happen.*

She hurried to the door of the den. Marcie looked up from the computer screen.

"Darling, I want to talk to Angie." Kathy contrived to sound casual. "I'll pick her up at her office."

"Mom, you know Scott said you weren't to leave the house alone." Hate mail, nasty phone calls still arrived. And traffic past the house was far heavier than normal. The curious were eager to see the murder site – where the accused was holed up on bail. "Besides, Angie will be here in a couple of hours."

"I want to talk to her now," Kathy insisted. "I'll call her to come over and pick me up," she compromised.

"Where are you going with her?" Marcie was alarmed.

"It'll be all right, Marcie. Angie will go with me. It's something I have to do."

193

Twenty-Five

Angie swore at the slow flow of late afternoon traffic, then chuckled at her scatological language.

"Joe taught me to swear under stress," she told Kathy. "My language never exploded like this when we were younger."

"It's part of the times," Kathy consoled. "Most of us use language that would have shocked the hell out of us twenty years ago." But she, too, was annoyed by this tie-up.

"You're sure you want to do this?" Angie seemed uneasy.

"I'm sure." *I have to make something positive happen for Marcie.*

"You said Scott insisted it would be useless to go to the District Attorney with what you have."

"We're not going to the District Attorney," Kathy hedged. "We're presenting our facts to his ADA – Lee Ramsey."

"Which isn't saying much." Angie grunted contemptuously. "It's weird to call her – think of her – as Lee."

"To us she'll always be Leslie. We can't make the jump over thirty-one years."

"She's not going to help Marcie." Angie's impatience surfaced. "All she's thinking about is what a conviction will do for her career-wise."

"I want her to understand that Eric was there in that room before Marcie arrived," Kathy insisted. "I want her to investigate Eric. That'll be a beginning."

"You're spinning your wheels." Frustration lent harshness to Angie's voice.

"Not if I can make a deal with her."

"What kind of a deal?"

"Just go along with me. OK?"

"OK," Angie agreed. "We'll do like you said – sit at the side of the road near her house until we see her car turn into her driveway."

Ten minutes later they saw Lee's Acura Legend pass them, swing into the driveway of the stately Georgian house where she lived with

194

her father. They waited for her to emerge from her car and go into the house before they followed.

"She may refuse to see us," Angie warned as they approached the stairs.

"She won't dare." For all Lee's bravado, Kathy surmised, she wanted to steer clear of any ugly disclosures.

When a woman whom they gathered was the family domestic greeted them at the door, Kathy asked to see Lee.

"Tell her it's two old friends. Kathy and Angie," Kathy said. Lee would understand she was here with back-up.

Moments later Lee confronted them, dismissed the domestic.

"I told you, Kathy. I can't help you." Lee appeared cold, yet Kathy sensed that Angie's presence was unnerving her.

"We have to talk." Kathy's eyes dueled with hers. Let Lee realize she wouldn't be brushed aside. "It's urgent."

Lee hesitated a moment. "Let's go into the den." She thrust open a door at the right of the foyer, walked with Kathy and Angie into the elegantly furnished room, closed the door and swung around to face the other two women.

"I've told you Kathy. I'm acting as prosecuting attorney. I have to carry out my obligations."

"What about friendship?" Angie flared, forgetting her plotted role as silent supporter. "Have you forgotten how we put ourselves on the line for you?"

"That's history," Lee dismissed this. "Nobody would believe you if you tried to revive it."

"We won't do that," Kathy told her. "Never. But I want you to investigate Eric Matthews. Marcie knows someone was in the room where Frank was killed just moments before she came in. Nobody in the house smokes – but the room reeked of heavy Turkish cigarettes. Scott Lazarus found grey cat fur on the rug – but Frank and Marcie never owned a cat. Eric Matthews smokes Turkish cigarettes. He has a grey cat. He reads a novel that police authorities know is like a textbook for violent paramilitary groups. He—"

"I can't order an investigation on that!" Lee stared at Kathy with scorn. "You're wasting my time."

"Maybe not." All at once Kathy was deceptively calm. "Maybe we have information that could bring Eric Matthews up on other charges. We know that a South American drug lord – with a warrant out for his arrest in Miami – is right here in Madison."

That snapped Lee to attention. "He's staying with Peter James. They've been in heavy conferences with Dan Reagan and Madison Central Bank." She paused, allowing Lee to absorb this. "And with Eric Matthews. The South American drug lord is wanted on charges of money laundering."

"Who is he?" Lee's voice was electric.

"It would be a terrific deal for you to break up a major money laundering operation involving this South American, Paradise Estates and a local bank," Kathy pointed out. "It would make you look great in the eyes of Madison residents."

"Who is this man?" Lee tried – unsuccessfully – to appear amused. Kathy knew she was churning for action. "Or is this just some wild scene you've dreamt up?"

"The South American was recognized by a foreign correspondent – a friend of Ellen's." There – another jolt for Lee. "He and Scott Lazarus trailed him to James's home. They saw him with this man and Dan Reagan and Eric Matthews. Ellen's friend checked with a contact in Miami and learned about the warrant. Also," Kathy pursued, "it's likely Torres supplied arms to the True Patriots. They're the ones probably responsible for the drive-by shooting at my house."

"What's his name?" Lee demanded again. "This South American drug lord. I'll have to check with the Miami police—"

"How can I be sure you'll implicate Eric?" Kathy challenged.

"Because I'll want to bring in everybody involved." Lee tried to conceal her excitement. "Give me his name, Kathy – unless you're bluffing."

"His name is Juan Torres. Miami police will confirm what I've told you. He's staying at Peter James's house. He travels in a black Rolls Royce with a chauffeur who wears a shoulder holster." Kathy paused, all at once breathless. "Call the Miami police!"

Lee gazed from Kathy to Angie with a sudden, piercing intensity.

"Why did you stop writing to me? All of you—"

"We didn't." Kathy turned to Angie for confirmation. "We wrote – the three of us – and our letters were returned. Just after the Christmas holidays. We figured you'd left that boarding school—"

"I left it, yes. I wrote each of you to give you the address of the new school." Lee seemed to be groping for an explanation. And all at once, they knew, she'd arrived at a bitter conclusion. "I guess my father forgot to mail my letters." Because – except for Ellen, whose father had been a paediatrician – they didn't meet Mr Hilton's social standards.

With an enigmatic smile Lee crossed to the phone. "I'll check with Miami."

An hour later Scott and Joe listened in astonishment while Kathy reported on her encounter with Lee Ramsey. Marcie moved about the dining area, setting the table, moving Chinese take-out into bowls. She had heard this earlier. In the kitchen the tea kettle whistled. She rushed to silence it.

"You two women are amazing." Scott exchanged an awed glance with Joe. "You went there to face Lee Ramsey with a bargaining chip she couldn't resist."

"We were acting on instinct." Kathy managed a shaky smile. "Once Pam told us about the warrant, I knew we had to move fast. Before Torres left town."

"Feminine intuition." Joe nodded in respect. "But how do you know Lee Ramsey will follow through on this guy Torres?"

Scott chuckled. "Lee Ramsey will play it for all it's worth. It's terrific for her career-wise to have spotted this guy. She'll take all the credit, of course—"

"Just let her involve Eric in the money laundering," Kathy said passionately. "The whole scam – including the tie-in with the True Patriots – will begin to unravel!"

"Bill Collins is taking another whack at them in the next issue of the *Guardian*. But let's be realistic." Scott was apologetic. "We still have a way to go to clear Marcie."

"Frank's parents must be ripping me to shreds on that TV program right this moment," Marcie reminded from the dining area.

"We won't listen." Kathy hadn't been able to bring herself to tell Marcie that Glenn, too, would be discussing the case on national television.

"Come on, let's eat before the food gets cold." Angie rose to her feet. "Marcie may not be home free yet – but we're on the home stretch."

But unless they proved Eric Matthews killed Frank, Kathy taunted herself, Marcie could be convicted for a crime she didn't commit.

Kathy was imprisoned by a mesh of impatience as they waited for

Lee Ramsey to act. *Was Juan Torres still in town?* If she didn't move fast, he could disappear.

"Mom, it takes time for the District Attorney's office to check facts, put through whatever papers are necessary," Marcie said while her mother paced about the living-room. "Scott's sure she won't waste a minute. This is important to her."

"But suppose Torres takes off?" Kathy was growing distraught. "We talked to her twenty-four hours ago!"

"Joe just told you. He drove by Peter James's house twenty minutes ago – and the black Rolls Royce was sitting in the driveway."

"Right." Kathy sought for calm. And Joe had also told her he'd seen Eric and a workman piling bags of fertilizer into Eric's car at the Paradise Estates temporary office area. Was that fertilizer going to Eric's house – or to the farm to be made into a bomb?

The phone rang. Kathy reached for it – as always these days, wary about the caller.

"Hello."

"Turn on the TV," Scott ordered. "There's a news bulletin! I'll hang on."

"Right." She swung around to Marcie. "Switch on the TV!"

"Just thirty minutes ago," a newscaster was announcing excitedly, "Lee Ramsey, an assistant district attorney, noticed the presence of a black Rolls Royce in town. Curious, she did some checking. But here's Lee Ramsey to tell you herself."

The TV cameras moved back to include Lee, wearing a beautifully tailored red coat-dress, her make-up and coiffeur perfect.

"I noticed the black Rolls, a rare sight in this town," Lee said crisply. "I did some follow-up – not liking what I learned. I spoke with police chiefs in several Florida cities. Photos were faxed to me. I discovered that Juan Torres, a notorious drug lord, is the house guest of Peter James, head of Paradise Estates. And that both men have been conferring with Dan Reagan, president of the Madison Central Bank." Kathy's eyes were glued to the TV screen. *Why didn't she mention Eric Matthews?* "Juan Torres is wanted on money laundering charges in Miami. We're looking into possible similar charges here in Madison. Peter James and Dan Reagan are being held for questioning pending an investigation of the Madison Central Bank."

"Thank you, Lee Ramsey," the announcer wound up. "And now . . ."

"Why didn't she bring in Eric?" Kathy railed, turning off the TV. "That was our deal!"

"Talk to Scott," Marcie urged.

Kathy went to the phone table, picked up the receiver.

"Scott, she didn't say a word about Eric!"

"She probably needs more evidence before she can bring him in," Scott soothed. "We'll just have to give her time."

"She doesn't give a damn about bringing in Eric!" Kathy's voice soared perilously. "All she cares about is nabbing Juan Torres! He's the one who'll give her headlines. She lied to me, Scott!"

Twenty-Six

S cott sat in a lounge chair before his television set and watched the ten p.m. local news round-up – which, he suspected, was creating an avalanche of shocks around town. Torres, Peter James, and Dan Reagan monopolized tonight's round-up. Lee Ramsey had acted with amazing speed, he conceded – but nowhere was Eric Matthews mentioned.

Enough of the news, Scott told himself when the newscaster moved to another subject, and rose to switch off the television. The phone rang. Probably Jake, he surmised, and reached to respond. Jake hadn't checked in yet today.

"Hello."

"Hi." It was Jake. "I told you – I've gotten chummy with Matthews's secretary. She said he'd be leaving at seven a.m. tomorrow morning for a business meeting in some little town near Albany. I'll be right behind him."

Signals shot up in Scott's head. "If you see him making the round of banks, buzz me right away – at the office or on the car phone." Torres was in jail, Peter James and Dan Reagan held for questioning. With the others out of the way was Eric about to cash in a bundle of drug money for his personal use? "Try to find out if he's buying cashier's checks."

"Gotcha," Jake said.

Scott debated for a moment. It was late to be calling Kathy, but he wanted to report this latest move on Eric's part. He crossed to the phone – knowing she'd be pleased to hear from him.

"Hello—"

"Kathy, I just spoke with Jake." He repeated their conversation. "I may be way off base, but the hairs on the back of my neck are standing up straight. I suspect Eric is out to make a killing for himself – and this could trip him up."

"Oh Scott, let this be it!"

"It still doesn't set him up as the murderer," Scott reminded. "But each small step we take in that direction makes me feel better."

Off the phone, Scott went to his bedroom. He'd try to focus on reading for an hour or so. Sleep was always elusive these nights. He settled himself in bed, reached for the suspense novel Marcie had loaned him. He read longer than he'd anticipated. Finally – slightly after one a.m. – he fell asleep. His last conscious thought was that rain was hitting the bedroom windows.

He awoke with a start when lightning flashed across the sky, invaded his bedroom. Then thunder pierced the night, demonically repetitive. A taunting power that seemed invincible. Most times storms with that kind of clout fascinated him – but not tonight. He squinted at the clock. It was barely five a.m. He turned over, clutched his pillow in a hazy need for sleep.

He awoke again seemingly only minutes later – though a glance at the clock told him he'd slept for an hour. Now he became aware of the insistent ringing of the bedside phone. Who the hell was calling him at this hour? *Kathy? Had something happened at the house?*

"Hello—"

"Mr Lazarus? Scott Lazarus?" A brisk male voice.

"Yes." Alarm catapulted him into full wakefulness.

"This is the Madison police, sir. I'm sorry to have to report this – but a bomb exploded in your office about twenty minutes ago."

"Good God!"

"There's been considerable damage but no fire. We're at the site now. We'd like you to come down and talk with us."

"I'll be there in ten minutes!" *A bomb in my office?*

Scott tossed aside the sheet, began to dress with obsessive speed. This had to be the work of the True Patriots – their reaction to Torres's arrest, the questioning of Peter James and Dan Reagan. They'd been promised good jobs, he guessed – and now those seemed to have been snatched away by government forces.

Somebody in the District Attorney's office must have leaked word that Kathy was responsible for the arrests. They couldn't bomb Kathy's house with the security there – but his office was a sitting duck.

He drove with unaccustomed speed to his destination – through streets that were barren of cars and pedestrians at this hour. Approaching his office he saw hordes of people milling about the immediate area. In his troubled sleep the sound of the explosion had probably blended with the rumble of thunder – but people close by had rushed to the scene. Nothing like this had ever happened in Madison.

What seemed to be endless yards of yellow tape cordoned off the site of his office. He felt sick as he stared at the gaping hole in the front wall of what had been his reception room. Debris was scattered about the sidewalk. Pam's computer and printer – of which she was so proud – lay on the sidewalk in barely recognizable form.

He left his car, stopped dead as his eyes focused on the yellow painted design on a segment of the sidewalk. *A swastika in Madison?* He'd come here for peace, a quiet unpressured life. Anger welled in him that such ugliness had erupted in what a little while ago had seemed an oasis in a troubled world.

"The damage was confined to the front area, Mr Lazarus." A detective walked towards him with a conciliatory air. It always amazed him that so many local people knew him by sight. Probably because of the *pro bono* work he did for various groups. "After you've had a chance to inspect the premises, we'd like to talk to you."

"We can talk now." Scott was unconsciously brusque.

"Have you any suspicions who might be responsible for this?" the detective asked and beckoned to another to join him.

"Oh yes." Reined-in anger colored his voice. "This has to be the work of the True Patriots. They're responsible for the drive-by shooting at Marcie Loeb's house and for this." It was time to rout out these homegrown terrorists. This was where he wanted to spend the rest of his life.

The two detectives exchanged an uneasy glance. Damn it, didn't they understand what was happening in this town?

"*They exist.*" Scott was abrupt. "A private investigator employed by me heard extensive shooting on a farm eight miles out of town. He explored and encountered six guys in camouflage and carrying assault rifles or 9mm semi-automatic pistols." That snapped them to attention. "He pretended he thought they were ROTC on training maneuvers – and, thank God, they believed him. And that farm," he pursued, "is the property of the father-in-law of Peter James. Who, as you know, is being questioned on charges of money laundering."

"What's the connection with the so-called True Patriots?" one of the detectives asked dubiously.

"My office was hit by a fertilizer bomb?" Scott's gaze moved from one detective to the other. He read immediate confirmation in their eyes.

"It could have been," one detective hedged. "We don't know for sure yet."

"It'll be confirmed," Scott said. "Just recently Peter James bought fertilizer from half a dozen supply houses in the area – enough to handle Paradise Estates's needs for a dozen years. If you search the farm now, you'll find—"

"We can't ask a judge for a search warrant on what you've told us." Yet Scott intercepted a silent communication between the two detectives.

"I'll give you the names of the supply houses," Scott rummaged in his shirt pockets for paper and pen. "The tax office will confirm that the farm is owned by Peter James's father-in-law – who lives in Miami. Where Torres established residency."

"Here—" The detective who'd first approached him extended a notebook, folded to a clean page, handed over a pen. "We can't promise anything, but we'll see what we can do."

Scott scribbled down the information, handed notebook and pen back to the detective. Now he braced himself to inspect the premises. He walked into the shell of what had been his office's reception room – his throat tightening at the sight of its destruction. It hadn't been a powerful bomb. Probably crudely put together. But enough of this. As soon as the police gave him the go-ahead, he'd ask Joe to take charge of the repairs.

Scott headed across the street to the coffee shop that was just opening up for the day. Have some breakfast to clear his head. Try to piece together what had happened. Pray the police get a search warrant! Let them link the bombing to the True Patriots – and to the Paradise Estates set-up. And somewhere along the line he must connect Eric Matthews to the whole deal.

Inside the coffee shop – deserted except for a pair of truckers at the counter – Scott went to the public telephone at the rear. Call Pam, warn her about what had happened. The office, of course, would be closed for the day. The police were still moving about in search of evidence.

"I just this minute heard on the radio news!" Pam was shaken. If it was on the morning news already, Kathy knew. He must call her. "I couldn't believe it—"

"Believe it, Pam. Police are swarming all over the place. There's no way we can open up today."

"What about our files?" Pam wailed. "All our records?"

"Just the reception room was damaged, plus some windows on the side. My office and the conference room appear intact. We'll operate from there as soon as we're allowed."

"Have the police any ideas about who did it?" Pam was simultaneously alarmed and furious.

"I've put some possibilities into their head," Scott admitted. "Let's see if they follow through."

Off the phone with Pam, he called Kathy, explained what had happened.

"You're all right?" Kathy sounded terrified.

"I'm fine," he soothed. "It happened almost two hours ago – I was home asleep when the police phoned to tell me." He took a deep breath. "Whoever did it left a greeting card. A yellow swastika painted on the sidewalk in front of the office."

He heard her gasp. "I never thought something like that could happen here." Kathy's voice was hushed. "It's something you read about happening in other towns."

"You never thought there'd be violent extremists here in Madison," he said gently. "We're living in insane times. And yes, I'm sure the True Patriots are responsible."

"Why don't the police search that farm Jake talked about?" Kathy demanded. "Are they waiting for somebody else to be murdered before they take action?"

"I'm working on that, Kathy." Yet he felt a painful frustration as he remembered his conversation with the detectives. They'd made no commitment. "I'll talk to you later, okay?"

He'd finished his stack of pancakes and was on his second cup of coffee when his cellular phone rang. He picked up.

"I'm on Matthews's tail," Jake reported. "He's been into two banks already in this burg, and I suspect it's the beginning of a tour. I'll—"

"Where are you?" Scott broke in, and Jake told him.

"Matthews is carrying this attaché case – and I figure it's stuffed with twenty-dollar bills. He's bought a cashier's check for two thousand dollars in each bank. And when he left the house this morning, he threw a large valise into the trunk – probably with more bills."

"Stay with him, Jake!"

"Funny thing," Jake said. "His car stinks like hell. He must have driven over a pile of horse shit – or fertilizer."

"Give me the names of the two banks he's visited so far." The noose was tightening about Eric Matthews. He wasn't yet about to be accused of murdering Frank – but the missing pieces in the puzzle were growing smaller. He glanced at his watch. *Call Lee.*

He left the coffee shop, returned to his car. Every nerve in his body tingling in anticipation, he called the District Attorney's office, asked to speak with Lee Ramsey.

"I'm sorry, she's in a meeting." The voice at the other end didn't sound sorry at all.

"This is Scott Lazarus. I have something urgent to report to Ms Ramsey. Can't you bring her out for a minute?"

"No, I can't." Impatience slithered through to him. "We don't interrupt meetings in this office."

"Tell her, please, that I called on an urgent matter." He strained for politeness. "I can be reached at this number." He gave her the number of his cellular phone.

The phone on the seat beside him, he reached for the ignition. He'd go to Kathy's house to wait for Lee Ramsey's call. Kathy had sounded so frightened when he told her about the bomb. Let her see that he was all right.

"Tim, let's stop at the post office to pick up the mail," Grace Mitchell ordered her husband as they drove into town.

"It'll just be a load of bills," he grumbled. "I don't know why they can't wait." Grace was still teed off because he hadn't gone with her on the cruise to Nova Scotia – though everybody in town thought he had.

He'd holed up in the house until it was time to pick up Grace and drive up to the cabin. He'd *enjoyed* being alone in the house – reading what Grace called his 'crappy mystery magazines' or just lying around doing nothing. He couldn't watch TV or listen to the radio because nobody was supposed to know he was home. Grace had this nutty idea that folks in town expected them to spend all their vacation time together.

Tim parked in front of the post office. He and Grace went inside to collect the mail that had been held for them for the past three weeks. The postal clerk – the grandson of a local plumber

Tim and Grace had known for over forty years – greeted them warmly.

"You sure picked the right time to go on vacation," he said, bringing the pile-up of letters, catalogues, and magazines that had accumulated in their absence. "You missed all that craziness next door to you – the murder and the drive-by shooting and all. Then the bombing this morning—"

"Back up there!" Tim ordered. "What are you talking about?"

"Hey, this town has been making national news! The place is crawling with reporters and TV crews and—"

"We've been out of touch with TV and radio," Grace interrupted nervously. "Ten days in Nova Scotia, then up at our cabin in the mountains. What's been going on here?"

Tim and Grace listened – the color draining from their faces – while the postal clerk brought them up to date.

"Marcie Loeb's out on bail now – but the DA's office is yelling for the death penalty. It might be the first case since Governor Pataki went for it."

Tim reached for Grace's hand as he shook his head in disbelief.

"Frank dead? And Marcie accused of his murder? How could anybody in their right mind believe that? Marcie adored Frank."

"Let's go home." Grace's voice was choked. "I want to see Marcie and Kathy. I know Kathy's here with her."

Tim's hand was trembling as he groped for his car keys. He was one of the cautious townspeople who'd stopped leaving keys in the ignition – even to run into the post office.

"Grace – you know when I was hiding out in the house while you went off on the cruise—" He took a deep breath. "I heard Marcie scream late that afternoon it happened – just before I conked out for a long nap. I figured she'd seen another waterbug." He and Frank used to tease Marcie about the way she screamed every time she saw one.

"You mean you think she found Frank – murdered – and screamed? But it was over – you couldn't have saved him."

"I may have seen the murderer." He clutched Grace's arm. "Let's talk to Marcie."

"Now don't start up something you can't finish," Grace warned. "You weren't supposed to be in the house. Everybody we know will think you're making this up to help Marcie. The police won't believe you."

"Get in the car." His voice was terse. "I have to talk to Marcie."

Twenty-Seven

Kathy hovered beside Scott while he talked with Lee on his cellular phone. From Scott's comments she assumed Lee was about to issue orders for Eric Matthews to be picked up at what was now the fourth bank on his tour – where Jake had reported he was opening up a savings account. Jake remained on his trail. Eric was unaware that he was under surveillance.

But what about the farm? Kathy fumed. When would the police go in and confirm that the True Patriots had built the bomb that exploded in Scott's office this morning? The evidence must be there. She flinched, remembering Scott's description of the devastation the bomb had wrought.

"Here's fresh coffee—" Marcie came into the living-room with a tray. Kathy gestured for silence.

"It's Lee Ramsey." Kathy's mouth framed the words.

"No question about it, Lee," Scott wound up – his eyes telegraphing his excitement. "Eric is making the rounds with a valise stuffed with cash – Torres's drug money. I suspect huge sums went through Dan Reagan's bank – which you must have discovered by now." He listened to Lee's response, pantomimed his amusement at her stalling. Scott said the bank records would open up the whole deal, Kathy remembered.

A moment later Scott was off the phone.

"Local police will move in to grab Matthews at the bank as soon as Lee gets her call through." He reached for the mug of coffee Marcie extended. "The Madison police are about to get a warrant to search the farm. They'll discover ammonium nitrate fertilizer and diesel fuel – which, put together, make powerful bombs. In Eric's car they'll find traces of the same fertilizer. There's his link to the True Patriots. But let's not forget," his eyes were apologetic, "We still have to prove he killed Frank."

"This bears out what Marcie has said all along," Kathy reminded.

"We're getting closer, Kathy – but we're not there yet."

"I want Frank's killer caught." Marcie's hand trembled as she handed her mother a mug of coffee. "It has to be Eric! I want him to spend the rest of his life behind bars!"

All at once they were aware of argumentative conversation outside the house. Kathy darted into the foyer.

"Tell Marcie and Kathy it's Grace and Tim." Grace's voice was shrill. "We live next door! We're close friends!"

Kathy pulled the door wide. "It's all right – let them in, please."

"Kathy—" Grace reached to pull her close. "We've just got back from the mountains. We heard at the post office—"

"I don't know whether it'll help," Tim said, following the two women into the house. "But there's something I have to tell you—" He paused as Marcie rushed to greet them.

For a few moments the living-room reverberated with the sounds of Tim and Grace's grief for Frank, their outrage that Marcie was accused of his murder. They knew Scott by sight, as most Madison residents did. Now Kathy introduced them to him.

"First I was on that cruise to Nova Scotia," Grace explained, sitting on the sofa at Kathy's prodding. "Then Tim and I were holed up at the cabin. You know how it is out there—" She turned to Marcie and Kathy for confirmation. "No phone, no television, no radio. We don't bother reading the newspapers. We just go up there to fish and unwind."

"But I didn't go on the cruise to Nova Scotia." Tim shot a sheepish glance at Grace, settled himself beside her while Kathy and Marcie sat on flanking chairs. "I don't mind fishing at the lake from a canoe – but big ships and the ocean scare the hell out of me. Kathy, you remember how you used to tease me about that."

"Where were you?" Scott remained on his feet. Kathy knew that – like herself – he was anxious to learn what Tim was trying to tell them.

"I was in the house until it was time to pick up Grace in New York and head for the cottage. We like to drive real late at night – when the roads are empty. Nobody was supposed to know I was here because Grace wanted them to think that I'd gone with her on the cruise." He shook his head. "She's a pip about some things. Anyhow, we pretended the house was closed up. I kept the shades down, I didn't play the TV or the radio. We had the timers on – the way we always do when we go to the mountains. I didn't use any other lights. The living-room lights came on about six p.m., went off at ten p.m., then the bedroom lights—"

"Tim, stop the yammering and tell them what you told me," Grace interrupted.

"Well, I was upstairs in our bedroom and just dozing off. And I heard Marcie scream. I figured she'd seen another waterbug. I went off to sleep for the next four hours."

"When was this?" Scott leaned forward, his eyes holding Tim's.

"It – it was the day Frank was killed. But I didn't know it then."

"When Tim sleeps, nothing wakes him up," Grace broke in. "I mean, there must have been police cars arriving—"

"About eleven p.m. when I figured nobody would see me – I headed for where I'd parked the car until it was time to leave for the city. In the Wilson's garage. They're away until Labor Day weekend – I knew they wouldn't mind."

"Tim, why do you feel it's important to tell us you heard Marcie scream?" Scott strained for patience.

"Because a couple of minutes before that I'd glanced out the window for a second – and I saw a guy coming through the backyard – like he was leaving the patio. I figured it was kinda funny – but folks do strange things. He wasn't a workman – he was wearing a business suit and a tie."

"It was Eric!" Marcie told Scott. "The way you said it could have happened! He heard me coming towards the den and went out through the patio slider!"

"Did you recognize him?" Scott asked Tim.

"I don't know his name—" Tim squinted in thought. "But he looked awful familiar."

"All right, let's follow this up." Scott was striving to appear calm, but Kathy sensed his inner tumult. "I want to get a photo of the man we believe you saw." He was at the phone now, tapping what Kathy recognized as Bill Collins's unlisted number.

Moments later Bill picked up.

"Bill, this is Scott. Would you have any photos of Eric Matthews in your files? It's important." He nodded to the others. "He's checking."

"Tim's nearsighted," Grace warned.

"Not as bad as I used to be," Tim said triumphantly – though Grace shook her head in disbelief. "I only wear glasses now for reading."

"If Bill doesn't have a photo, I can check out the *Daily News* and the *Journal* at the library," Kathy said. *Could this nightmare be over – or is this a false lead?* "Eric's been so involved in local campaigns there must have been photos in the newspapers."

"Let's see what Bill comes up with," Scott began, then focused on the phone again. "Yeah, Bill . . . Great! Could you have somebody rush it over to Marcie's house? We may be on to something." He put down the phone, took a deep breath. "We'll have two photos in ten minutes. I'll tell the security guard we're expecting a messenger from the *Guardian*."

The atmosphere in the living-room was charged with suspense. Kathy was conscious of the pounding of her heart while she joined in the general conversation, meant to ease the painful wait.

The sound of the doorbell was a traumatic intrusion.

"I'll get it—" Scott charged into the foyer. After a brief exchange at the door, he returned to the living-room, pulled two glossy photos from an envelope. "Look at each one carefully," Scott told Tim. "No rush."

The others watched while Tim examined the first photograph. He squinted, sighed. "I think so – but I can't be sure." He was upset that he couldn't make a definite identification.

"It's okay," Scott soothed. "It's a group shot and out of focus. Now look at this one." He extended the second glossy to Tim.

"Oh, this is him!" Tim said instantly. "I'd swear to that on a stack of bibles."

"Tim, will you go with me to the District Attorney's office and swear to Lee Ramsey – the prosecuting attorney in this case – that you saw this man emerging from the Loeb's backyard a couple of minutes before you heard Marcie scream?"

"You bet I will." Tim rose to his feet. "Let's go."

"Will it – will it be enough?" Marcie asked.

"I don't know." Scott was candid. "But it should be grounds for questioning Eric about the murder. He's already involved in money laundering."

"Let me go along!" Kathy acted on instinct. "Please."

"Good thought," Scott agreed. "You gave Lee Ramsey her money laundering deal. That should buy us some good will."

Twenty minutes later – after a brief wait in the District Attorney's reception area – Scott, Kathy, and Tim were seated in Lee's small private office. Lee appeared cool, impersonal – yet Kathy sensed that her own presence was disturbing. Lee wasn't sure what she might do in her desperation to clear Marcie.

While Lee listened with barely concealed impatience, Tim repeated the meandering account he'd given Scott earlier.

"You're willing to give us a written statement?" Lee asked Tim when he was at last silent.

"Yes ma'am, I am." Tim was emphatic.

"Eric Matthews is your murderer," Scott said with quiet conviction.

Lee frowned. "We have a long way to go before we can charge him."

"We've brought you a witness who places him at the scene of Frank's murder!" Kathy was outraged. "He was there just minutes before Marcie walked into the den. He—"

"You're having Matthews brought in on suspicion of money laundering," Scott broke in. "Right?"

"Yes." Lee was terse. "But that—"

"And you know he's part of the whole Paradise Estates picture," Scott forged ahead. "Which includes the True Patriots – who bombed my office this morning. I'll lay odds that if Eric is questioned about Frank's murder, Peter James's fancy team of lawyers will make sure he and Torres co-operate with you. They won't want their clients to be indicated as accomplices in a murder case. That's a lot rougher than money laundering or placing a bomb not intended for personal injury. And James and Torres won't be happy to learn that Eric Matthews was trying to abscond with their funds. They'll talk, loud and clear."

"They might talk," Lee said after a moment. "If I give them the right picture." Fleetingly her eyes met Kathy's. This was the pay-off that Lee felt would liberate her from the past, Kathy interpreted. So be it. "But their attorneys may realize I have no grounds for questioning them about Frank Loeb's murder."

"Make sure they understand that Eric Matthews was picked up trying to launder a valise loaded with twenty-dollar bills," Scott told Lee. "He was opening a savings account with those cashier's checks. I'll be much surprised if Torres and James don't admit they knew that Eric killed Frank – but not on their orders."

Scott's eyes held Lee's for a traumatic moment.

"I'll play the scene that way," Lee agreed. "But I can't promise that it'll work." She turned to Tim. "Mr Mitchell, I'll have someone take down your statement."

*   *   *

211

At Angie's insistence, Kathy allowed her to help Marcie clear away the dinner dishes. They'd eaten extremely late, lingered at the table, ignoring talk about what monopolized their thoughts. Was Scott right? Kathy asked herself while she walked with Scott and Joe into the living-room. *Will Torres and James make the statements that will clear Marcie?*

She could hear the TV in the living-room of the two hostile sisters next door. They were deliberate in keeping the volume unconscionably loud. She was grateful that the TV voices were muffled, yet she knew they were listening to Glenn being interviewed. Linda had called ten minutes ago – when the program began.

"It was insane to listen," Linda had admitted, "but all I had to hear was Dad's opening comments and I felt sick. I never want to see him again!"

"You'll see him," she'd told Linda gently. "But you'll never respect him again."

It was strange how – at last – her rage at Glenn was dissipating. Finding Scott had accomplished that. She sat on the sofa beside him and reached for his hand. No need to mask their feelings for each other. Marcie knew. Angie and Joe knew.

"We might not hear anything tonight," Joe reminded, his eyes compassionate as they rested on Kathy.

"I know." Ellen and Phil were standing by out at Montauk, she remembered. '*Call us no matter what time the word comes through,*' Ellen had ordered. They weren't sure that Scott's scenario would play, she warned herself yet again.

"Maybe we should call it a night," Scott said.

"Not yet," Kathy pleaded. "You said the questioning could continue till all hours."

"I'll stay," Scott told her. "I left instructions to call me on my cell phone – so I could be reached wherever I happened to be – at any time of day or night. Lee knows that. The police know that."

"Joe, you and Angie go on home," Kathy urged. "I know you're up for work early in the morning."

"Angie may want to stay—" But Joe was already suppressing yawns.

"We're cutting out." Angie came into the room with a determined smile. "Your alarm clock will be going off at five twenty a.m.," she told Joe. "If any word comes through, Kathy will call us."

Best Friends

Marcie followed Angie into the living-room. She looked exhausted, Kathy thought. Her poor, sweet baby.

"I don't know about the rest of you," Marcie said with contrived flippancy, "but I'm not going to bed before I have a slab of that strawberry shortcake Fiona left for us this morning." She winced in pain. "Poor Fiona."

Only Marcie would think of Fiona Matthews at a moment like this. Married to a money launderer and a murderer – but the world had yet to be convinced of that.

Everyone froze at the shrill ring of Scott's cellular phone – waiting in readiness on the coffee table. Scott picked it up, his face tense.

"Hello . . . Yes, this is Scott Lazarus."

Her heart pounding, Kathy darted to his side. Angie reached to pull Marcie close – as though, Kathy thought subconsciously, to protect her against bad news.

"Okay, Torres and James blew their stacks." Scott frowned impatiently. "Did they *talk*? Did Matthews confess?" Scott was listening now. His face relaxed. He murmured something under his breath while Kathy's eyes searched his. "Congratulations, Lee." A touch of humor in his voice. "Your stock in this town has jumped sky high."

"Eric confessed?" Kathy's eyes clung to Scott's.

"After Torres and James agreed to co-operate with the DA's office," Scott told them. "Eric admitted to founding the True Patriots here in town – for a total membership of nine. All of them expecting good jobs at Paradise Estates. But Eric implicated James as having bankrolled the group. The plan was to have the True Patriots handy if pressure was needed to put through the re-zoning deal. Eric had bragged to James and Torres about a group he'd been part of before he moved here. That group had hounded a judge out of the county, threatening kidnappings and even murder. He spouted the usual boast of these extremist groups: *'If we can't beat you at the ballot box, we'll beat you at the bullet box.'* But Torres and James didn't order Frank's murder – and they wanted no part of that charge."

"You're off the hook, Marcie," Joe said gently and reached to embrace her. "All those candles Angie lit helped some."

"It wouldn't have happened without you," Kathy told Scott – her eyes glistening with tears of joy. "At last we can live again."

Kathy knew that Marcie would grieve for a long time. She, too, would grieve for Frank. But Scott would share her life from

213

this point on. From all that horror had come something beautiful.

After a long, shockingly dry summer Madison was enjoying a beautiful early autumn. The trees that shaded the expansive lawn of the Frank Loeb Senior Citizens Center were garbed in red and gold and tawny browns. Only Marcie's tragically young widowhood marred this day, Kathy thought as she walked into the huge Georgian house that had been converted into Madison's new Senior Citizens Center – financed by the insurance money Frank had left to Marcie. Masses of autumn flowers in yellow and burgundy – plus the armloads of white Montauk daisies that Ellen and Phil had brought from the beach house – lent an air of festivity to the occasion.

"There're Ellen and Phil with Angie and Joe." Scott pointed towards the far side of the opened-up lower floor. Ellen and Phil had come for the dedication of the Center and for Kathy and Scott's wedding tomorrow morning. Phil's mother was staying with the grandchildren in the Manhattan apartment. Later today Linda and David would arrive with Joanie, the baby, to be here for the wedding. "They're holding seats for us."

Kathy and Scott threaded their way through the growing assemblage to their seats. Marcie was off in a corner in conversation with the Mayor, who was to speak. Subdued but determined to be here, Fiona – who was to be Marcie's assistant in managing the Center – was distributing programs.

"There's Bill," Kathy told Scott and waved a warm greeting.

The room ricocheted with high spirits. Photographers from the two dailies and from the *Guardian* were snapping pictures. Bill Collins made his way across the room to chat with Kathy and Scott and Angie and Joe. He'd been so helpful to Marcie, Kathy thought gratefully. He was so like Frank.

"We're running the final story on the True Patriots next week," Bill told them with satisfaction. "Even the Madison Militia were relieved to see them flushed out. They were scared to death they'd be linked with the other group. 'Hey, we're not loose cannons. We just want to make people understand the need to protect their rights – warn them not to give up the freedoms the Constitution demands,'" he mimicked. "But it's a fine line between such groups as the Madison Militia and the True Patriots. So easy to cross over that line."

"Look who's just arrived," Angie whispered and the others turned to see Lee Ramsey, pushing her father's wheelchair.

"She's about ready to announce a run for the State Assembly," Bill said. "And she'll win," he predicted drily. "Guess who's claiming all the credit for putting Madison on the map? She caught notorious money launderers, tracked down a murderer, and cleared this town of a violent extremist group. She's after every photo opportunity, straining for every vote."

"But she'll never be truly sure that we won't bring up what happened thirty-one years ago," Angie whispered to Kathy. "It'll haunt her on the long, savage climb to the top. She'll never be a happy woman."

"That's not Leslie Hilton," Kathy said quietly. "That's Lee Ramsey. Leslie Hilton died a long time ago."

"Sssh," Scott ordered, dropping an arm about Kathy's shoulders.

Marcie had moved towards the improvised, flower-banked podium. Her face was luminous as she began to speak.

"We're here today to dedicate the Frank Loeb Senior Citizens Center. Frank would be so happy to know that his dream for this town is being realized . . ."

Tears blurred Kathy's vision as she listened to Marcie. Her sweet, precious baby who had suffered such a terrible loss. But tomorrow would be better for Marcie – and for herself. Tomorrow morning – when she married Scott – there would be three generations in the family house plus cherished friends. She was rich – in the ways that counted.